## THE DURAND CHRONICLES:
## BOOK THREE

# LARK
# BRENNAN

Also by Lark Brennan

The Durand Chronicles
*Dangerously Yours*
*Irresistibly Yours*

Diversion Books
A Division of Diversion Publishing Corp.
443 Park Avenue South, Suite 1008
New York, New York 10016
www.DiversionBooks.com

This is a work of fiction. Names, characters, places and incidents either are the product of the author's imagination or are used fictitiously. Any resemblance to actual persons, living or dead, events or locales is entirely coincidental.

For more information, email info@diversionbooks.com

First Diversion Books edition August 2017.
Print ISBN: 978-1-68230-323-8
eBook ISBN: 978-1-68230-322-1

To my dear friend, and critique partner, Sarah Andre.

Thank you for always knowing when to pat me on the back,
kick my butt, or talk me off the ledge.

What a long, strange trip it's been!

# CHAPTER ONE

Seven Years Ago – London

Normally the fog and drizzle would have irritated Tanner. So would standing for hours in a tight alcove just across from the embassy, waiting for action. But tonight he had a companion, and was just fine spending time alone with her.

His cell phone buzzed.

"The guards inside are rotating," Javier said. "Be sure Chantal pays attention to anyone approaching the gate on foot, even if they don't stop."

"What do you think we've been doing for the last five hours?" Tanner snapped. "If a Dissembler's walking down the next block, she'll smell him."

"Don't let her get distracted." Click.

"Fuck you," he muttered at his phone. He and Javier had been trained to detect a Dissembler assassin at close range, but Chantal Durand could smell their foul majik from a hundred yards or more—which was why she and Tanner were outside in the elements instead of sitting in a warm surveillance vehicle.

"Javier's an ass," Chantal said. "I don't understand how he can be your best friend."

"He's a good guy, even though you two don't get along."

"I'm not the one with the problem. He hates me and resents all the First Order."

She was right. When no one else was around, Javier frequently bad-mouthed the First Order Durand—Adrien, the future head of the family, and his first cousins, including Chantal. Tanner had figured out long ago that his friend was jealous of the First Order's wealth and superior psychic abilities.

Chantal rolled her shoulders and stretched. "I almost wish something would happen."

Her auburn hair glistened in the gold streetlight, and the faint scent of expensive shampoo and even more expensive perfume floated to his nose. Chantal, the wild child, had grown up to be a stunning woman without shedding the daredevil nature that had drawn him to her so many years ago. At twenty-two, the three-year age difference between them no longer made her off limits, even if her birthright did.

She shivered and wrapped her arms around herself.

"Cold?" he asked.

"And hungry. How about we blow this gig for a nice English breakfast at Claridge's?"

"Come here." Tanner opened his wool trench coat and pulled her back against his body.

As he folded her into his coat and into his arms, she smiled at him over her shoulder. "Better not let your compadre catch you consorting with the enemy."

"He can mind his own damn business." Javier would give him hell if he caught them together, but luckily he was posted in the guardhouse at the other entrance.

She rested her back against him, her curves fitting perfectly. "This waiting is pointless. It looks like Javier's intel was crap. Again."

The heat of her body warmed his blood. Over the past three days, something between them had shifted—a look here and a touch there. He wanted more.

"Once it gets light, we'll leave," he said. And go their separate ways again, each on a new Protector assignment. For now she was cocooned in his coat, against his body, and he couldn't bear to let her go. He'd wanted her for too long.

"Why don't you come to Turkey with me?" she said. "Adrien

ordered me to leave tomorrow to check out some artifacts that surfaced after the last earthquake. A couple may have mystical properties, so he wants me to read their history. You might be able to pick up information from the site's energy."

"Mark wants me in Guatemala by the weekend." He wasn't excited about reading the residual energy of a bizarre mass execution, but that was his psychic ability and his role in the war against the Durand's ancient enemies.

"So it'll be another year before we work together again." The disappointment in her voice matched his.

"Chantal," he murmured into her hair. "I wish we had more time."

"Me too." She turned in his arms and angled her face up to him. Her cheeks were rosy, and her eyes shone blue even in the dim light. Her lips were so close and inviting.

He brushed her mouth with his, and her breath hitched. Then he kissed her in earnest, tasting lemon on her tongue as it met his. Her arms slid around him and he held her tightly.

Her lips were soft, plump, and delicious. He devoured her mouth—tasted, explored, claimed it—and she met his invasion greedily. Her hands snaked around his neck and her fingers tangled in his hair, holding him fiercely. When her teeth raked his bottom lip, he groaned, "You make me crazy."

"Let's get out of here." She stepped out of the warmth of his coat and took his hand. "Nothing's going to happen."

Tanner barely rebuttoned his coat when the thunder of an underground blast shook the building at their backs and they rushed into the street. "What the hell was that?" he asked.

"This way." Chantal dropped Tanner's hand and took off running in the direction of the explosion.

He kept up with her, but as they passed by the guardhouse, he glanced over at the location where Javier was stationed. It was empty.

In the next block, they saw the chaos. People were writhing on the ground crying, others running is every direction, screaming. Smoke poured out of the underground entrance along with soot-covered commuters. In the distance sirens wailed and a few police were already on the scene.

Chantal slowed to a walk. "A bomb. Probably more than one."

"So many injured. We should help."

"We are." She stopped and inhaled deeply. "That way." She pointed down a side alley. "Two Dissemblers."

They took off again, weaving through the crowds. The trail zigzagged through narrow streets and alleys to an old warehouse district. Around a sharp corner stood Javier, cell phone in hand. He started when he saw them and pocketed his phone.

"They went through that door," Chantal said.

"I know," Javier sneered. "I tracked them here."

The brick building was smaller than its neighbors. Someone had jimmied the lock.

Tanner checked the side of the warehouse—no doors. "Have you called Adrien?"

"We can handle this." Javier glanced at Chantal. "You stand guard outside while Tanner and I go in."

"That's not how it works," Chantal said. "We call Adrien, give our position and assessment, and *he* decides whether we go in or not."

"Adrien isn't here, I am. I say we go in before they get away."

Chantal stepped forward and glared at Javier. "The two Dissemblers from the subway have powerful majik. You're no match for them."

"Fuck you, Chantal. I'm sick of you and the rest of the First Order. We're going in. You stay out here to make sure nobody else shows up." Javier headed for the door. "Tanner, let's go."

Tanner hesitated.

"Don't follow him," Chantal pleaded.

"I can't let him go in alone. Call Adrien and wait here."

She nodded and he followed Javier into the building.

The only light in the hallway came from a filthy low-watt bulb that hung from the ceiling. They crept silently down a dusty corridor that reeked of mold and rodent droppings. Cover was limited to stacks of wooden pallets, discarded office furniture, cardboard boxes, or rusted equipment.

Fluorescent light radiated from the management office at the other end of the open space. Once, the foreman or manager would have monitored the workers through the huge window. Now the glass was broken and the voices of four men inside drifted indistinctly in their direction.

"Take cover here," Javier whispered. "I'm going to work my way over to the stairway and try to get a height advantage. Don't fire until I do."

Tanner watched his friend disappear, then found a vantage point where he could see the terrorists. The police might capture the two non-psychic *ordinaires*, but the authorities would be powerless against the two Dissemblers' psychic abilities and dark majik. They had to be stopped now.

Crouched on one knee, he waited and listened. Somewhere water dripped. The scratching sound in the trash was probably rats. His guns were ready and he had extra clips of ammo in his front pocket where he could get them. He was so intent on Javier's position to his right he didn't notice the movement to his left until the report shattered the quiet.

Three shots in quick succession—two men in the office went down—and all hell broke loose. Tanner started to fire, but the men had already taken cover and were firing back with much heavier artillery than he packed. The wall of pallets in front of him took enough assault rifle fire to begin collapsing, but he didn't dare leave its safety.

Chantal darted from her original position and threw herself behind a pile of furniture anchored by an old desk and some file cabinets. She was fast, but not fast enough. A bullet caught her calf and she cried out.

What the hell did she think she was doing? He and Javier had had a plan. His hands shook with fury. She'd had her orders and still came in and started a shit storm. A bullet whizzed by his shoulder and he pulled back. He listened for Javier, but there was no way to tell who was firing.

The explosion came a moment later. Debris pelted Tanner's toppling cover and rained down on his head until he covered himself with his jacket. Smoke filled the air and a fire crackled to his right. A quick glance confirmed the source—the stairway where Javier had taken cover was gone and the building was ablaze.

"We have to get out of here," Chantal called to him.

"Javier's in there. We have to pull him out."

"Nobody could survive that blast or the fire. We need to go." She tried to stand, but her left leg wouldn't hold her weight.

His training kicked in, and he went into action, picking her up and carrying her out the way he'd come in. When they got outside, he set her on her feet and looked around.

"That way." She pointed down the street opposite the subway bombsite. They took off, her leaning on him, his arm circling her waist. At the end of the second block, a familiar black Range Rover stood parked at the curb, but its driver was gone.

"Adrien will be back in a few minutes," Chantal said. "Would you help me into the back seat?"

Tanner opened the door, his hand trembling. Grief and fury churned in his chest. "He's dead because of you. Javier is dead. You couldn't do what he asked. What possessed you to barge in there and start shooting?" She started to speak and he raised his hand to stop her. "No, don't tell me. You couldn't take orders from him, so you took matters into your own hands. Now my best friend is dead."

She stared at him defiantly. "That's what you think?"

"I was there." He turned his back on her and walked away.

# CHAPTER TWO

Present – Somewhere Over Montana

Chantal Durand peered out of the window of the Gulfstream at the tree-covered mountains and deep rocky valleys—so different from the Australian Outback where she'd spent the last three years working on an archeology dig. And the last four weeks in jail.

She shuddered. Thanks to her cousin, Mark, that ordeal was over, and a payback assignment lay in her immediate future. As Field General of the Durand Protectors his message had been clear—you owe me. So here she was, about to land god-knew-where, to do whatever she was told.

The plane made a smooth landing and coasted down the runway. As it approached a weathered hangar, Chantal searched the tarmac for her brother, Victor. Mark had ordered her here by text while she was en route—catch the Durand Tech jet for Montana and meet Victor. At the time she'd been relieved to have an assignment, instead of returning home to Paris in disgrace. Now? Maybe she should have asked more questions.

The flight attendant opened the rear door of the aircraft, allowing icy air to blast into the cabin. Chantal shivered and buttoned her jacket. It had been spring when she left Sydney two days ago. God, she hated the cold.

She pocketed her ComDev—a Durand Tech Communications Device—and opened the luggage storage compartment.

"Do you need help with your bags?" the attendant asked. "I don't want to rush you, but a team is waiting for a pickup in Denver."

"Thanks. I can handle them myself." She pulled out her duffle and backpack and hoisted the strap over her shoulder. "I appreciate the ride."

The young man nodded stiffly. "Just following orders. Have a good evening, Ms. Durand."

She descended the stairs onto the runway, her eyes tearing in the chilly wind. Her winter jacket was packed in her duffle along with a cashmere scarf. She'd expected her obsessively prompt brother to be there waiting. So where was he?

Dusk had fallen and night wasn't far behind. Aside from the sparse runway lights at either end of the private landing strip, the only sign of life was a glow in the window of a low metal building a couple of hundred yards beyond the hangar. Her knee-high Chanel boots weren't designed for hiking, but they'd make it just fine if necessary. And the weight of the Glock in the inner pocket of her jacket reassured her.

"Do you need for us to wait with you?" the copilot called from the door of the plane.

"No, go on. My ride will be here any minute."

Without hesitating, he pulled up the stairs and closed the door, leaving her alone. She headed for the hangar and out of the way of the jet engines just as they roared to life. A minute later, the Gulfstream was gone.

The hangar was locked up tight. She tucked into a doorway out of the wind and retrieved her ComDev from her pocket. "Call Victor," she ordered. His voicemail answered.

"Damn it! Where are you?" She shivered as she pulled her winter jacket from her duffle and put it on.

A pair of headlights appeared in the distance heading her way. Relief washed over her. Gathering up her bags, she began walking toward the oncoming vehicle. It was moving fast over the rough road, its headlights bouncing as it took the ruts. The hair on the back of her neck prickled. This wasn't her brother's white Macan.

She dropped her duffle, drew the pistol from inside her jacket and slipped it into the right-hand pocket of her coat.

A dark-colored Tahoe ground to a halt twenty feet in front of her, blinding her in its high beams. She shielded her eyes and waited for Victor to get out. Several seconds passed and nothing. Something was very wrong. Using her psychic ability and Protector training, she scanned the vehicle. She detected a shielded mind, which meant another psychic. Great. The driver was either on her side or she had a fight on her hands. With no cover. In Chanel boots, damn it.

She slipped her hand into her picket and closed her fingers around the handle of the Glock. If the driver was a Dissembler, she'd know the moment she caught the scent of dark majik.

The truck door opened and a man got out. Every muscle in her body tensed for action, as she tasted the air. No noxious stench of the enemy. Still, something wasn't right. Even in the dark, she could see the man's head topped the SUV by a couple of inches. Her heart pounded and she cocked the pistol as he stepped from behind the door.

"Are you getting in or not?" His voice was deep, American-accented, and irritated.

Her hand clenched the handle of the Glock. "Who are you? Where's Victor?"

His chuckle startled her. "That son of a bitch didn't tell you."

The stranger stepped into the light. Chantal gasped. Her brain reeled. *No. Anyone but him.*

He'd changed in seven years, filled out and hardened. But it was him all right. Tanner Hays. The last time she'd seen him, he'd accused her of killing his best friend and walked away.

"Get in the truck," he said. "We have work to do tonight."

She didn't move. "Why did you agree to this assignment?"

"Orders."

"You knew you'd be working with me?"

"Yeah. Now get in the fucking truck."

Heat rushed through her body and her hands trembled. How

could Mark do this to her? He knew Tanner hated her and how devastated she'd been that he'd never given her the chance to explain. She glanced around. They were alone with nothing but black wilderness in sight. She had no choice but to go with him.

She picked up her bags, stalked to the SUV, and tossed them in the back seat. He was already in the driver's seat when she climbed in.

"Dressed to impress as usual," he said as the Tahoe started to move. "Hope you brought something besides those ridiculous boots."

"My work clothes are in my duffle. Victor said he was picking me up." Her brother would have appreciated her attire, not criticized it. "Where is Victor, anyhow?"

"Something urgent came up. He was at my place in Jackson for the last four days and had to leave early this morning—a stolen relic or amulet or something. He didn't fill me in on the details."

No, he wouldn't have. For security, Protectors operated on a need-to-know basis. "Where are we headed?"

"To a cabin I rented. A local archeologist called me about a clay tile one of the Blackfeet elders found in the intestines of a bear. You're here to read it."

"Of course," she muttered.

"The Blackfeet are close to the natural world and attuned to its energy. When one of them senses power in an object, we check it out."

He was right. This was what they did. Just not together, not for a long, long time.

"Can we call a truce?" she asked. "Neither of us wants to be here."

"Wrong. I like being here. I just don't want you here."

"Not your call or mine." Neither of them would ever refuse Mark's orders, but for very different reasons.

She stared out the window into the darkness for several minutes. The night was black and no signs of civilization lit the road ahead or behind. The dashboard lights threw a glow on Tanner and she finally gave in to the temptation to study him.

His face had lost its youthful warmth, transformed into a dark, brooding maturity that emphasized the high cheekbones and strong features of his mother's Native American ancestry. His dark hair was shorter than it used to be, just skimming his collar. And the scar was new. The angry line from the corner of his right eye to his jaw didn't so much disfigure his face as turn up the wattage on the masculine danger he exuded.

Warmth pooled in her stomach and she looked away. He'd grown into a handsome man, but that didn't change a thing between them. Still, she couldn't help remembering the way he'd kissed her—a kiss she'd never been able to forget.

# CHAPTER THREE

The rustic log cabin was charming, especially with all the modern conveniences. Chantal carried her bags into her bedroom and threw some water on her face. She started to change her boots then blew it off. If Tanner didn't like them, she sure as hell wasn't going to change. Besides, the heels reduced his height advantage—only by four inches, but every inch counted.

When she returned to the living room, a fire blazed in the stone fireplace, throwing cheery shadows on the floor and ceiling. With a different companion it could have been a romantic hideaway. However, the scowl Tanner threw her as he unpacked takeout from a greasy brown bag turned it into a battle zone.

"I got you a grilled tomato and cheese sandwich, coleslaw, and fries," he said. "Homemade brownies for dessert."

"Thanks." At least he'd remembered that she was a vegetarian like most of her first cousins, some of whom were animal telepaths.

While Tanner sat down at the table and began to unwrap the food, she got plates and silverware from the kitchen. There was even a bottle of Pinot Noir tempting her on the counter. That, she'd save for later.

She sat across from him and started to eat. "How do you know the guy who gave you the tile?"

"Hank and I worked together on a dig up here a couple years ago. He was born and raised on the Blackfeet reservation. Knows everyone around these parts—is related to most of them."

She was distracted by a puckered scar across the top of his right hand, a burn mark still pink against his tanned skin.

"Why did he call you?"

"He knows I'm interested in objects that are reported to have supernatural or mystical power. Three weeks ago, an elder named Johnny Hawkswing shot a black bear he thought was killing his goats. When he butchered it, he found this in its stomach." He opened a small white cardboard box—the kind earrings or a pin might come in—that was on the table next to him and pushed it in front of her. "Johnny said when he touched it he got a vision of snow and felt the cold down to his bones."

Inside, on a bed of cotton was a piece of clay about an inch square and a quarter-inch thick.

"Then what?" she asked.

"He took it to Hank."

"Did Hank have a vision too?"

"Didn't touch it except with tweezers. Do you recognize the markings?"

"They look like hieroglyphics." She studied the piece of clay, first from above, then squinting at it from different angles. "They're almost familiar, but not quite. Very delicate and detailed for the medium. The clay has been fired, not just dried, and it has a lot of silica in it. What's the clay like in this area?"

"Mostly brick red and loose, I think. Not dark gray."

"So probably not from around here." She didn't have to touch the tile to sense its power. Whatever it was, she picked up enough energy to know it packed quite a punch. "And he didn't mind if you borrowed it?"

"He gave it to us. He doesn't want it back. Johnny thinks it's cursed, so nobody around here wants it."

"Interesting. I'm surprised the tribe would give a piece of their heritage to outsiders."

He shrugged. "We're not sure it is their heritage or where this came from. That's why you're here—to read it."

"Can this wait until tomorrow? I only arrived in Los Angeles from Sydney this morning and hopped the flight here. The jet lag is catching up with me."

"No. We need to do it now. If something comes up that needs to be researched someone at headquarters can be on it overnight."

"You're not the one about to be tranced. I'd rather get some sleep first."

"Sorry." His tone said he wasn't in the least. "Where do you want to do this?"

Nowhere at the moment, she thought. The grilled cheese weighed a ton in her stomach and dread squeezed her chest. She was about to make herself completely vulnerable in front of a man who hated her. "On the sofa, I guess." She moved to the couch and settled into the oversized cushions. The fire danced merrily, or perhaps ominously.

Tanner dropped into the chair beside her and held out the box.

"If this thing kicks my ass..."

"I won't let it get out of hand," he said. "We've been here before. I know what to do."

She felt the heat rise on her face. The last time she'd trusted him, he'd been her friend and more. Their eyes met and she searched for any sign of warmth.

His sapphire eyes hardened and he handed her the little cardboard jewelry box. "The tile."

Wiping her hand on the leg of her jeans, she mentally fortified herself, cleared her thoughts, and opened her mind's shield.

"Here goes," she said and dumped the tile into her palm.

The jolt was instant and violent. Places, people, objects, and energy machine-gunned through her mind in a collage of information too rapid and vivid to sort through. Time swirled into a helix of present and past, churning in a maddening pattern that her psychic subconscious absorbed without understanding. It was as though her brain splintered into a dozen receptors, each operating by its own laws with its own software.

Her body shook uncontrollably with the cold. She just let it all happen. Then, abruptly, the deluge halted and her vision cleared. She blinked down at her lap which was now covered with a sofa pillow holding the tile, then up at Tanner. He'd planted the pillow and tilted her hand, so the tile fell onto it, ending her trance.

He watched her intently. "You okay?"

As usual, her mind's intuitive processor worked on the data with no conscious effort on her part. How that happened was as much a mystery to her as it was to everyone else. The psychic trip always heightened her senses. The fire crackled and flared while Tanner's steady breathing four feet away brushed her sensitized skin. Her head filled with the scent of leather, cedar, and the earthy male spice that was distinctly him.

"Wow." Oddly, the experience had given her a second wind. "Powerful little item your friend found."

"Executive summary?"

"Origin? Hard to say. The energy is too old and diluted to see its beginning—a couple of thousand years, I'd guess."

"So could you read any of its history?"

So much was fuzzy. She closed her eyes to let the impressions clarify. "It was hidden or lost for many centuries until traders sold it to the Shalamov."

"The Shalamov?"

"They control the delphic energy Source in Siberia, which explains the cold Hawkswing felt."

"I know who the Shalamov are," he said. "I'm just surprised it found its way here. When was that?"

"The Shalamov aren't much for keeping track of dates or time. I'd guess the twelfth or thirteenth century. It was a part of a larger structure—a box or container of some kind—that was created with an ancient protection ward." Other pieces of data sorted themselves out as she spoke. "Flight."

"As in air travel?"

"No, running away. A long journey, maybe five or six hundred years ago. An *ordinaire* priest and his son to his son's son and so on made their way east, living amongst the people of the land for years at a time, enduring cold and hardships until driven by the urgency to move on. Finally, the last caretaker—a priest or holy man of some kind—grew old without offspring and knew it was the end. He decided to hide the burden in a place where he believed it would be safe forever."

"What do you mean by burden?" he asked.

"I got the sense that whatever this thing was, it was awesome and fearful."

"Evil?"

Closing her eyes and concentrating, she tried to pinpoint the correct impression. "Of great power. Could go either way, I think."

He tilted the cardboard box next to the tile and used a Swiss army knife to prod it back onto the cotton. "Any idea where the hiding place is?"

Closing her eyes, she tried to sift through impressions to see the tile's journey backward. "The bear's animal energy and another animal energy—a fish, maybe—that's recent, then nothing for a long time except insects."

When she opened her eyes, he was staring at her thoughtfully without his usual disdain. "So the bear ate a fish who ate the tile?"

"Seems plausible."

"And before that?"

"It was a part of the box or container. The priest put it in something else before carrying it to its final resting place. I only get impressions of human or animal energy—mostly thoughts and feelings—when the being is actually in contact with the object. The man who hid the box knew enough about its power to protect himself from leaving a trail on it."

"So it could be anywhere." He glanced down at the tile, then at the fire. "Maybe it's just as well the damned thing stays hidden."

If they left it where it was, in a couple of days she could be in Paris, having dinner at L'Atelier with Adrien and his wife, Tate. "The last place I saw was a steep cliff, mountains on three sides, and a swiftly running river. The priest was deciding on how to descend to a sacred cave."

He snapped to attention. "In all the time I spent here, I would have heard of a sacred cave in the park. It must be hidden. Would you recognize this place again?"

"It was a long, long time ago."

"Would you recognize it?"

"If I saw the scene from the same place, maybe. But it could be anywhere." The trip from Australia was catching up with her again and she wanted to sleep. She stood up. "Let's talk in the morning. After coffee."

"You're going to bed now? We need to report in to Mark."

"He can wait. I'm beat."

Her ComDev began playing Queen's "Princes of the Universe" in her pocket, and she groaned. Her cousin was telepathic, but surely he wasn't omnipotent.

"Hello, Mark. We were just about to call you."

# CHAPTER FOUR

"Bottom line, Chantal." Mark Durand stood by the window of his Paris penthouse and watched the traffic on the Place Charles de Gaulle. It was just after 5:00 a.m. and still dark, but the city was already waking for the day. "Good or evil?"

"Maybe both," she replied. "The tile has incredible power. The bad news is, it's only a piece of a larger container, which is still missing."

"Explain."

Mark listened while Chantal and Tanner filled him in on what she had discovered, taking turns to add details and observations. His shoulders relaxed a fraction at their professionalism. He'd had reservations about sending them out together. The animosity between them wasn't a secret among the Protectors, but Mark knew Chantal had stormed into the warehouse in London all those years ago on Adrien's orders. He'd intentionally kept them apart since, but on this assignment he needed their combined expertise and psychic abilities. So far they seemed to be doing their job professionally, but how would they handle themselves if things got rough out there? If they needed to cover each other's asses?

"Have you ever heard of the Shalamov ridding themselves of an artifact or a cursed object?" Tanner asked.

"Or that some power object went missing?" Chantal asked. "Maybe Kirill mentioned a legend or myth."

Mark winced at the mention of the Shalamov heir. They'd been friends—Adrien, Mark, and Kirill—until that horrible day in Siberia when Irina Demidova betrayed both Adrien and Kirill. Adrien had been crippled and his friend's mind destroyed. Mark shut down the memory and reached for his coffee. "I don't remember anything about a power object, but there were family secrets he never shared."

"Then we'll post the question on the Protector board and see what we can find out."

"No. See what you can find out about the marking and the material." Mark raked a hand through his short blond hair. "Don't you have a friend in research who specializes in symbols and hieroglyphics?"

"There's a woman who's done some work for me," Chantal said.

"Contact her, but don't mention the object's history. As far as anyone knows, you're investigating claims of supernatural activity at an Indian burial site."

"Will do," Tanner said. "Chantal had a vision of where the box might be buried."

Chantal snorted. "Yeah, a couple hundred years ago. Nobody has found it in all that time. I say let's leave it for another few centuries."

Mark grimaced. That would be his choice too, but once something powerful surfaced, trouble always came out of the woodwork. "Do you think you could find it?"

"Maybe," Tanner said.

"No," Chantal protested. "The park is huge and my vision wasn't that clear. At best, it's a long shot."

"We know a bear ate a fish that ate the tile," Tanner said. "Hawkswing found it in the bear's intestines. Maybe we could find out where the bear caught his last meal and go from there."

"And how's that going to work?" Chantal asked. "Lay my hands on a bear carcass? Hawkswing probably butchered and ate him by now. That, or the meat's in a freezer and the innards long gone."

"We can talk to Hawkswing," Tanner snapped.

"And trying to find the box or whatever it is will still be a shot in the dark," she grumbled.

Mark sighed. "Combine your talents and look for it. Tanner, if Chantal says it's powerful, it is. You need to follow your instincts on this. I'd rather leave the thing buried, but there's always the chance it could fall into the wrong hands. If there's any way to find it, then bring it in."

Tanner swore. "There's going to be some radical climbing in frigid temperatures. I'd be better off on my own."

"No, you wouldn't," Mark said. "This is your first assignment since Mexico—you don't know how your injuries will affect you in harsh conditions. She's got better covert operations training than most of the US military. You're agents on a mission, so work together." He waited for Tanner to argue. Only silence. Whether he was resigned or fuming, it didn't matter. He owed Mark his life and wouldn't refuse a direct order.

"Should I call in for equipment and supplies?" Tanner's tone was resigned.

"Buy what you need locally. If there's something you can't get, I'll have it overnighted to you myself. Talk to the old man and see what you can find out, but don't give out any more information than necessary."

"We'll go see him tomorrow," Tanner replied.

"Then both of you drop off the radar. That's an order."

"Is there something you're not telling us?" Tanner asked.

Mark hung up.

# CHAPTER FIVE

The fire had burned out during the night. Tanner lit some kindling and threw on a couple of logs to take the chill out of the living room. He'd tried to sleep—even drifted off a couple of times—but mostly he'd stared at the ceiling, planning their next move and trying not to think about the woman in the next room. They'd track down Johnny Hawkswing and ask him about the bear and his vision. Then they'd have to find the place Chantal had seen.

As much as he hated to admit it, she was right. The relic had been hidden for a few hundred years and might stay that way for many more. But his gut told him once the tile made its way back to the world, the game changed. Rumors spread quickly among the locals and superstition would escalate the interest. He couldn't help believing if one tile had surfaced, then there were more pieces out there.

He prodded the fire until it flared and quietly replaced the poker in its stand. They had next to nothing to go on and yet he felt in his bones he could do this. He had to do this. If they could find any part of the route taken by the person who'd hidden the object, he might be able to follow the energy trail.

The white cardboard jewelry box waited on the dining table. He reached for it. His gift was reading the residual energy left by humans in places, not on objects. Still, he could sense the tile had some kind of mystical property. After a moment's hesitation, he dumped it in his hand.

Revulsion surged into his stomach and he dropped the tile. Immediately the nausea receded. He swallowed hard and drew in a deep breath to clear his head. There had been no vision and, yet, he knew there had been a reason for his physical reaction—some magic that repelled him. He studied the symbol.

Javier would have been able to read the spell—or part of it—in that symbol with a touch. Old anger and grief weighed in his chest. If it weren't for Chantal's recklessness, Javier would be alive now. Countless times over the past seven years, those five minutes had replayed in his head—the gunfire, the explosion, the inferno that incinerated his best friend.

He couldn't think about that morning now, or at all until this assignment was over.

The bedroom door opened. He clenched his teeth and focused on his java, unable to greet her like a civilized human being.

"Coffee smells good," she said, in a sleep-husky voice that twitched his groin. His survival instinct took a cigarette break and he glanced over his shoulder. *Damn.*

Her faded blue jeans sat low on her slim hips and the yellow turtleneck was loose enough to be comfortable, but still called attention to her firm breasts. With her auburn hair down and no makeup, she reminded him of her teenaged self—the girl who could never resist a dare. He'd liked that girl. A lot.

"I slept like the dead." When she ran her fingers through the crown of her shoulder length hair, a flash of flat stomach peeked between her sweater and jeans. "Only good part of jet lag."

Instinct returned and he opened his laptop just as the familiar scent of French rose soap wafted his way. He breathed through his mouth while she made a cup of coffee and took a sip.

She moaned in approval. "Damn, that's good."

His body reacted instantly. All those months isolated in his cabin had affected his brain, not to mention other parts of his anatomy.

"Want some eggs?" she called. "I can make an omelet or frittata. And what do you know, this looks like homemade bread."

"I'm trying to work." His voice sounded like forty-grit sandpaper.

"Your laptop's still booting. What's your problem?"

He glanced back, prepared to lash out, but the words caught in his throat. "My problem is you," he said through his teeth.

"Is that supposed to be a news flash?"

He clenched the mug. "Forget it. We have a lot of research ahead and without tapping into Durand Tech resources…"

"Big deal." She shook her head. "I've been in the Australian Outback for three years working with *ordinaires* and we did just fine without all of Mark's high tech toys. You boys in the home office have lost your edge."

"Bullshit. If you did just fine, why'd you spend a month in jail?"

"For shooting a son of a bitch in the ass, as if you didn't know. Be careful, Hays, or I may put some lead in that tight little butt of yours. You want breakfast or not?"

Keeping his jaw from dropping took some effort. He remembered her cooking, almost as good as her mother's world-famous cuisine. Yeah, he wanted breakfast. "Three fried eggs and a couple pieces of toast."

"*Please.*" A sweet smile spread across her face, but her eyes still threw daggers at him.

"Please."

"That's better." She turned her back to him and he forced his gaze back to his laptop.

Google Earth showed the general geography of the area—mountains, valleys, lakes, and rivers. If the box was hidden in the park, hundreds of square miles of wilderness fit Chantal's vague description. They needed to find evidence that would reduce the scope of their search. They needed more information about the bear.

He was still clicking away when a plate clinked on the table next to his arm. "Eat up while it's hot." She plopped herself and her plateful of frittata across the table and began to eat. He'd have taken issue with her bossy attitude had his rumbling stomach not seized command.

He scarfed down the eggs in a couple of swallows and finished both pieces of toast. As he pushed back his chair to make more, she flipped one of her slices onto his plate.

"I sent photos and a material scan of the tile to Kara at DT last night," she said.

"Kara Hagen?"

"Yes. Do you know her?"

He picked up her toast. "She's done research for me a few times. I've suspected she hacked into classified and private databases more than once." And got him information no one else had been able to, so he hadn't complained.

"She messaged this morning that she didn't recognize the exact symbol, but said it looked Sumerian or Mesopotamian. She's going to get back to me as soon as she has more."

"How did it end up with the Shalamov and why would they rid themselves of it?"

"We may never know that," she said. "So what do you want to do next?"

"I'm going to call Hank and see if we can visit Hawkswing. He might be able to tell us more about the bear and the fish."

He shoved the last bit of toast in his mouth, took out his ComDev, and tapped the screen. A moment later the call connected. "Hey, Hank, this is Tanner."

"Where are you?" his friend asked warily.

"At a rental cottage near the lake."

"Whitefish Lake?"

"Yeah. Is something wrong?"

"What can I do for you?" Hank's tone wasn't friendly.

"Can you set up a meeting with Johnny Hawkswing? We'd like to ask him about the bear."

"Well, that's going to be tough. Something killed him early this morning."

*Something killed him.* The words echoed in Tanner's head and a cold dread crept through his chest. "An animal attacked him?"

"Put it on speaker," Chantal hissed.

He tapped the speaker icon. "Hank, are you still there?"

"Yeah."

His friend's silence worried him. "What do you mean something? A bear or a wolf?"

"No. His grandson said a spirit sucked the life from his body. There were no marks, no blood. He crumbled to the ground dead."

Tanner huffed in exasperation. "He probably had a stroke or a heart attack. Did the coroner examine the body?"

"His grandson saw what happened. Johnny was on the rocks by the river and the moonlight was bright. Jason saw the spirit, but was paralyzed and unable to help the old man."

Tanner shook his head. The kid had probably been asleep or frightened and made up the whole story. "Would it be OK if we talked to the boy?"

"Boy?" Hank asked.

"The grandson."

"Oh, he isn't a boy. He's a surgeon in Salt Lake City."

Chantal pulled her chair closer to the ComDev and leaned in. "Hi, Hank, this is Chantal Durand. I think you know my brother, Victor."

"Sure. He's a good man."

"I know it's a bad time for the family, but can you please tell us how to contact the grandson? It may not be connected, but we'd like to learn more about how Mr. Hawkswing found the tile."

Tanner frowned at her and whispered, "What are you doing?"

She lifted her pointer finger to signal him to wait. He wanted to bat it away.

"You think Johnny's death might be connected to the tile?" Hank asked. "How?"

"We don't know one way or the other," she replied. "We just want to eliminate the possibility it is."

"How would you do that?"

Tanner leaned into her space and glared. As usual, Chantal was opening doors that should be left closed.

"Look, Hank," he said, eyes still boring into her, "All we want to do is ask the grandson if Johnny told him anything about the bear—where he shot him and anything unusual about the stomach contents."

Hank cleared his throat. "I probably should have told you more when you picked up the tile. Johnny's story just sounded so far-fetched."

"How about you tell us now," Chantal said.

"I'm not sure exactly where Johnny shot the bear. He claimed to be near Doris Creek Campground, but I'd guess it was someplace he shouldn't have been. He said when he slit open the animal's stomach he found two trout; one was partially digested and the other looked as if it had just been swallowed alive. Of course, that was unlikely, but when he pulled it out of the bear's stomach, it seemed to glow and wriggle in his hand for a moment before stiffening. He cut the fish open and that's when he found the tile in its stomach." Hank paused.

"Was he near a lake?" Tanner asked.

"Doris is next to Hungry Horse Reservoir," Hank said. "I didn't believe the trout was still alive, but I humored him. He was an old man and sometimes told fantastical stories."

"What happened next?" Chantal asked.

"He said when he touched the tile he was transported to a world of ice and snow so frigid he thought his heart would stop. He lost consciousness and when he woke the tile lay next to him on the ground. He wanted to get rid of the thing, but was afraid someone else would find it and die."

Chantal's expression was unreadable, her mouth tight and her eyes riveted on the ComDev. "Anything else we should know?"

"That's all I can tell you," Hank replied. "Maybe I should have told Tanner more when I gave him the tile, but Johnny was a superstitious old man with a lively imagination. I wasn't sure what was true and how much just made it a good story."

"We'd still like to talk to his grandson," Tanner said.

"It's a bad time. The family's pretty broken up."

"We won't push," Chantal said, "But if there's any connection…"

There was a pause. "Okay. The grandson's name is Jason."
Hank rattled off a phone number.

"Thanks," Tanner said. "And we're sorry about Johnny."

"Me too." Hank clicked off.

Chantal crossed her arms over her chest and glared at him.
"Why didn't you ask more questions when you picked up the tile? It
sounds like it almost killed Johnny."

"You were waiting on the runway to be picked up." He crossed
his arms over his chest. "I figured you'd be able to tell me more than
Hank could."

"And it kept the bloody fish alive. That would have been good
intel to have before I let it trance me."

"Johnny didn't have a shield."

"I opened myself to its energy."

"That's why you're here. To find out what we're dealing with."
And yet, he'd insisted she read the tile when she was tired and not
a hundred percent. Too bad. It was what they did, and he'd been
right to push her. She, however, had been out of line. "Why the
hell would you tell Hank the old man's death might be related to
the tile?"

"Because it might be."

He glared at her. "How do you figure that? Is the tile so powerful
it conjured up spirits?"

"How should I know?"

"But you went there with Hank."

"What if it wasn't a spirit? What if it was a Dissembler with
mind control magic?"

"In the middle of nowhere at night?" He laughed at the
absurdity of her suggestion. "Okay, why would a Dissembler kill an
old man?"

# CHAPTER SIX

"Why do they do anything? Power." Although Tanner had been a Protector a year longer than she had, Chantal had a known about the covert war between the Durand Protectors and the Brazilian Sentier—currently Tolian—and his Dissembler followers when Tanner was still a clueless kid playing in the cornfields of Nebraska. "Murder, terrorism, violence, chaos—it's what they do. If a Dissembler got wind of Johnny's find, invading his mind and killing him in the process is just part of the job."

"They aren't everywhere."

Her eyebrows rose. "You were in disguise and still they recognized you in Mexico. All the First Order assumes Tolian's keeping tabs on us and any other Protector his underlings have identified—which you were years ago."

He winced. "You're paranoid. They can't be everywhere."

"No, but fifty years ago they had to track the Durand with feet-on-the ground surveillance. Now technology does a lot of the legwork for them."

"I'm not buying that in this case. How would a Dissembler learn about the tile?"

"Same way you did. Somebody called him."

His thoughts played out on his face—skepticism dissolved into concern. "Are you saying someone else may know about the box or container or whatever it is?"

"Not about the box specifically. Without the tile and the ability to read it, they couldn't. But they might suspect it's part of something bigger and more powerful."

He let out a long breath. "Then we'd better find it quickly and get out of here."

"So let's call the grandson."

Tanner picked up his ComDev and she rattled off the number Hank had given them. "Put it on speaker."

He set it on the table close in front of him. "Keep your mouth shut this time."

Her face heated, her hands itched to conk him on the forehead with her ComDev. In four rings, a man answered, "Jason Hawkswing."

"My name is Tanner Hays. I'm a friend of Hank Morris. He gave me the tile your grandfather found in the bear."

A short pause. "We don't want it back."

"I know. My colleague and I just wanted to ask a few questions. She's an anthropologist and I'm an archeologist, and we investigate unusual incidents attributed to ancient objects."

"My grandfather is dead. The family is preparing to lay him to rest."

"We don't want to intrude, but if you could give us a few minutes of your time we'd be grateful," Tanner said.

"Did Hank tell you how he died?" Jason asked.

Tanner glanced at her questioningly. She shook her head. A firsthand account would be far more valuable than Hank's.

"He mentioned you were there," Tanner said. "Anything you can tell us would be helpful."

A woman's voice called from the background. "My aunt needs me," Hawkswing said. "I have to go back to the campsite to pick up some gear I left behind. If you want to go, I can meet you at three o'clock. There's a barbecue joint called Sister Lil's on Highway 2 about a mile before you get to Flathead River."

"I know it," Tanner said.

She waved her hand to get his attention. This might be their only chance to meet with Hawkswing and they had to get as much as they could from him. She whispered, "Ask if he was wearing gloves when he died."

He nodded. "Was your grandfather wearing gloves when he died?"

"Sure. It was cold last night."

"Could we borrow them for a few days?" Tanner asked.

"Why?" Hawkswing asked.

"We have an experimental device that detects traces of all kinds of substances. We might find a clue to what happened."

"I saw what happened." The doctor's voice hardened.

"We just want to eliminate every possibility, sir."

"Fine. I'll bring the gloves."

"Thanks for the help. We'll see you at three."

He ended the call and stared at the ComDev for a moment before looking up. Chantal met his dark gaze all too aware they were wading into dangerous territory. Together. Again.

"Are you sure you want to read the old man's death gloves?" Tanner asked.

She shrugged, pretending the prospect didn't frighten her. "At least I know what I'm in for."

He rose and pocketed his ComDev. "Don't take dangerous chances, Chantal. We don't know that Johnny's death is connected to the tile."

"Thanks for your vote of confidence."

His voice hardened. "I've seen you in action."

But he'd never let her tell him her side of the story.

• • •

"*Merde.*" Chantal froze in the doorway of Sister Lil's and gawked. Tanner's hand on her back felt more like a shove into the dimly lit bar than a courteous guiding. Then again, her feet refused to budge when she spotted all the huge elk heads hanging on the walls. They looked like a herd had poked their heads through the clapboard to watch the patrons eat brisket. Her family had the largest collection of taxidermy animals in Europe, but those were entire animals. The disembodied heads were just wrong.

"Go with it," Tanner hissed. "This is hunting country and trophies are a big draw to this place."

"Tell me someone ate the meat."

"And tanned the hides most likely."

She moved to the bar and automatically scanned the room for anyone who might pose a problem; she noted Tanner doing the same. They'd both been through the rigors of Protector training, heightening their ability to detect malignant psychic forces as well as dark magic. The dozen or so patrons checked them out then went back to whatever they were doing.

"Tame crowd," she muttered, then noted the blond cowgirl behind the bar giving Tanner the once over. "The bartender looks like she'd have a piece of you, though."

He threw the woman a sexy smile. "I'll keep that in mind."

The wooden tables and chairs could have been right out of an old western movie, and the bar was stacked logs with a single slab of wood for a counter.

A stocky man in a denim jacket, plaid shirt, and jeans entered from a side door and headed their way. "Tanner Hays?"

"Yes. Dr. Hawkswing?"

The doctor's eyes crinkled when he grinned. "Around here I'm just Jason."

Chantal liked him right away. "I'm Chantal Durand. We're sorry for your loss. Thanks for meeting us on such short notice and at such a difficult time."

Jason's face sobered. "Thanks. He was a good man. Ornery as hell, but his heart was always in the right place."

"Can we buy you lunch?" Tanner asked.

"Sure. There are picnic style tables in the back room or we can order at the bar and eat in here."

"Here's good," Tanner said. "How about the table in the corner?"

They ordered from the bartender who flirted with Tanner while she filled pint glasses with beer from the tap.

Beers in hand, the two men headed for a table and Chantal

followed. Where Tanner was six foot three inches of lean muscle, Jason couldn't be more than five foot nine and had the thicker body of a weightlifter. Both had black hair, but the doctor's was short and straight while Tanner's had a slight wave and licked his collar. And yet their angular features and chiseled bone structure clearly proclaimed their shared Native American heritage.

When they reached the table, Tanner claimed the chair with its back to the wall and Jason seemed to remember her existence and his manners.

"Where would you like to sit, Ms. Durand?" he asked, flashing her a charming smile.

"Just Chantal, please." She crossed to the seat to Tanner's right, which was closer to a side wall and had the second best view of the front door. "This is fine."

The doctor held her chair for her then sat down next to her with his back to the room. He took a gulp of beer and set his glass down. "So what do you want to ask me?"

Tanner planted his forearms on the table and leaned in. "What do you know about the bear your uncle shot?"

"Black bear about, six and a half feet, five hundred pounds. They're common enough around here."

"What about the fish with the tile in his stomach? Any idea what it was or where it might have come from?" Tanner asked.

"Yeah. That was kind of odd. It was a Westslope Cutthroat Trout, but it hadn't been digested."

"Why is that odd?" Chantal asked.

"Because the trout in the lakes around here are all stocked lake trout. The Westslope requires pure, cold water for survival, and a secure habitat protected from the bigger, stronger, non-native species. If the bear ate it from one of the remote lakes where they generally live, it would have been digested by the time Johnny shot him."

"Maybe he stole it from some fisherman who caught it in a remote lake," Tanner suggested.

Chantal nudged Tanner with her foot and subtly shook her

head when he glanced at her. No human could have caught the fish or she would have sensed the human energy in the tile.

"How far do these bears roam?"

"Can't say I've ever thought much about it," Jason replied. "I'm sure someone in Fish and Wildlife could tell you."

Tanner pulled a map out of his jacket pocket and opened it on the table. "Do you know where your grandfather killed the bear?"

Jason studied the map for several seconds then put his finger on a spot in Flathead National Forest. "About here."

"And where did he die?" Chantal asked.

This time Jason didn't hesitate. "Here."

The two spots were at least eight miles apart. They sat in silence, studying the map until a teenaged girl plopped a tray of food on the edge of the table and everyone claimed their order.

The discussion went on hold until Tanner and Jason had made a serious dent in the mountains of brisket and ribs and set down their knives and forks. A second round of beer was delivered and the table cleared.

"What happened last night?" Tanner asked.

Jason glanced around the bar, which had cleared out except for two old coots at a table near the door. "If you're ready to go, we can talk in the truck on our way to the site."

"Sure," Tanner said. "We can take our Tahoe."

She nodded to him. The vehicle was standard Protector issue, which meant it had been retrofitted to be faster, sturdier, and more powerful than anything Chevy had ever produced. It was also bulletproof and had secure storage for valuables, weapons, and equipment. Mark hadn't been amused when she mentioned the fleet was a drug smuggler's wet dream.

"The road gets pretty rough and narrow. You sure you want to risk your shocks and paint job?"

"No problem," Tanner assured him as he signaled the waitress for their check. "It's her cousin's hunting truck; it's had some hard use."

Chantal would have preferred the front seat, but Tanner insisted

Jason ride shotgun to give him directions, which would give her a chance to record the conversation discreetly on her ComDev.

About five miles from the bar, they turned off the main road onto a well-maintained gravel track that quickly began to climb through the pine forest. She caught glimpses of snow-capped mountains in the distance and shivered. There was no way she was sticking around until it started snowing in the lower country. The further they drove, the rougher the road became, and the more uneasy she felt. "So what happened last night?"

Jason glanced at her over his shoulder and nodded grimly. "Johnny called me around two in the afternoon and asked me to ride out to the rocks where we used to fish when I was a kid. I was in the hardware store buying a new kitchen faucet for my mother, so I asked him if we could go today instead. He didn't want to wait. It was almost dusk before we set out. The full moon lit the way and the trail's well marked. Johnny rode a mare he swore was the reincarnation of my grandmother. I rode my uncle's buckskin stallion because he needed the exercise."

"Was that unusual?" Chantal asked.

Jason nodded. "My grandfather was ninety-two years old. We hadn't taken horses out there for years. I told him it was a bad idea and his bones would ache for a week. He wouldn't listen, the stubborn old man. Said he missed the old ways when our people were connected to the earth."

"Did you sense anything unusual during the ride?" Tanner asked. "Anything that felt threatening or off?"

Jason laughed. "You're talking to the wrong guy. I've never had an ounce of intuition. Take after my mother that way. When I was a kid, Johnny and my father tried to teach me to sense things—an animal approaching, danger, even spirits—but I never felt anything. They decided I didn't have the gift and gave up on me following them as tribal leaders."

"So you became a doctor, a man of science." Chantal opened her psychic senses to read his energy and had to agree; he had no psychic abilities whatsoever, which made her observation of his grandfather's death even more puzzling. "Why did Johnny want you to go out there with him?"

Jason's gaze fixed on the road ahead. "He said death was watching him from the shadows and he wanted to meet it in the open, not wait for it in his bed. I told him that was nonsense. He was still a healthy man." He took a deep breath and slowly let it out. "Obviously I was wrong."

"Maybe not," Tanner said. "Could you have been followed?"

Jason frowned. "Not easily, but I guess it's possible. The trail's too narrow and winding for cars and trucks, and I think I would have heard an ATV or motorcycle."

"You weren't listening," she said.

"No, and between us talking and the horses tromping along the dirt road, we made a fair amount of noise. Come to think of it, Vegas—my mount—was more skittish than usual. I figured he smelled bear or something. Once we got to the campsite, I tied the horses in the clearing, close enough to the fire pit to keep them safe, and gathered some wood while Johnny climbed the boulder where we always sat to fish."

"How far away was he?" she asked. "Could you see him from where you were?"

"Him, the creek, the path from the woods. It couldn't have been twenty yards, and the clearing was lit up by the full moon." He pointed to a fork in the road ahead. "Go right."

Tanner veered right and the Tahoe bounced down a rocky incline to a large clearing along the river.

"Park here," Jason said. "The campsite is on the other side of that line of pines."

As Tanner parked, Chantal wanted to ask what he was picking up. Obviously, he wasn't any more eager to get out and read the place where Johnny died than she had been to read the tile the night before. Once those visions invaded your head, they were there forever.

Despite witnessing his grandfather's death in this place, Jason had no reservations about getting on with their errand. He got out and headed for the fire pit in the center of the dirt clearing.

When he was out of earshot, she studied the tension in Tanner's face. "You okay?"

He shook off whatever was bothering him and threw her a cocky half smile. "This is what we do. Let's do it."

Jason's gear—an electric lamp and a Yeti cooler bag—sat on a bench fashioned from a split log spanning two stumps. He paused near the burned-out fire and squatted to examine something in the dirt. As Tanner and Chantal approached, he reached for it.

"Don't touch that," Chantal said sharply.

"Find something?" Tanner asked.

Jason pointed to a white circle with a flat round stone about two inches in diameter. Half was painted red and half black. "What do you think this is?"

Unconsciously, she wrapped her arms around herself and tucked her hands in her armpits. Crouching, she examined the circle drawn with fine white crystals.

Tanner knelt beside her. "Salt?"

"Probably." She braced herself, licked a finger and reached out her hand.

Tanner grabbed her wrist. "Don't touch it. Let me."

The warmth of his skin on hers felt intimate and his voice held a note of concern she hadn't expected. Her gaze flipped to his and for a moment she could almost believe he didn't hate her.

He turned his attention to tasting the white stuff. "Yup. Salt."

She took a picture with her ComDev. "We need to take the stone. These will protect you." She held out gloves and a pouch— they were made of a fiber that shielded the wearer from psychic energy and magic.

"Ancilon?" he asked.

"Yes."

He put on the gloves but still used his hunting knife to pick up the painted stone and drop it into the pouch.

"Where were you standing when your grandfather was attacked?" she asked Jason.

The doctor glanced around the clearing, pausing on the fire pit to his right and a pile of cut logs behind him. "Just about here. Funny, I didn't notice the circle last night."

"You weren't meant to."

"Were any of the emergency personnel who came out here last night in this area?" Tanner asked.

"Yeah. The fire was roaring by the time they arrived and it was a chilly night. I had coffee in my pack and one of the guys made a pot for the sheriff's men. They stood around while the coroner and his assistant examined my grandfather."

"Would you tell us exactly what happened?" Tanner asked.

"I was here feeding the fire to get a blaze going and Johnny was on the rock over there." Jason pointed to a gray, flat-topped rock the size of an RV.

From where she stood the sides looked vertical. "How'd he get up there?"

"There are stepping stones and footholds on the river side." Jason shoved his hands in his pockets.

"Pretty impressive for an old man," Tanner observed.

Jason nodded. "The fire had finally caught on and I was going for a couple more logs when he cried out. I looked up in time to see a dense fog envelop him. I tried to help him, but my limbs wouldn't move and even my voice locked in my throat. I watched him struggle to get free, but the fog sucked the spirit from his body, and he crumbled to the ground." His voice trembled, then cracked. "After a minute or two, the fog dissolved and the paralysis drained from my body. When I finally reached him, Johnny wasn't breathing and had no pulse. I called 911 and tried to revive him. I did everything I could, but by the time help arrived, he was gone."

"He was an old man," Tanner said gently.

"And I'm a doctor. I should have been able to save him."

Tanner glanced at her and their eyes locked for several seconds. Neither of them was a telepath, but they'd always had an uncanny ability to sense each other's thoughts. In their world, the line between life and death often blurred, and he was about to straddle that line. The resolve in his eyes was tinged with dread and she understood how he felt.

"We can take Jason back and return tomorrow morning," she said.

Tanner shook his head. "We're here. I'll climb the rock. Why don't you and Jason check out the nearby campsites for recent activity?"

In other words, get the *ordinaire* out of range in case things get weird. Trancing in front of *ordinaires* was never a good idea. The less they knew, the better.

"Will do," Jason said and headed for a cluster of lean-tos and picnic tables tucked in the woods.

When Jason was out of earshot, she asked, "Are you sure you want to do this?"

Tanner shrugged. "Are we ever sure?"

He'd been there to break her trance the night before. Tanner reading the death site alone—anything could happen. "No, but that rock's pretty high. Should you fall…"

"I'm a good climber and I won't let down my shield fully when I'm up there. The residual energy will tell me what killed Johnny."

The sun dropped behind a mountain and the temperature seemed to plummet ten degrees. A shiver rolled up her body. "Be careful."

He nodded, his expression grim, then turned to scale the monolith.

# CHAPTER SEVEN

The huge block of sandstone hadn't seemed so imposing from across the clearing. Up close, the thing was almost three times Tanner's height with rough, vertical sides. He slowly circled its base until he reached the river side. What Jason had called "steps" were no more than a series of footholds and indentations—adequate for a seasoned climber in his prime, but crude for a ninety-two-year-old man to navigate.

As he grabbed the first handhold, a wave of nausea rolled over him, and his foot nearly lost its purchase. The residual energy of malevolence. Swallowing hard, he reinforced his psychic shield and ignored the barbecue roiling his stomach. The climb took less than a minute, but by the time he stood at the top, sweat that had nothing to do with exertion rolled down his back, plastering his shirt to his skin.

The air carried the putrid odor of terror, and death still clung to the rock. He didn't need to fully open his psychic senses to know how Johnny had died.

Jason had been partially correct, the life had been sucked out of the old man, but not by a spirit, by a telepath who had used a powerful mind control spell on the doctor to cloud his perception.

All the signs were there, including an oddly shaped red stain about the width of an orange. Tanner squatted and studied the spot. Blood. He removed his glove and carefully brushed his fingertip over the rock. Even with his psychic shield at full strength, a jolt of terror convulsed through him and he yanked his hand back. His heart pounded. The terror had been soul deep, the old man's fear of something more horrifying than death.

Tanner's memory flashed back to his own excruciating ordeal in the Mexican dungeon almost two years ago—the engrossing pain that wracked his body and mind when he was tortured by the drug lord's thugs. That evil had almost extinguished his will to live and would have killed him had Mark not shown up and gotten him out. He shuddered and forced himself back to the present. Johnny's death had been mercifully quick, but Tanner had no doubt that his murderer had invaded his mind before ending his life.

Tanner pulled his ComDev from his pocket, photographed the spot, then rose and took pictures of the rock and the camp clearing below. From this angle, he could see that the lines etched in the dirt, though trampled, formed a pentagram. Not a common Indian symbol, but not unknown among the tribes either. The painted stone and salt could have anchored Jason within the star shape, and yet, the logistics of the spell were impossible unless the intruder knew ahead of time where Johnny and his grandson were headed.

A telepath could have read Johnny's mind or maybe Jason's. That meant someone had followed one or the other. But why?

On the far side of the clearing Chantal and Jason were deep in conversation. As if she felt his gaze, she looked up and gestured at him with the universal hand signal for "Okay". He gave her a thumbs-up and she nodded.

Concern? Camaraderie? Both were dangerous when applied to her, and forgetting that could get him killed. He turned away to climb back down the rock.

The descent was quick and by the time he reached the others, he'd almost shaken the effects of the malevolent energy. The crisp air cleaned the foulness from his lungs and cleared his head.

Chantal stood next to Jason, her arms wrapped around her body. "Sure gets chilly when the sun goes down, doesn't it? Have you seen enough, Tanner?"

"Yeah." More than enough.

"Then let's go," Chantal said. "I could use a cup of hot chocolate."

"Or a shot of tequila." Leaving this place behind could only improve his dark mood.

Jason picked up his lantern and cooler bag. "Got what I came for, so I'm ready to go."

As they approached the Tahoe, Tanner's ComDev vibrated. He checked the screen, which read: INTRUSION WARNING

"Hold up," he said and stopped.

"What is it?" Chantal asked.

"I don't know." He tapped into the Tahoe's monitoring system and watched the motion-triggered surveillance video on mute. Two men on foot approached the truck and tried to pick the locks. These guys were amateurs and no match for Durand Tech security. One swung a tire iron at the driver's side window. He obviously hadn't expected bulletproof glass. They seemed to argue, then scurried off the way they came.

Chantal cleared her throat loudly. "Want to share?"

"Someone tried to break into the Tahoe."

"Your phone told you that?" Jason asked. "Where do I get one?"

"It's just some app I downloaded, Watch My Car or something like that." Chantal rolled her eyes at him.

"Cool," Jason said, then glanced around the parking area. "It wouldn't tell you if they're hiding in the bushes, would it?"

"No, so let's get out of here."

A half hour later, they pulled into Sister Lil's parking lot. The drive back had been awkwardly quiet. With the *ordinaire* in the Tahoe, Tanner couldn't tap into its monitoring system and Chantal was absorbed in something on her own ComDev.

She swore under her breath. "You knew, didn't you?"

Wasn't too hard to figure out what she was talking about, but he ignored her for the time being. "Where's your truck?" he asked Jason.

"The red pickup over there."

Tanner brought the Tahoe to a stop next to the truck. "Thanks for your help, Jason."

"I appreciate the ride and the company. I borrowed the cooler from my brother-in-law and he had a fit when I came home without it. Said he paid three hundred bucks for it. I wasn't looking forward to going back out there alone." Jason opened his door.

"Oh," Chantal said, "I almost forgot. Did you bring the gloves?"

Jason shook his head. "Nobody knew where they were. My mother said he wasn't wearing them when the ambulance arrived at the hospital. Sorry."

"No problem," Tanner said. "You be careful, man."

They watched Jason climb into the Chevy pickup and pull out onto the road before Tanner opened his door. "I'll just be a minute."

He circled to the back wheel-well and groped around for the tracker stuck there with a magnet. It wasn't much bigger than a quarter—something easily purchased online. He surveyed the vehicles in the parking lot until his attention landed on a U-Haul truck towing a Honda Civic with North Dakota plates. Hopefully, these people were moving to a warm climate, far south. With a quick glance around, he planted the tracker on the truck and headed back to the Tahoe.

No sooner had he opened his door than Chantal laid into him. "How long did you know we were being tracked?"

He started the truck and slowly made his way to the highway.

"Damn it, Tanner, answer me."

He pointed to a small icon on the screen of what looked like a satnav system. "Since we left here the first time." Tapping the icon pulled up a video of the small boy who planted the tracker. "Figured someone paid him to tag us and letting them follow us would tell us who."

She crossed her thickly padded arms over her chest and glared at him. "You should have told me."

"You're armed and you have lightning responses. I'm armed and had an eye out for them. We were covered."

"We're a team here. You still should have warned me."

"They weren't after us. They wanted to search the Tahoe."

"For the tile?"

"I don't think it was any secret that Johnny found it and Hank gave it to an outsider. We show up the day after Johnny's death and meet Jason. Maybe they were following him?"

She nodded thoughtfully. "Any guess who 'they' might be? Not Dissemblers."

"No. You didn't get a whiff of Dissembler majik, did you?"

"No. Then who?"

"I don't know," he said.

"Did you pick up anything on the rock? Maybe who killed Johnny?"

"Whoever it was is a telepath with dark majik. He terrified the shit out of the old man before he died. I wouldn't be surprised if Hawkswing's heart just stopped, or maybe he had a stroke from fright."

"It wasn't a death touch, was it?" Her voice held an odd undertone.

"You don't believe there *is* such a thing, do you?"

"I know there is."

"How?"

She shook her head. "Just trust me. There is."

Her certainty sent a shiver through his gut. "It was like the guy scrambled the energy so I couldn't read it."

"Is that even possible?"

"Apparently."

"Did you pick up anything inside the pentagram?" she asked.

"You saw that too?"

She let out an unladylike snort. "Who do you think you're working with, some clueless distant cousin just out of basic? Don't insult my competence."

"Nobody's insulting your competence."

"Fine. So we know whoever killed Johnny wields some serious magic to do the deed and cover his tracks. Where do we go from here?"

"We only have one solid clue," he said. "The stone."

"That's a clue to Johnny's death. Our priority is to decide whether to search for the box."

"I think Johnny was killed by someone who suspects the tile is tied to something else. If that's true, he may know something we don't."

"Like what's in the box?"

He shrugged. "Maybe."

"If he's willing to kill for it, we need to find it first."

And transport it to the Durand version of Fort Knox, where no one could ever exploit its power.

Tanner turned into the main street of Whitefish. "Tomorrow we can start by talking to the park rangers about fish and park geography. Tonight we try to figure out who killed Johnny."

# CHAPTER EIGHT

Chantal examined the pile of clothes and boots on the checkout counter of the sporting goods store, resigned to extending her stay in Montana indefinitely. Tanner had insisted on stopping on their way back to the cabin and choosing the wilderness equipment they'd need.

In the back of the store, Tanner was in deep conversation with a grizzled old man who'd introduced himself as the owner. He laughed at something the older man said and she remembered the sixteen-year-old boy he'd been, arriving at Valtois—the exotic animal sanctuary outside of Paris where she'd grown up—so serious and proud and bewildered by the Durand family who had claimed him as one of their own. Most of that summer they'd explored the estate on horseback and she'd introduced him to the animals—lions, giraffes, ostriches, zebras. Did he remember all the crazy stunts she'd pulled to get his attention? Or that she'd been the only person who could make him laugh?

He glanced her way and she gestured toward her pile. He nodded before returning to his discussion. He'd insisted they provision up tonight so they could leave early in the morning for the ranger station. She just wanted to get back to the cabin and open the bottle of Pinot Noir.

She pulled out her credit card and the teenaged cashier checked her out. While she waited for Tanner, she called her cousin Lex in Anegada. "Hey, girl, you still disgustingly happy?"

Lex laughed. "Yup. Amazing, isn't it? What are you up to?"

"Mark sent me on an assignment to some tiny town in Montana. With Tanner."

"Shit. Are you kidding?"

"No. He's being almost civil, but I'm ready to wrap this up and get out of here." She noted that Tanner was finally headed for checkout, his cart loaded with gear. "I'm calling to see if there's any way I can get access to the data from Bodie's scanner."

"He's right here. Ask him yourself."

Chantal smiled. Lex's husband was intimidating and brilliant, and he adored his wife, which was why Chantal loved him.

"When are you coming to visit us?" Bodie's voice was deep and as huge as he was.

"As soon as I finish my current mission, which is why I need your help."

· · ·

Tanner's attention was riveted on the road ahead, as though Chantal wasn't even there. He flicked a switch on the dashboard and a green light came on. "The weather is supposed to turn cold in the next couple of days and there's a chance of snow. The faster we get in and out, the better."

An involuntary groan escaped her. Temperatures already skirted freezing. "How much colder?"

He grinned. "In the twenties. Maybe teens. You can head back to California if you can't take it."

"I can take it. I don't have to like it." And she'd hate every minute, especially the part where he gloated. She pointed to the green light. "So what's the light you turned on?"

"A jammer in case someone tries to track all our electronics."

"And follow us?"

"Probably not, but why take the chance?"

Besides being the Durand Field General, Mark was also the founder, Chairman, and CEO of Durand Tech, which was rivaled only by Microsoft and Apple. DT, however, was privately owned, and outfitted the Protector organization with vehicles that were a combination of a tank and a high tech command center. There were all kinds of special equipment concealed in the Tahoe. Three years off active duty left her with some catching up to do.

"Where did you stow the tile?" she asked.

"The reinforced safe under the back seat. It's safer there than anywhere else."

She stared out the windshield. "I just can't understand why it was necessary to kill Johnny. A telepath could read his thoughts without being detected."

Tanner slowed the SUV and tapped the monitor on the dashboard until the data from the surveillance cameras he'd set up earlier confirmed no one had approached the cabin. "True, but a telepath gets more details and sensory feedback from direct invasion than by catching random thoughts, even in a direct interrogation. Maybe the killer saw something he didn't want anyone else to know about."

She shuddered. "Johnny's vision?"

"That would be my guess." Tanner pulled up to the front door of the cabin and killed the engine. "Let's just hope he thinks the tile is the object. Finding that box will be dangerous enough without a telepathic murderer on our tail."

"I thought you said there was majik involved. A telepath who also wields powerful majik sounds formidable. Could it be a new type of Dissembler? Someone who has enough psychic power to tap into some other kind of majik?"

"Can't rule it out, but…"

She waited while he formed his thoughts. Her impression of the site of Johnny's death didn't include the Durands' ancient enemies either. She'd sensed the echo of dark majik, but with a different taste and frequency from any Dissembler she'd ever faced.

"There was a lone wolf quality to the obsession I sensed." He glanced out the side window of the truck. "Let's talk about this inside. I could use a beer and a warm fire."

The night hung densely around them—pitch black from the cloud cover and frigid. A shudder rolled through her. Hot soup and a cheery, well-lit room would do a world of good for her morale.

The icy wind whipped around them, biting her cheeks and ears as she helped him carry their purchases inside. She was conscious of Tanner moving around the room, an oddly comforting awareness that almost felt domestic. He removed his jacket and opened a bottle of Budweiser. As he leaned against the countertop and crossed his arms, he looked about as hot as any man she'd ever seen. Even the scowl that creased his forehead amped up the sexy factor.

He watched her take off her jacket and, for an instant, she would have sworn she saw a flash of desire in his eyes. Her heartbeat ramped up and warmth pooled deep in her belly. He'd always had this effect on her and her body's treachery pissed her off. "Unless you're planning to cook, get out of my kitchen and stoke that fire."

• • •

They hadn't talked much during dinner. Drying his hands on the dishtowel, Tanner studied Chantal working on her laptop at the dining table. She pulled her weight today investigating Johnny Hawkswing's death. At no time had she played the First Order Durand card and been a prima donna. It had been a long day, but their work still wasn't finished. "Have you found out anything about the painted rock that was in the salt circle?"

She blinked her azure eyes before focusing on him. "Haven't looked. I've been working on something else. Bodie gave me access to the data from his scanning system. Look what I found."

He studied the screen of her laptop. "What am I looking at?"

"It's a topographical map of the park showing the distribution of delphic energy. That's the purple overlay."

"Bodie can measure it?" He sort of knew what delphic energy was, but the science of it was vague.

"Yes. His monitoring system is top secret because it shows concentrations of delphic. Only a few Durand know about it."

"What are you looking for?"

"You know that delphic energy originates from one of the six Sources, and over countless millennia has flowed over the earth's surface, right? It's what allows our senses to operate on a psychic level."

He nodded.

"Bodie's been studying its distribution around the world and identifying where there are unexplainable concentrations. See this?" She pointed to an area of the park that was a darker shade of purple than the rest. "There's no reason these mountains should have more delphic energy than anywhere else within a hundred miles."

"A mini-Source?"

"That's what I thought, so I messaged Bodie. He suggested it might be a power point that's collected delphic over time. He noted other examples—Lourdes, the Potala Palace in Lhasa, the Luxor temple..."

"Those are all religious sites. None are in the wilderness."

She leaned back in her chair and stretched her arms over her head. "The park is 1500 square miles. If we're looking for an ancient, sacred cave, it's at least a starting place."

"A 300 square mile starting point."

She grinned. "See, we're already making progress. We can talk to the park rangers tomorrow and see if any spot in that area is similar to my vision."

"I guess that's better than nothing," he admitted.

"Damn right. You're welcome."

"What about this thing?" He picked up the pouch with the rock from the sideboard and dumped it out on the table. It was shaped like a river rock, about two inches in diameter, round, and flattened. The black and red paint had been sloppily applied. "You want to read it?"

"Absolutely not." She waved a hand over the rock and pulled it back. "I can tell from here it's got bad majik. I'd rather send photos and a description to headquarters and let someone there research it."

He poked it with a penknife. A weak charge tingled through his hand. "Wonder what the paint is."

"If it's paint at all. Majik uses a lot of substances that aren't found in a hardware store. You could scan it and see what happens. You have your equipment with you, right?"

"Of course." He retrieved a handy little device Durand Tech had developed for Protector fieldwork. It could determine the substance of organic materials, their age, and orphic fingerprint—the last particularly valuable because the nature of the orphic energy would tell them the degree of evil cast into the stone. The data would then be sent to his ComDev for analysis.

He sat back down and turned the scope on. Immediately, it emitted a warning buzz that got louder as he held it over the rock. "What the hell?"

Chantal slid her chair closer so she could see the screen of his ComDev. "That's disgusting."

He read the analysis. The paint was, in fact, human blood and wolf feces mixed with an oil-based pigment. Age: recent. Orphic reading: evil. "But not Dissembler majik. I've never heard of Blackfeet practicing dark majik. Their medicine men practiced nature-based rituals for healing and protection, not destruction."

"An outsider?"

"Maybe. Maybe not." He turned off the scope and the buzzing stopped. "What if the murderer used telepathy to compel Johnny to go to the campsite last night? He could have set everything up and waited for him and Jason to arrive."

"That would make the murderer someone he knew." She shuddered.

"At least someone he'd encountered."

"And someone we may have encountered." She moved her chair back in front of her laptop. "The bartender at Sister Lil's gave me the evil eye. Might be her."

He started at such a ridiculous suggestion then realized she was teasing him. "Naw. She was way too hot to be evil. Besides, she was especially nice to me."

She snorted. "Men. A big chest and a nice ass fool you every time. The woman is evil. Now be quiet so I can work."

He suppressed a smile. Chantal Durand was jealous and he

couldn't help but be amused. Except, she was right—they might have encountered the murderer. He stared at the stone. Human blood and wolf feces—a far cry from the herbs, sticks, and feathers of Blackfeet magic. Even the stones and bones the medicine men used weren't employed for sinister purposes.

"Send me the stone's data from your ComDev," Chantal said. "I'll send that, along with the photos of the stone, and the spell where we found it, to Kara. She can run it through the Durand search engine and see if we have anything similar on record."

He emailed the data and her laptop dinged when it was received. "What should we do with the stone?"

She typed for a moment then looked up. "It's too dangerous to send to DT or headquarters, but I'm not keen on having it here."

"Bury it outside in the pouch?"

"No. An animal might dig it up." She stared at the thing; repugnance etched on her features. "We need to destroy it."

"How?" Messing around with majikal objects wasn't his specialty, and this one was more odious than most.

She closed her laptop. "The safest way is to drop it into a furnace. A fireplace is a poor substitute, but the only option immediately on hand."

"I can get the blaze going strong, make it as hot as possible."

"Do that."

Fortunately, he'd brought in a large pile of wood when they arrived. Soon the blaze raged in the fireplace, throwing heat out into the room.

Chantal stared at the stone. "Too bad the fireplace doesn't have a door."

"Why?"

She shook her head. "Just thinking out loud."

He reached for the stone.

"No. Let me. I've done this before." Gathering the pouch around the stone, she managed to get it inside without it brushing her fingers. Her hands trembled.

"You okay?" he asked. "You don't have to do this."

"Yes, I do. Stand back. The kitchen will do."

"Why?"

"Damn it, Tanner. Just do what I ask. If anything goes wrong, you need to be ready to step in."

If her warning was meant to frighten him, it did. "Let me throw it in," he said.

"No. I'm pulling rank on this. Get back."

She crossed to the fireplace, shoulders squared, and head high. The flames roared, silhouetting her slim frame. Her arm swung forward and the pouch flew into the flames. Then everything seemed to happen in slow motion. She leaped backward, just as the rock exploded, blowing Chantal and flecks of molten shrapnel far into the room. Tanner rushed forward, stamping out sparks that landed on the rug and caught fire.

Chantal lay near the sofa unconscious, her face drained of all color. He lifted her onto the cushions and felt for a pulse, his fingers shaking. A steady rhythm thrummed against his fingertip. *Thank God.* But her skin was cold and clammy, and perspiration glistened on her forehead.

He rubbed her icy hands between his to warm them. "Come on, Chantal, wake up."

She didn't move. Pulling a wool throw from the back of the sofa, he wrapped it carefully around her, and propped a pillow behind her head. A lock of hair fell across her eye and he gently brushed it away, his fingertips skimming her brow. He stroked her cheek and leaned his ear to her lips to listen for her breathing. A warm wisp of air caressed his skin.

"Please be okay," he murmured. "Wake up and be okay."

Minutes passed. Call 911? Call Mark? Terrible things bounced around his head as adrenaline surged through his body. Her pulse beat at her neck, too quickly perhaps, but it was strong. He brushed his fingers across her lips—her breath warmed the tips.

Her eyes fluttered open and she gasped. He jerked back.

"How long have I been out?" she asked.

"Three, four minutes maybe. How are you?"

"I feel like I've been kicked by a horse." She tried to sit up and he stilled her.

"Relax. What happened?"

"When the stone exploded it released the spell which hit me hard. Luckily, I was ready to repel it, but the force of the orphic energy threw me..." She glanced around. "All the way back here?"

"Almost. You were on the floor. Did you pick up anything more?"

"No. Just icy cold malevolence." Her teeth chattered in spite of the wool blanket. "It feels like I'll never be warm again."

"I'll be right back." He hurried to his room and pulled the bottle of cognac Victor had given him in Jackson from his duffle. It was a very old bottle from the Durand cellars. Ordinarily, he might begrudge sharing it with her, but snuggled under the blanket, eyes closed, she looked tiny and fragile. He wanted to gather her in his arms and hold her. He was losing it.

Instead, he unceremoniously thunked the bottle down on the coffee table. "Cognac."

"There is a god," she moaned.

He went to the kitchen for glasses, then dropped into the armchair and poured them each a generous amount.

She took a sip and her soft moan of pleasure sent a jolt of arousal straight to his cock. Damn, why hadn't his body gotten the *"This is Chantal, the same Chantal who got Javier killed"* memo?

"You have to taste this," she said.

For several minutes they sat silently savoring the cognac and gazing into the fire. The tension in his neck and shoulders melted away and for the first time that day, he let himself relax.

"Throwing that stone in the fire was dangerous," he said. "Why did you insist on doing it yourself?"

"One of us had to, and I've destroyed spells before and lived. The majik was noxious and focused, but nothing I couldn't handle."

He studied her. "When we go after this thing, you can't go doing anything crazy. Both of our lives depend on clear heads and cooperation. Risk your life and you also risk mine."

"Then I need to ask you a question," she said.

"All right."

"Are you both mentally and physically recovered from Mexico?"

The scar along his face seemed to pull at his skin. He swallowed the scathing reply. It was a fair question, one he'd asked himself for months. He just didn't like her asking it. "Why would you even ask me that?"

"My life's at stake."

"Mark wouldn't have sent me here if I wasn't ready."

"You haven't answered my question. Are you physically recovered?"

"Yes."

"No PTSD for me to worry about?"

"No," he hissed through gritted teeth. "I've been cleared by the Durand shrinks and DT psych board."

"Good." She took another sip of cognac. "Johnny's death complicates our mission. Whoever killed him knows we have the tile."

"Do you think he knows about the box?"

She shook her head. "He wields majik and may have telepathic abilities, but he doesn't have our talents. Besides, Johnny didn't know about the box."

"So he wants the tile."

"Probably. But why didn't he steal it from Hank?"

Good question. Hank knew everyone around here and his comings and goings would have been easy enough to monitor. Why wait so long to make a move? "Maybe he isn't local. Whoever killed the old man on that rock was much too..." How to verbalize the deep repugnance he'd felt. "Too psychically *large* to blend into a close community like this."

She nodded. "Unless he has ties here. We're probably looking for a telepath who arrived within the last couple of days."

"Arrived or returned. He has at least two local accomplices, so maybe he grew up here or has family here."

"Should we ask Jason or Hank about any recent newcomers?"

He took another sip of cognac. "We don't want to look too interested."

"I thought you wanted to find Johnny's murderer."

"I do, but as far as anyone around here knows, I'm just an independent archeologist with some Indian blood and an interest in unusual artifacts. We need to concentrate on the box. Tomorrow morning you can describe every detail of the landscape from your vision to a park ranger and maybe we can narrow the search area down."

"Then what?"

"We check it out."

"On all-terrain vehicles?"

"If accessible. If not, on foot."

Her grimace told him what she thought of that idea.

"Mark said you aced survival training."

"The operative word is *survival*. Don't worry, I'll do my job." She reached for her ComDev. "Are we ready to call Mark?"

"You got any details for him? Because I don't."

She frowned. "No."

"We aren't green Protectors anymore, Chantal. We can handle this on our own for now."

# CHAPTER NINE

Aaron Greywolf slammed the phone into the cradle. "Fucking idiots." All he'd ordered his cousins to do was break into a parked SUV and find the tile that Hank had given away.

He swiveled his chair to stare out the window at the courtyard outside the Department of Native American Studies Building. In September, students had filled the space each evening. Now there were less than a half dozen of them hurrying down the sidewalk toward home, or their rooms, or wherever students went these days.

He rolled his head to stretch his neck. Too many hours in the car had left him stiff, but he'd gotten what he wanted—Johnny Hawkswing's vision. Too bad the old man had recognized him. Killing him had been necessary, but not a pleasure. Collateral damage in an epic quest. Aaron had grown up with the legend— inherited his father's secret obsession. And now he knew he was close to discovering the treasure.

A knock on the door startled him. He glanced at his watch. Almost nine o'clock. He could guess who it was. "Come in."

The door opened and a plain young woman with long dark hair poked her head in. "I'm sorry to disturb you, Dr. Greywolf."

He stifled a groan. At least three times a week Maria Naranjo recited the same apology, but she appeared at his door nevertheless. "Yes, what is it?"

"I've finished the research you wanted. Do you want me to email it or print it out for you?"

"Email is fine. Did you find anything particularly interesting?" Grad students were useful when it came to digging for obscure information, and Maria was one of the few who didn't ask why he wanted anything. Her infatuation with him was a minor nuisance he could tolerate for her devotion. Plus, the girl was a whiz with Internet research and could hack into all kinds of secure databases, even email.

She plopped into his guest chair, her shapeless sweater pooling over baggy jeans. "I ran a search on Tanner Hayes. He's an archeologist who worked with Hank Morris a couple of years ago on the shopping center project that caused all the trouble near Whitefish. His email address—the one Hank used…" She paused for effect. "Is a Durand Tech account."

He straightened. "He works for Durand Tech?"

Her smug smile irked the hell out of him. "That's what's strange. He has a special account—very secure and routed separately from Durand employees and subscribers. It's unhackable."

"So?"

Maria's eyes sparkled with excitement. "The woman with him, I ran facial recognition on her and got lots of hits. She's a French socialite who spent time in an Australian jail for shooting her lover. Was just released last week."

"Cut to the point."

"Her name is Chantal Durand and she's a shareholder in Durand Tech."

Interesting, but was it relevant? "So the guy has a rich girlfriend."

"She's more than that. Chantal Durand is an anthropologist who studies mystical relics, religious practices, and aboriginal magic."

"Fuck," he muttered. How much did these people know? All these years of searching for any clue that the legend was true, and just when he had his first breakthrough these outsiders not only turned up, but took possession of the tile. He needed to call his boys again about keeping track of their whereabouts.

Maria watched him expectantly. "Do you want me to dig deeper?" She'd do whatever he asked, but he didn't trust her with anything beyond research and hacking.

"Find out what you can about the Durand connection and monitor Hank Morris's email. Can you hack his cell phone records?"

She shrugged. "I can give it a shot. What are we looking for?"

"Any calls to or from Tanner Hayes or Chantal Durand." Hank had called them for a reason and Johnny had told him about his vision. If Hank made a connection between the tribal legends and the mystical tile, he might tell his friends, which could become a serious problem. Aaron had spent a lifetime hoping for this break and no one was going to stand in his way now.

# CHAPTER TEN

Mark grunted under the weight Adrien had loaded on the leg press. He welcomed the burn and physical exertion, not to mention a quiet hour in his cousin's personal gym.

"What's the matter? You getting old?" Adrien said.

"Fuck you." He straightened his burning thighs and locked the machine in place. This shit wasn't as easy as it used to be, but he sure as hell wasn't getting old. "Could use a decent night's sleep, though."

"You're not going to get that in sex clubs."

"How would you know?" It had been years since Mark had hit Paris' finest, but Adrien knew he was a perverse son of a bitch. He wiped the sweat from his face and neck with a hand towel. "I've got to hit the shower and head over to the bank for a meeting."

"Not yet." Adrien leaned against the squat rack and studied him. "Why are you so interested in this tile? Wasn't sending Tanner and Chantal to pick it up overkill?"

He shrugged. "Neither had anything else to do. The guy who had it called Tanner because they'd worked together. Chantal could read the object and find out if it was anything worth investigating."

"Somebody else might buy that bullshit. Why are *you* interested in some piece of clay in Montana? Tanner didn't call you about it, did he?"

"He told Victor and I had a data scan run for legends and folk stories in that region. It came back with a Blackfoot legend of a powerful treasure buried hundreds of years ago."

Adrien laughed. "So you sent in two senior Protectors who hate each other to investigate based on a folktale?"

"The legend was recounted in a scholarly book by a professor of

Native American Studies at the University of Montana—a member of the Blackfeet tribe. I thought it was worth checking out."

"And it was. Sit down," Adrien said. "I've been thinking about the Shalamov connection. Something kept alluding me all night, but while I was on the treadmill it came to me."

Mark picked up his bottle of water and dropped his ass on a bench. "You've heard of this box?"

Adrien shook his head and sat on a bench opposite from him. "No, but I remembered a Shalamov legend I heard when I was visiting Kirill. Maybe creation myth is a better description."

"Go on."

"One winter day, a hunter is out in the frozen tundra and comes upon a female wolf who has just killed an ermine. He's about to kill the wolf, when she pleads for mercy, telling him she has four pups in a cave who will die without her. She offers the ermine in exchange for her life and tells him this particular ermine has great power. He's skeptical…"

"Because everyone knows wolves lie."

Adrien scowled at him. "But he takes mercy on her and lets her go. He then skins and guts the ermine only to find a ruby heart in the ermine's chest. As soon as he touches the ruby, he's filled with power. All his senses are preternaturally heightened and he's aware of an energy he never knew existed before."

Mark chuckled. "Ruby magic, huh? Happens in Cartier all the time."

Adrien grinned. "So I'm told. Anyhow, this hunter became the first Shalamov Sentier and the first man to control the Siberian Source."

"So where is this ruby now? Is it still the source of the Sentier's power?"

Adrien wiped a rivet of sweat from his neck. "I've never heard any hint of it. Not that anyone would tell a Durand about it. And, if it did exist, I doubt Kirill would have told me that legend."

"Okay, for argument's sake, let's assume the power object is the same ruby. Why send it half way across the world?"

"Power is dangerous," Adrien said. "Extraordinary power in the wrong hands…"

Their gazes met. As two of the most powerful psychics in the world, they'd both had to use their power in the Durand's covert war with Tolian, the Brazilian Sentier, and his Dissemblers—and not always in ways they were proud of. Mark's dark talent—a death touch—was one of the Protectors' greatest defenses and greatest weapons. And every time he used it, his soul died a little.

Mark rose. "I already told them to look for it."

Adrien glared at him. "If it's been buried for centuries, why not let it stay buried?"

"Once Johnny Hawkswing reported his trance and handed over the clay tile to Tanner's archeologist friend, the magic or power or whatever it is reentered the world. It would only be a matter of time until someone else took interest in the box—maybe our enemies."

"You believe that?"

"I do. And we can't risk letting a power object fall into the wrong hands." He swept a towel over the bench he'd being lying on. "Between them, Tanner and Chantal are our best chance of tracking this ruby—or whatever it is—down."

"If they fail, we let it stay buried," Adrien said. "Nobody else goes hunting for it. Is that clear?"

Mark bristled. Adrien was Sentier and gave direct orders daily—just usually not to him. "Understood."

"How are they handling working together?" Adrien asked.

"Tanner still blames her for Javier's death. Maybe it's time he knew the truth." A truth that should come from Adrien.

"Not now. We can't risk him losing his focus."

"Your call, A. But for the record, it's a fucked up thing to do to Chantal."

# CHAPTER ELEVEN

Chantal snuggled under the covers and tried to ignore the sounds of Tanner moving around the cabin. The clock on the bedside table read 7:08 a.m. God knew when she'd be cozy under a down comforter again. Probably not in the next twenty-four hours. And she didn't want to think about what they had to do before then.

He knocked sharply on her door. "Up and at 'em. We've got a long day ahead."

"Shove it," she muttered under her breath and dragged herself vertical. "Just getting in the shower. Be done in fifteen minutes."

It took her twenty minutes, but he didn't complain when she emerged from her room. He was working at the stove. She took a cup of yogurt from the fridge and a spoon from the drawer. "Are we going to call Mark this morning?"

"I sent him a report last night. He replied to be careful."

"So you're in charge now?" she snapped.

"This is my world. If we were at a Paris fashion show, I'd happily defer to you."

"Up yours, Hayes. I've been living in a tent in the Australian Outback. Not exactly a life of luxury. It's been a long time since I lived in Paris and you know it."

The muscle on his jaw next to the scar twitched. "And you wouldn't follow my orders anyhow, would you?"

So this was about Javier. She wanted to tell him she'd saved his ungrateful life. "Fine. You're welcome to take the lead for now. Once we find the box, we decide together how to proceed from there."

His brow creased. "We carry it out and call in for pickup."

"Until we know exactly what this thing is, we leave our options open."

He turned away, his posture stiff. "I'm calling Hank," he said as he walked away. "We head out in forty-five minutes."

• • •

Three hours and four cups of coffee later they climbed back into the Tahoe. The retired park ranger Hank had sent them to had been helpful. And very talkative. He'd suggested five possible locations for their "hike" although only two fit all the criteria—next to the water, inhabited by Westslope Cutthroats, down a steep cliff, and having a view of a jagged mountain formation to the right. Chantal had found the old man charming and accepted the refills he poured into her coffee cup. She was glad she'd used his bathroom on her way out.

Tanner had studied the map the ranger showed them and input the coordinates of each route into his ComDev. He pulled the first up on the screen and linked it to Durand Tech's satellite system. "We can hike into this one this afternoon. It's only about five miles off this access road."

She studied the image of the terrain. "Pull up the other coordinates."

He tapped them in and the image moved to another location and zoomed in. "This one's a harder hike—nine miles in with some climbing."

Her spirits sank. The shape of the river valley was familiar. She touched the screen and dragged the image to show the mountains in the background. Red rock. Three pointed peaks. "This looks more like my vision." She put her finger on a spot at the edge of a steep cliff. "From about here."

"You're sure?"

"That it's the place? No. That it's much closer to my vision than the other location? Absolutely."

He started the engine and put the Tahoe in drive. "Then let's get going. The temperatures are supposed to stay moderate until tomorrow morning, then they're predicted to fall. We can be in and out before then if we're lucky."

. . .

Tanner ran his hand through his hair, a gesture she realized he made when stressed. His mouth was set in a hard line and his attention riveted on the road ahead. This wasn't a happy man.

"Want to talk about it?" she asked.

"What?" he snapped.

"Whatever's bothering you. If we're going to hike into the wilderness and climb down that cliff, I need to know your head's in the game and not worked up over hating me."

He registered surprise. "Not everything's about you, believe it or not."

"Then what? Is this about Mexico?"

He winced.

Bingo. Shit. She'd heard he'd been half dead when Mark brought him and Luke out. And Luke had been much worse. She didn't blame him for being edgy as long as he could still do his job. "I know it was bad. If Mark didn't think you were ready to come back to work, he wouldn't have given you this assignment."

"Is this supposed to be a pep talk?"

"Yeah, it is."

A grunt told her what he thought about that.

"We're on the same team, and whether you like it or not, we have to trust each other." She hesitated. Bringing up the past would probably make things worse. "There was more to what happened in London than you know."

That earned her a glare. "Is that so?"

"Yes."

The Tahoe slowed and he pulled into a scenic viewpoint lay-by. He yanked the gearshift into park and turned to her, snarling. "I was there, remember? You were stationed outside to warn us of intruders and you left your post, came inside, and started a firefight that left my best friend dead. Are you telling me that's *not* what happened?"

"I killed two Dissemblers who would have gotten away."

"You don't know that," he snapped. "We had them covered."

"But neither of you took a shot. Why was that?" She willed him to see the truth she wasn't permitted to reveal.

"You burst in and started shooting before we had a chance. Then all hell broke loose and Javier was dead."

"He led you into a trap. That's why he didn't shoot."

"Bullshit." His hands gripped the steering wheel so tightly they had gone nearly white. "You fucked up. Own it."

Her throat tightened around a knot that had formed there. Their fragile détente had crumbled and she'd brought it on herself. She hadn't fucked up. She'd saved his life.

Tanner's eyes focused on hers. They were icy dark blue, the color Mark's had once been. "I need your word that you won't deviate from our plan if the situation gets ugly. That you won't go off on your own and make things worse."

She stared back at him. "I'll do my job and follow the plan unless something goes wrong and that plan needs to be adjusted. I won't go off on my own unless you're incapacitated or dead and I have no other choice." He flinched at that last part, but they both knew standard procedures. "I expect you to do the same if I go down."

He nodded and pulled back onto the highway.

Thirty minutes later he turned the Tahoe onto a dirt road that ended in less than a quarter of a mile in a small clearing. "This is as close was we're going to get in the truck. We have about three hours of daylight to make it to the ledge and set up camp."

"So we can start down the canyon at first light," she muttered, wondering why she'd agreed to this plan. Camping was bad enough, but having to share a tent with Tanner was going be agony. "I think I'll take my own tent for tonight."

He shook his head. "You need to carry water and equipment, not an extra tent. I'm not any happier about sleeping with you…" He froze, and a faint hint of color rose on his neck. "Sharing a tent with you. Since one of us will be on watch while the other sleeps, it won't be a problem."

The watch was unnecessary and they both knew it. He'd packed a sophisticated Durand Tech device that would detect and identify any life force in the area whether human, bear, deer, or even small mammals. If the mammal were large enough to be a threat, the device would let them know instantly.

"Let's get this straight, Tanner. I'm not sitting out in the cold when the DT scanner will keep watch much better than I can. If you want to, fine. Knock yourself out." She got out of the Tahoe and opened the back passenger door to retrieve her jacket and pack. The jacket was light but warm, and the pack was high tech and comfortable. She hoisted it onto her back and adjusted the straps, ignoring Tanner's grumbling at the back of the Tahoe. Finally, she pulled on her custom leather gloves—the ones with the Ancilon energy absorbing fiber lining to protect her from accidentally trancing.

"I'm ready," she called to Tanner. "Is there anything else you want me to carry?"

Slamming down the back of the Tahoe, he came around to her side. "Take this." He offered her a Sig Sauer and a box of ammo.

Chantal pulled her own Baby Glock from her jacket pocket. "A birthday present from Mark. I never leave home without it."

He turned her around and tucked the Sig Sauer and ammo in the side pocket of her backpack. "Doesn't hurt to have a backup." His hand on her arm was gentle, but firm. It shouldn't have felt commanding or intimate, but somehow it was both.

She pulled away. Letting her head go where it didn't belong would only make the next two days harder and the trek was going to be challenging enough. "You taking the lead or shall I?"

His glower was both macho and hot. "I'll go ahead and set the pace. Let me know if I need to slow down."

Death before dishonor. She bit back an anatomically impossible suggestion. "I think I'll manage if we can get moving before dark."

Another glare and he took off at a brisk clip that she had

no trouble matching. Her legs had been her main means of transportation in the hills of the Outback and she enjoyed the exercise as they hiked along the forest trail.

The terrain grew rockier and the trees thinned over the first couple of miles. She tracked their progress on her ComDev just as Tanner was doing, and noted the elevation slowly increasing. By mile five the climb steepened significantly and her calves began to burn. Twenty feet ahead of her, Tanner had slowed down and occasionally glanced back to check on her. Each time she grinned and gave him the thumbs up.

Underfoot the gravel was looser now and small boulders, which looked to be the result of recent rockslides, punctuated the path requiring her to climb over or around them. Their progress slowed even further when the trail curved around a cliff and narrowed to a ledge less than six feet wide. She peered over the sheer drop to woods far below and a fast moving river.

"You okay with this?" Tanner asked, "Would you be more comfortable going first?"

"You know heights don't bother me."

He flinched, remembering her climbing to the tops of the ancient oaks at Valtois while he'd stuck to the lower branches. "Just be careful. The footing may not be stable."

She gestured for him to go on and laughed. "Then if it holds you, I'm home clear."

He stepped carefully, testing the path as he went. She followed close behind, prepared to grab him if the ground gave way. Across the valley, the sun was quickly sinking toward the mountaintops and the temperature was dropping. Nevertheless, a drop of sweat rolled between her shoulder blades. She didn't dare look at her ComDev and didn't want to know how far they had to go on the damned ledge. Her boot slipped on sand and she had to grab a root sticking out of the stone cliff to keep from losing her balance.

She'd been through much worse than this—survival training in the Alps, a mission in the Andes. So why were her nerves so strung out now? Experience and instinct told her this was the easiest part of their mission. Whatever was in the cave somewhere below was a game changer they might not be able to handle.

"Only about thirty yards to go." A ray of the sinking sun hit the back of his head causing his hair to shine a freaky scarlet color and throwing his face into eerie, skull-like shadows.

She stared at him in horror and an instant later the bizarre trick of the light dissolved.

"What is it?" he asked.

"Nothing." At least nothing real. Her mind, however, was twisted up by what she'd just seen. A fluke of the sun or a premonition? The Durand didn't believe in prescience. No one could know the future. Still, was Tanner in danger? She shuddered. Because the only thing worse than being out here with Tanner Hays was being out here alone.

• • •

Tanner had sensed the change in Chantal, but sure as hell wasn't going to call her on it. They had about a half hour of light when they reached their destination—a clearing on the ridge overlooking the river valley that was their most promising lead. Chantal had volunteered to set up the tent and unpack the provisions. He'd backtracked on the trail to scout the area.

Campsites dotted the forest behind the clearing. He clicked on his flashlight and wandered along the path, opening his senses to the dusk. In the summer it was a popular destination for hikers looking to rough it in the wild. Families, couples, and groups of friends all left their energy in the earth. For the most part, the campers had been happy or at least content.

Leaving the path, he ventured into a secluded clearing that lacked the tree cover most of the sites enjoyed. Overhead, the stars had appeared in the night sky. He looked up at them as he strolled farther into the clearing. The vision hit him hard and fast, anchoring him to the spot. A couple making love on a blanket, their grunts and moans almost audible in the quiet night. Their pleasure echoed in his body and he began to harden. Abruptly, the vision shifted. A second man, demanding his turn entered the scene. A blow to the first man's head and he was on the woman. She scratched and screamed.

Tanner wanted to help her, rescue her from her attacker. The pain was unbearable. The fear, suffocating. His shield slammed in place and he staggered backward, panting. His heart raced and his head pounded. The attack had been recent, maybe as recent as last summer. Had the girl lived? Would she ever recover? He wanted to believe she would, but knew she'd be broken.

Shaken, he started back toward their campsite. In the lantern light Chantal crouched over a flat rock assembling two pouches for their dinner. His vision echoed in his head on a diabolical loop. The girl's screams rang in his ears. Under his clothes his skin had grown clammy, alternating hot and cold. He ducked into the tent and sat on a sleeping bag, his knees pulled up to his chest. Closing his eyes, he concentrated on his breathing. In for four counts, hold for four, exhale for eight. And again. But the vision refused to clear.

Suddenly Tanner was back in the Mexican hellhole. The young man turned to him and stared from Luke's beaten face, Luke's pleading eyes. The clean forest scent turned rancid with blood and sweat and urine and feces. The campsite and the dungeon were one, blaring with the screams, moans, and curses of beings condemned to hell.

"Tanner, wake up." Someone was shaking him. "You're trancing."

He groaned. "Vision. Woods."

She slapped him across the face hard—once, twice—and the pain was real and immediate. He concentrated on the sting and forced his eyes open.

A wet cloth dabbed at his cheeks and forehead. The woman again. "Come on back. Follow my voice."

Gradually his head cleared. He was lying on his side in a fetal position; Chantal knelt next to him stroking his face with a cool cloth.

"Welcome back." Her smile belied the concern in her voice. "What happened?"

"I came across the site of a recent murder and rape in the woods." He didn't have to explain further, she knew firsthand the effect of violent energy on people like them. She didn't have to know about the flashback.

"Is there anything I can do?"

"No. I'm fine now." A lie, but fine was relative in his world. "I'll be out in a couple of minutes."

She nodded, clearly not convinced, and ducked out of the tent.

Lying back down, he stared at the inside of the tent. The small light Chantal had hung in the top corner cast a cheery light. His flashbacks had stopped over a year ago. What had just happened made no sense. He'd have to be more careful not to fully open his senses as he tracked whoever had hidden the box. He couldn't afford to be taken by surprise again. His life and Chantal's life depended on it.

• • •

His vision had killed his appetite, but he attempted to eat the meal Chantal had prepared. After the first few bites, his stomach took over and insisted on finishing the tasty chicken and vegetable combination.

She tucked an errant auburn lock behind her ear and crumbled the parchment that had held her vegetarian dinner. She then rolled a metal-like fiber mat and slid it into a nylon tube about an inch in diameter.

He remembered seeing it with the equipment that came with the Tahoe. "What's that?"

"A prototype heat mat. I cooked dinner on it."

"How does it work?"

"DT magic, as far as I can tell."

"Not funny." The Durand never used magic to describe what they did—it was one of the many things that set them apart from their Dissembler enemies. "There has to be a power source."

"Of course, but I never figured out what it was in the earlier, bulkier version Mark sent me to test last year. Comes in handy when you can't build a fire." She slid the mat part way out of the sleeve and pointed to a red dot on one corner. "You pinch this to turn it on. The longer you squeeze it the hotter it gets—each pulse on your fingers indicates another twenty-five degrees."

"Ingenious." Like many other of Durand Tech's innovations.

"I kind of miss campfires," she said as she slipped the mat back into the tube. "When I'd visit Lex and her family in the States in the summer, sometimes we'd camp out at their summer house in Vermont. Georges would build a campfire and we'd toast marshmallows and make s'mores. It was all so beautifully normal."

He was tempted to point out that the summer-house in Vermont was a 500-acre estate with a manor house the size of a boutique hotel. Given that Chantal's parents lived in a chateau with an animal sanctuary outside of Paris, her normal wasn't even in the same universe as the two-bedroom ranch house in Nebraska where he'd grown up.

"My dad encouraged me to join the Boy Scouts." He still thought of Walt Hays as his father, even when he discovered his biological father was a distant Durand cousin.

Chantal grinned. "Like it?"

"Not much. My Indian quarter never quite fit in with the pink-cheeked Anglo boys."

"And your talent made it all more difficult?"

"Yeah." Dealing with their abilities as children was a subject they'd exhausted years ago. "Protector boot camp made up for washing out of scouts. Learning to make a campfire and read a compass and all kinds of nifty tricks."

"With the bonus of campfire songs in English, French, and Spanish." She wrapped her arms around herself and glanced away for a moment. "Did you bring the tile?"

"It's in the safe in the Tahoe."

She nodded gravely. "Good. In the morning we can walk along the cliff and I'll try to pinpoint where we need to start our descent."

"If we get close, I should be able to pick up the energy of

the person carrying it—if there's anything to pick up—unless it's become a major hiking path." And a couple of hundred years of dissipation should temper any radical shit. "With a little luck, we could track the energy to the box and hightail it out of there via the river route before the bad weather rolls in."

"Right." She pulled her ComDev out of her pocket and tapped the screen. "Assuming we find anything at all. The good news is, according to the weather report the snow should pass to the north of us."

"And the bad news?"

"It's going to get damn cold by tomorrow night." She glanced up and shuddered. "Unless we make it out before dark, that little tent you brought isn't going to cut it."

"We'll be fine. I've spent a lot of time in the wilderness."

"So have I, but it was a warm wilderness with rudimentary facilities in camp and natural materials for basic shelters in the bush."

"What were you looking for out there? I never heard anything about the project."

"Just that I put lead in Clive's ass." Her smile twisted something in his gut. "There's a rich aboriginal history in the desert that hasn't been explored by archeologists and anthropologists. That's what my team was trying to record and preserve. New Age quacks have found their way out there and hijacked the mystical aspect of the culture, not knowing that the Pitjantjatjara Source is an important part of the Sacred World of the Aborigine."

"And everyone else on the team was *ordinaire* and clueless." He'd done enough work with *ordinaires* himself and knew how hard it was to keep his knowledge of a place to himself when the head guys' theories were completely wrong. "How did you manage to get yourself engaged to the asshole?"

Her eyes sparkled in the firelight. "He was very handsome and charming and I've never been good at long stretches of celibacy. We started seeing each other and biology kicked in."

"Weren't you in love?"

There was something odd in her expression. "I thought I was. At least I wanted to be in love with him. It was complicated."

"Because he was *ordinaire*?"

"Partly." Her gaze drifted into the night and he read pain in her expression. "His father owned a huge ranch and wanted grandchildren. My bank account might have been an added bonus."

The knot in his gut loosened. Why the hell should he care if she was in love with some Australian? "You deserve better than that."

"In the end, he cheated on me and I filled his ass with buckshot. A colorful way to end a relationship, don't you think?"

He chuckled. "You've always had a flare for the dramatic."

"What about you?" she asked. "Why are you still single? There must be women all over Wyoming dying to warm your bed."

He choked then tried to cover it with a cough. "Busy. Traveling." Recovering from being tortured in a filthy dungeon. He swallowed and tried to form a full, coherent sentence. "Between my archeology work and Protector assignments, I haven't had much time for a relationship. I don't think I could handle getting involved with another Protector knowing she was going into danger with every mission and I don't lie well enough to date *ordinaires*."

An elegant eyebrow cocked. "But I do lie well?"

He hadn't meant his comment as a dig, but maybe it was better to put a little distance between them. Getting friendly with her was taking him off guard. "I want to check the area with the scanner, then do some work before we head down the cliff tomorrow. So if you'll excuse me, I'm going to set up inside."

"Me, too." She smiled sweetly. "You do remember we're sharing the tent, don't you?"

"Yeah." Side by side in sleeping bags. Surely she wouldn't strip down when there might be trouble. "I'm going to walk the perimeter first. I'll be back in a little while."

Hopefully she'd be asleep and snoring with drool running from her mouth by then.

# CHAPTER TWELVE

Lorraine Humphrey lingered in the doorway of the suite, the only occupied room in the sprawling lodge. "Let us know if you need anything, Dr. Greywolf. We usually go for food and supplies everyday during season, but not when the lodge closes. Mike's going to Saint Mary in the morning, before the storm sets in, so he can pick up anything you need."

The last thing he wanted was anyone coming to check on him. "The most important thing I need is quiet and solitude so I can work on my book. Everything else I brought with me."

"You'll get plenty of quiet here. Nobody around and not even a television in the room."

"I appreciate you letting me stay."

Lorraine grinned. "Hell, you're a local celebrity. We're honored you called us."

"I'd appreciate it if you didn't mention to anyone I'm here." He mentally pushed the request to make it a command. *Now leave and don't come back.* The telepathic directive worked. With a confused look on her face, the woman turned and walked away.

Local celebrity. She thought that was a compliment. If she only knew what he really was, the power he controlled. But the guise of an academic served him well and led people to underestimate him. And say and think things in his presence that had brought him here.

He took his cell phone from his pocket and checked for reception. One bar, rather, a dot. There was a phone in the room with directions to dial nine to make an outside call. This would be tracked by the lodge's phone system so using it would be a last resort.

Wandering around the suite, he located a spot with three bars and figured that was the best he was going to get. He tapped the screen and his cousin answered.

"Where are they?" Aaron asked.

"Camped on a bluff in the middle a nowhere." And if Tom said, middle a nowhere, it must be a remote spot. That boy had been roaming the park all year round since he was ten. "Hiked out there with a lotta gear. If I was a gambling man, I'd bet they's planning to go down into the canyon."

"Why climb down? Why not just take the easy route along the river?"

"Beats me, doc. Trail's shit, what there is of it. I ain't bothered with it fer years. Not since that mud slide."

"Keep out of sight and text me when they move in the morning." For Tom, a night in the woods was second nature—like he'd been raised by wolves, or was channeling their Blackfeet ancestors. "You have everything you need for a few days out?"

A deep chuckle echoed through the line. "You think I need fancy gear to spend a couple nights in the woods?"

Aaron glanced around his rustic "suite" with its very basic furnishing and lack of luxuries and realized how soft academia had made him over the past decade. For him, this was as close to camping as he wanted to get. "Just be careful and keep alert. Hayes is smart and part Indian himself, and there's no telling why he brought the girl. I want to know where they're going and why—that's it."

When he hung up, Aaron sat down at the old pine desk, opened his laptop and pulled up an aerial view of the area where the two strangers were camped. The photo was nearly a year old, but not much changed out there in a year or two. He zoomed in on the cliff and the canyon below. What were they looking for? Sure, there were outdoors fanatics who hiked and camped in the park all year long, but he'd bet his tenure these two weren't in that category. They were looking for something, and that something was related to the tile Hank Morris had given them. The same tile that caused Johnny's vision.

He took a joint from his shirt pocket and lit it. The first hard toke settled his nerves and cleared his head. This was locally grown marijuana, not that designer shit they sold in the city that fucked you up and turned you into a blithering idiot.

He leaned back in his chair and concentrated on his breathing. Within minutes his mind began to float and tap into the energy in the room, then expanded beyond its walls, and the walls of the lodge, and into the night.

# CHAPTER THIRTEEN

Chantal pretended to be asleep when Tanner shifted against her back and unzipped his sleeping bag the next morning. The tent was designed for subzero temperatures and had been warm and cozy last night. Knowing they'd be warned of any person or large animal's approach, she should have slept more soundly, but the even rhythm of Tanner's breathing next to her and the clean woodsy scent of him had inspired erotic dreams she couldn't shake.

The dreams had been so vivid she'd almost come from the intensity. Even now, as he pulled on outer clothes and boots, her body ached for his hands on her breasts, his mouth devouring hers, his cock pumping inside her. Last night she'd almost believed he was warming up to her, or at least thawing. Then he'd closed off and left.

Crawling out of the sleeping bag, she fumbled around for her clothes. Thankfully, today would be physically challenging and there wouldn't be the time or energy to waste thinking about him as anything but a mission partner.

She dug in the side pocket of the backpack, found some wipes Lex called "Bath in a Pouch" and freshened up. With any luck, they'd be back at the cabin by dark and she could take a long bubble bath. Yeah, that would suit just fine. She pulled on long underwear made of Ancilon protective fiber and layered clothes on from there. She didn't mind being a bit too warm, but too cold? No way.

After packing her belongings in her backpack, she rolled up her sleeping bag and snapped it to her pack. Tanner's things were already gone so she threw hers out of the tent and began to disassemble their cozy sleeping quarters.

The sun hadn't risen above the mountains yet, and clouds hung low and dense as far as she could see. Not exactly a cheery morning, although the weather wasn't nearly as gloomy as her companion was. Tanner sat on a rock drinking coffee and gazing out over the canyon.

The coffee pot sat on the cooking mat. She poured herself a cup and joined Tanner on his rock. "G'morning. Good java."

He grunted.

Deep shadows obscured the canyon floor and the riverbed. She sipped the coffee—thick and strong. In the early morning light, the walls of the canyon seemed even steeper and rockier than they did last night.

"Second thoughts?" she asked. "We could go back and come along the shore of the river."

"No. If we came in by the river we wouldn't have a trail to follow. If the box is in a cave, the entrance has to be hidden. Too many people use this park each year for it to remain uncharted otherwise."

"Then we better get going." She pushed herself to her feet.

He nodded, but didn't move. Whatever was bothering him was beginning to worry her. They both needed their heads in the game if they were going to make it down the cliff in one piece.

• • •

In less than a half mile's walk along the cliff, Tanner came to a halt. He stood in place for a full minute while Chantal studied him. His gaze was frozen, while the muscles in his face flexed and twitched. She'd seen him like this before—he was reading the ground below his feet and from his facial expression it was an interesting history.

His breath came fast and hard, and his arms and shoulders began to spasm. She pushed him away from the sheer drop and he landed on his ass in the low brush.

A moment later, he shook his head and focused. "Enjoy that?"

"My other option was pushing you off the cliff. You're welcome." She reached out her hand to him. "What did you see?"

He ignored it, stood, and dusted dead leaves off his jacket. "Just like your vision, I also sensed the man with the *burden* was a priest, and he didn't come here alone. He came with a local Indian to guide him, and the man's son. The priest was an *ordinaire*. The Indian and his son both had psychic abilities although I couldn't get a clear feel for what they were. The guide was the tribe's medicine man."

She whistled softly. "Did you pick up anyone's thoughts or intentions?"

"The priest had wrapped the *vessel* in elk skin and tied it to his back. He just wanted to get rid of it somewhere it would never be found. He trusted his guide, but the shaman wanted the power for himself. He planned to take the priest to a cave down there." Tanner nodded into the canyon. "And then come back later for the treasure."

"Why not just kill the priest and take the box?"

"Superstition? I think he was afraid the holy man would haunt him and all his descendants. Apparently the priest was popular with the tribal leaders. I'm guessing more so than the shaman."

"And the boy?"

"Curious and wary of his father. Respected the priest."

"Are you reading all this or drawing conclusions?"

"Both."

"Are you sure you're not picking up any other human energy here? You're reading people who were here briefly a couple hundred years ago. We're way off the beaten path, but this park gets a lot of hikers."

He glared at her. "So your visions are clear and true, and mine are muddy and suspect? Oh, right. You're First Order Durand and I'm a distant bastard cousin."

"That's not what I meant. I've always respected your talent, and you wouldn't be here if you weren't the best at what you do."

"Then trust me. Three people went down into this canyon. Whatever happened down there, we won't know until we get there." He shifted his pack and took his ComDev from his jacket pocket. "Their energy trail goes straight over the edge of the cliff which means the path they took eroded and no longer exists. There's a spot ahead that leads down and back this way. Let's go that way and see if I can pick up their trail."

The wind had picked up and the temperature was dropping. Chantal adjusted the scarf around her neck and checked to be sure her jacket was zipped to the top. "Sounds like a good plan. Lead on."

The path turned out to be more of a series of inclined ledges than a flat track they could hike down. Had the weather been good, she would have enjoyed the challenging descent. Tanner was a strong climber and had packed all the right equipment, plus he was surprisingly nimble for a man his size. She watched him go down a particularly steep rock face, noting where he found foot and handholds.

"This would have been a lot easier if we'd repelled down," she called to him.

He scowled back up at her. "And how would I track the priest's energy dropping straight down to the canyon floor? We're already a couple hundred yards north of where we started our descent."

"Details," she muttered. He was right, but repelling was so much faster and much more fun.

Ten minutes later, they came to a shallow cave, about ten feet into the cliff. A light sleet had begun to fall, making the rocks slippery and hard to hold on to, and the wind whipped the frozen rain into their faces.

"How about we rest for five minutes," Tanner said. "The cave's dry and out of the wind, and I could use some water."

She nodded and ducked in, out of the elements. The cave wasn't any warmer temperature-wise, but without the ice and wind it felt downright cozy. She unhooked her pack and dropped to the dirt floor, her back to the rear wall. Pulling off her leather climbing gloves and rooting through the front pocket of her pack, she found chemical heat packs and pulled one out. Within moments, it grew warm and then hot. The heat stung her freezing hands and she had to wrap the pack in her scarf until her fingers thawed.

"Want to use this?" She offered the heat pack to Tanner.

He took it and pulled off his own gloves. "Thanks. It's always a tough choice between warmth and safety, isn't it? DT needs to come up with some self-heating gloves thin enough for bad weather climbing."

"I'll pass that suggestion on to R&D." She took a drink from her water bottle. "Have you sensed our friends lately?"

"They stopped here briefly. So have a lot of other people. I'm getting a vague impression of fatigue and impatience from our guys, and not much else."

Outside of their sheltered nook, the wind drove the sleet horizontally against the rock face. There were only two choices—go on or go back and she figured they were about at the halfway mark. "Remind me why we had to go after the box today," she muttered.

"Because someone killed Johnny—maybe because of the tile—and there's a blizzard coming the day after next. This place could be under a few feet of snow until spring." He handed the heat pack back to her and she tucked it in her jacket pocket.

"Then I guess we'd better get going." She adjusted her pack and snapped the front clasp in place.

# CHAPTER FOURTEEN

Mark read the final paragraph of the report from Durand BioTech a second time then closed the file. The fifth failure in eight months. Shit. And the worst part was having to tell Adrien. Now that the Sentier had been married for over a year, the rest of the family had begun hinting it was time for an heir and, not very subtly, checking Tate's slim waistline for any expansion. No one but Mark and Tate knew Adrien was sterile, which left the problem of fertilizing Tate's egg with Adrien's genetics on Mark.

Although the sofa in Adrien's study was as comfortable as a piece of furniture got, his back had stiffened with the stress of the last five hours. He rolled his shoulders and stretched his arms over his head. He should go back to his penthouse in the 16th arrondissement, but the Zen ambiance of Adrien's personal library felt more welcoming tonight than his own flat.

"Thanks for waiting," Adrien said. "Tate's parents finally went to bed." He entered the study and crossed to his bar. "What can I pour you?"

"Scotch." Whatever his cousin had would be old, fine, and smooth.

Adrien poured the drink and handed it to him, then poured a cognac for himself. He dropped into an oversized chair across from Mark and propped his feet on the matching ottoman. "You look like shit."

"I need to talk to you."

"You've heard from Tanner and Chantal?"

"Just a couple texts that they were following a priest's trail down into a canyon. Turns out the priest wasn't alone."

Adrien's eyebrows rose. "Who was with him?"

"A local medicine man and his son." He took another swallow of liquor and set the crystal glass on the coffee table in front of him. "The box was hidden a long time ago. There's always the chance both it and its contents are long gone."

Adrien studied him. "Would you be disappointed if they were?"

His cousin knew him like no one else. The question was one he might have asked himself if he hadn't had other pressing matters on his mind. "We've gone to a lot of trouble and expense…"

Adrien snorted. "Like you give a shit about the expense, and Tanner and Chantal both love a good physical challenge. You're personally interested in this object. If you weren't, you'd let them do their job without constantly checking on them."

Resentment reared its ugly head and Mark stopped himself from making a scathing reply. He never lied to Adrien—left out sordid details at times—but never lied. Adrien was more than his cousin; he was his best friend, and his Sentier. Adrien was also his conscience. "I don't want a powerful talisman falling into our enemy's hands."

Adrien's only reply was a cocked eyebrow.

"And yes, I want to see this object myself, to find out what it is and what it does. We need to determine if it is a weapon that can even the playing field in our war with Tolian and the Dissemblers."

"No."

"No? What the fuck is that supposed to mean?" Anger rolled through his body—anger, and guilt. He wanted to test the power, to find out what it could do.

"It goes into the vault with everything else. If the Shalamov sent this *thing*, whatever it is, to another continent, they had a damn good reason." Adrien's expression softened and his voice dropped the tone of command. "Let this go. You've been through enough."

Mark had no intention of letting the talisman or whatever it was go. He couldn't, but he wouldn't argue about it with Adrien now. They had another matter to discuss, one Adrien wouldn't welcome.

He reached for his glass and drained it. "Before you came in I finished the report from Biotech. Do you want to read it or just hear the bottom line?"

Adrien's face muscles visibly tensed. "A summary now and then send it to me."

Mark drew in a long breath. "The experiment went perfectly in every way but one."

Adrien nodded, sadness seeping into his expression. "The genetic sequence that determines psychic abilities didn't hold up. Again."

"Cloning an *ordinaire* is no problem. One of us? The DNA disintegrates as soon as it's frozen or manipulated. We've even tried fresh sperm and egg, but within twenty-four hours the DNA that makes us what we are breaks down. I'm sorry."

"The family has been watching Tate—Adele asked her last week when we're planning to start a family. Even her mother asked her if we were trying. She's been a good sport, but I can see she's uncomfortable. I hate to see her blamed when I'm the one who's the problem."

"We aren't giving up. Our people just don't know where to go from here. Someone will come up with a breakthrough. Tate's only thirty-three. You have plenty of time to make an heir and a spare."

"Have you reconsidered our other solution? Tate and I both think it's the best option we have." Adrien asked warily.

Even though he'd expected the question, it still hit him like a punch in the gut. "Off the table. You don't want your kid inheriting my ability."

"We both know it doesn't work that way. There's no way to predict what the baby's abilities will be."

"Right. But even with an outside risk, it's still an unthinkable risk."

"You're the strongest psychic of all the cousins and the only one who knows our situation. We're willing to take that risk."

Mark ran his fingers through his hair. He'd never refused any of Adrien's requests, no matter the danger to himself or people he loved. Telling him no now was killing him and yet, that was the only answer he could give. "Could you really sit by while I jerked off in one room and in the next, some doctor injected my sperm into your wife? I know you, man. It would kill you."

Adrien shook his head. "I can endure what needs to be done

to protect the family and the Source. I'm asking you to reconsider. I won't say you owe me. We both know you did what was necessary to save my life."

"Damn straight." Mark had negotiated with Bogdan, the previous Shalamov Sentier, for Adrien's life after his cousin's tragic psychic duel with the Shalamov heir. The exchange—Adrien's heirs for Bogdan's.

"I'm just asking you to reconsider."

And if the sperm donation didn't work? What would Adrien ask of him next? He shuddered. There were too many threats to everything the Durand stood for these days. If Adrien's dilemma was leaked, the family might panic. No one but Adrien could hold the Source alone and now, even he needed his wife to fully control the power.

"We'll find another way." As much as Mark hated to bring it up, there was a child they couldn't ignore. "Irina's son is over a year old." The son of Adrien's illegitimate older brother, now dead, and Irina Demidova, the current Sentier of the Shalamov Source in Siberia. The boy might be considered the rightful Durand heir if he could develop the power to channel the Durand Source.

"Time flies."

"She's remarried—to Kirill's cousin Yegor Shalamov. And she's pregnant again."

Adrien's eyes widened. "Yegor is a powerful enough psychic on his own to be the Sentier, if he had a ruthless bone in his body. And the Shalamov are loyal to their own."

"I have spies that will keep an eye on your nephew. If I think he's in danger, I'll do what needs to be done to keep him safe."

*Do what needs to be done*—that brought him full circle to the box in Montana. He'd stayed in Paris too long. First thing in the morning he'd fly his new custom Dassault Falcon back to New York, then decide where to go from there. If Tanner and Chantal found the box, he could fly to Montana and pick it up himself. No matter what Adrien said, if this object was as powerful as he imagined, using it couldn't be taken off the table.

# CHAPTER FIFTEEN

The icy wind stung Tanner's face. He grunted as he landed hard on the flat ground. The final drop had only been eight feet, but his legs ached from his old injuries, as well as the three-hour descent from the top of the cliff. A dull pain throbbed in his left shoulder—the one the Dissemblers had dislocated in the Mexican dungeon—and sweat plastered his undershirt to his chest in spite of the cold. The physical exertion was only part of the drain. The residual energy of the priest and shaman had become increasingly agitated—both men wary of the other—and the closer they got to the bottom, openly hostile. Only the boy remained calm.

"Get out of the way so I can jump," Chantal called down to him.

He stepped aside and watched her hand-over-hand down the sandstone and leap the last five feet. Mark had been right. She was an excellent climber and fearless. Few women could pull off some of the tough drops she had. Few men either, for that matter.

"Think there's a bar around here?" she asked. "I could use an Irish coffee about now. Even better, a hot tub."

He chuckled.

"Whoa, Hays, better be careful or you might catch a sense of humor."

"Fat chance." He scowled at her without conviction.

"That's better," she said. "Now where do we go from here?"

He dissolved his shield and let the life energy resting in the earth flow into him. Emotions and impressions swirled in his head until a jolt of aggression hit him in the chest and knocked the breath out of him. He tried to sort the mess out—who was the attacker and who the victim. The churning of something more clouded his perception. Close. They were close to their destination, but there was one last obstacle in their path. Arguing. Resistance. The river. Tanner's body shook violently. Terror. Not his.

Suddenly the trance broke and he was pinned against the wall of the cliff. Chantal held him there by both shoulders as the trembling lessened and stopped.

She let go. "What happened?"

He shook his head to clear it or maybe to process what he'd read. "They fought here over crossing the river. The priest was terrified—probably couldn't swim—and the medicine man struck him. I think the object in the box had something to do with the hostility. Feeding it, maybe? It affected the boy and the shaman, but not the priest."

"Because the two Indians had psychic abilities and the priest didn't?"

"Makes sense." He pushed himself away from the sandstone and scanned the opposite shore for a cave of any kind. The sleet had stopped and the cliffside was clearly visible for fifty yards in either direction. Nothing looked like the mouth of a cave or a good hiding place. "I'm going to walk up and down this shoreline and see if I pick up their energy. Tag our position with your ComDev and find us a route out of here."

"Should I send Mark our position?"

"Not until we find something." Assuming there was something to find.

He made his way north along the rocky riverbank opening his senses for signs the threesome had gone in that direction. On his right the river rushed by, swirling around the rocks and boulders in its path. Hikers, lots of them, had used the rocky trail—but not the priest and shaman. He turned around and backtracked to where Chantal was busy with her ComDev, then headed south. Again, plenty of foot traffic, none of it from the men he was tracking. The only alternative was obvious. They'd crossed the river.

The big difference between then and now was the season. The

weather had been warmer, summer maybe. The good news was, this time of year the precipitation in the mountains froze where it landed, rather than filling the tributaries that fed into the lakes. The river wasn't very deep or wide. The bad news was, the water flowing by was icy cold and they didn't have waders to keep them dry to the other side.

"So where did they go?" Chantal asked when he returned to his starting point.

He nodded toward the opposite shore. "They crossed here."

"Damn."

"Yeah." He scanned the river, assessing the depth and speed of the water. "We can wade or try to cross on the rocks ahead. Looks like there was a mudslide to the north at some point that deposited some decent-sized rocks. They'll be slippery."

She grimaced and slipped her ComDev back into her jacket pocket and zipped it. "Wading we're sure to get wet. I'm voting for the rocks."

"Rocks it is."

They set off, her taking the lead and nimbly navigating the stony shoreline.

"This looks like the best spot to cross," she called to him. "Except for a leap at the other side, we can walk across."

He reached her and studied the river. "That's a pretty long leap. We can walk further and see if there's a better spot." A glance told him they'd have a long walk before there was any possibility of a better crossing point.

"I checked the weather while you were scouting the shoreline. The storm is ahead of schedule. If we don't get out of here in the next few hours, we may be trapped." She adjusted her pack and readjusted it before taking it off. "This is a little heavy and the sleeping bag skews the balance. I'd be more confident of that last jump without it." She removed the rolled sleeping bag attached to the bottom of her pack and stuffed it under a bush.

"Does your ComDev say we can make it out before nightfall?"

"If we follow the river, we should be able to reach shelter in a couple hours. There's a lodge about eight miles from here and it isn't all uphill."

They both knew her guestimate was optimistic, especially since they still had to find the cave and the box. "Fine. I'll go first and test the stability of the rocks."

"I'm right behind you."

The rocks were worn smooth by the water, but stable. Tanner carefully chose the largest and flattest for his footing. His hiking boots gave him good traction, and the tension in his back eased a bit when he neared the far shore. As he stepped onto the last rocks, the distance across the open water seemed to double and it was much deeper than the rest of the river. "Damn." He could make it with a running start. Standing still? It was iffy.

Behind him, Chantal gingerly stepped from rock to rock, sometimes following his path, sometimes not. They could return to the other bank and look for another crossing spot, or he could go for it and hope he didn't land in the water.

Chantal stepped onto the rock next to him and whistled. "That's one hell of a standing long jump. Think you can make it?"

"Yeah. You?"

"Probably." She studied the stones at their feet. "There aren't enough footholds for a running take off, but if we start there…" She pointed at a flat stone behind him. "We can get a little momentum."

He hoped so. "I'll go first." Unhooking a line from his backpack, he handed her one end. "If I miss, drop your end, so I don't pull you in with me."

She stepped out of his way. "Mark owes us both a get out of jail free card for this." He didn't point out that Mark had already gotten them both out of jail.

He backed up and drew a deep breath. "Here goes."

Shifting his weight to his back foot, he took two powerful steps forward and launched himself toward the riverbank. His flight seemed to take forever, or maybe, time stopped while he hung midair. And then the frozen bank came up to pound his knees as he toppled forward onto his hands. He gasped for air, relief washing over him.

"You okay?" Chantal called.

"Yeah. Fine. Be careful of that last rock. It's icy."

She saluted him and stepped back for her approach. One step, two step, three. Her foot hit the edge of the last rock and it tipped. His heart stopped as she flailed her arms like featherless wings and flopped into the frigid water.

"Chantal!" The rope in his hand tensed and tugged from the current carrying her downstream. He tried to pull her in, but the line had snagged on a rock or branch under the water. Quickly, he knotted the line around a small tree trunk and scrambled over the boulders along the bank to follow her downstream. She wouldn't survive long in the icy river. He had to reach her and pull her out quickly.

Unfortunately, whatever snagged the line held her in the middle of the deep current, "Can you stand up?" he shouted.

"No." She tried to swim to the shore without letting go of the rope, but the water moved too swiftly for her to make headway.

He had another rope, but it was much shorter than the first. He'd have to wade into the water for it to reach her. As precious seconds ticked by, he quickly unhooked it and threw his pack into the bushes out of the way. "I'm going to throw you another line so I can pull you in."

Knotting both ends to make the line easier to hold, he braced himself, and waded into the water. The icy river immediately soaked his boots and pants to the knee. He gasped, but didn't hesitate to move deeper, close enough to toss the rope to Chantal.

She missed on the first attempt. He quickly hauled it back in and tried again, aware that every moment in the icy water threatened her life. This time she caught the line and started to pull herself toward shore. He scrambled for the bank, planted his feet in the sandy soil, and hand-over-handed the rope until he could grab her arm and drag her to shore. As he held her upright, water drained from her clothes and hair. Her face was so pale and her lips were a deep purple.

She pushed against his chest, teeth chattering. "Don't get any wetter than you have to. One of us needs some body heat."

"We need to get you warmed up."

She laughed without humor. "Where's the hot tub when you need it?"

"When we find the cave we can build a fire and use those chemical heat packs."

"I-i-i-f I d-d-d-d-don't expire of h-h-hypothermia first."

Extracting his pack from the bushes, he took her arm and helped her walk along the bank. Within fifty feet of where they'd crossed the river, he picked up the trail of the priest, shaman, and boy. In another hundred feet, the trail stopped abruptly at the side of the cliff, as though they'd walked right into the rocky wall.

"It's here." Tanner began rolling away the small boulders that had covered the mouth in a mudslide or avalanche. His gloves were wet and his hands so cold they were almost numb.

"Here, try this." Her shaking hand held out a small pick that had been attached to her pack.

He worked frantically, the effort increasing his blood flow and body temperature. He could do this. He had to do this. A hard blow of the pick threw him forward as the rocks tumbled into empty space.

"H-h-hot d-d-damn!" Chantal cheered. "You f-f-found it!"

Relief crashed over him. He could get her out of the cold and warm her up. Another half dozen hard blows with the pick and he was able to kick away the debris and create an opening big enough for them to crawl through. "I'll go first," he said, pulling out his ComDev and turning on the floodlight app. "To be sure it's safe."

"Anyplace is s-s-safer than out here. Hurry, d-d-damn it."

He took off his pack and wriggled through the opening, catching himself with his hands as his hips and legs followed. The floor was flat and the ceiling tall enough for him to stand. "All clear. Push the packs through then come on yourself headfirst. I'll catch you."

His pack came through the hole then hers. Hers was dripping water so he set it out of their way. "Now you."

Chantal's head and shoulders appeared, shaking violently. "I'm out of energy," she wheezed. "P-p-please…"

Carefully placing his hands under her arms, he eased her into the cave and held her up while she found her footing. She fumbled her ComDev from her pocket and turned on the search-light. Between them, they lit up the narrow passage that opened into a cavernous cave.

"L-l-looks like there are a couple t-t-tunnels into the mountain," she stammered.

"We can explore when we get you dry and warm. Let me help you get out of these wet things." He pulled off his gloves and started to work on the zipper of her jacket.

"I can't feel my fingers. I think they're gone." Her words were slurred, a sure sign of hypothermia.

Adrenaline surged through his body and his heart felt like it was going to pound out of his chest. He yanked the jacket from her shoulders and dragged it down her arms, then reached for her hands. "Let's get those wet gloves off."

Past the point of shivering, she didn't protest as he carefully undressed her. Her breathing was too shallow and she had to hold on to him to keep from falling. He got down to a soaked undershirt and silky long underwear pants and paused. "I'll get some dry things out of your pack."

"Hot bath," she mumbled. "Some nice tea. Do you have any tea?"

"Soon as you're dry, honey." He shook himself. He'd just called her *honey*? He was losing it too.

Their packs were water repellent, but hers had been submerged in the river. All her clothes were soaked except for a tee shirt, a change of long underwear and a pair of socks sealed in plastic.

"Need to go to sleep." She started to crumble.

He caught her. "Not yet. Stay with me."

He held her up with one hand and grabbed the sleeping bag attached to the top of his pack with the other. Awkwardly, he managed to unroll it and lay her down. He went back to their backpacks for the chemical heat packs and the cooking mat.

The heat packs were intended for hands, but they'd have to do. At least the cooking mat would stay hot for several hours. Turning it to high, he set it about six feet from the sleeping bag and started to remove Chantal's clothes. Her skin was a pale blue under her tan. He managed to get her in the dry long underwear and socks, then unzipped the sleeping bag and maneuvered her inside. The heat packs went in next to her chest before he covered her.

"Stay with me, Chantal. Stay with me." Peeling off his wet pants, he ignored the chattering of his teeth and the aching in his bad leg. Luckily, he had a dry pair of pants in his pack for later. He threw his wet scarf next to the cooking mat until it started to sizzle then patted it on his legs and feet to warm them up. He repeated the process, and by the third time, his skin was almost to its normal temperature. He pulled on dry long underwear pants and socks, and stripped down to a tee shirt. Unlike Chantal, he'd never lost his core temperature.

The heat mat would dry out some of her clothes. He propped it against the cave wall and rigged the line between the packs to drape the clothes over it, making sure nothing would catch fire. The air temperature around them would warm up a little, but not enough to counteract the effects of the icy river. Chantal hadn't moved, which was a bad sign. She was too far gone for her body to warm itself, even with the chemical heat. She needed help. Now.

He kneeled next to her, carefully lifted the edge of the sleeping bag and slipped in. She didn't stir. Shifting her so her back was to him, he wrapped his arms around her and drew her against his body. She was so cold, only her breathing and weak pulse told him she was alive. Entwining her legs with his, he tried to ignore the taut muscle and soft curves of her thighs and calves. Sharing body heat. That was all that was happening here. The goal was saving her life, nothing else.

Minutes went by and gradually Tanner relaxed. Once she warmed up, they'd look for the box and get back to civilization. The sleeping bag was cozy and her breathing seemed to be less strained. There was nothing more he could do for her. His mind began to drift. A short nap wouldn't hurt, especially since they had a long trek back to civilization. A few minutes were all he needed.

. . .

Chantal floated back to consciousness cocooned in heavy heat. Someone enveloped her with powerful arms against a hard body. Warm, even breaths feathered against her cheek and her head filled with the woodsy, musky scent of...Tanner.

Her heart sputtered and kicked into high gear. What the hell was going on? She tried to remember where she was and how they'd gotten there. The last thing she recalled was talking about crossing the river. She'd crossed the rocks and...

The memory crashed over her—falling into the icy water and holding on. Everything else was a blur.

Tanner shifted and tucked her tighter along his body. She didn't move. The floor beneath her was hard and uneven, and the little she could see was indistinct with shadows. As much as she enjoyed being warm in his arms, the weight of his leg twisted her knee painfully, forcing her to shift to straighten it.

"You're awake." His voice rumbled against her back and he pulled away. "Feeling better?"

"I think so. Did I pass out?"

"Yes. You were unresponsive and having trouble breathing. The hypothermia had me worried."

"So you shared your body heat with me?"

He cleared his throat. "Survival 101."

She smiled to herself. "Thank you. You saved my life."

"My pleasure...duty. Hell. It's what anyone would do." He disengaged himself and crawled out of the sleeping bag.

She rolled over and watched him stand and pull on his pants.

"I set your clothes out to dry, but likely they're still damp."

"I can handle damp." She wrapped the sleeping bag around her and sat up. The only light came from his ComDev propped up next to the heat mat. "Where are we?"

"I followed the trail to the side of the cliff and we dug through to this cave. I'm sensing that the boy stayed outside while the priest and Indian headed back into those tunnels. I haven't had time to explore yet." He picked up his ComDev sending much of the cave into darkness and tapped the screen several times. "I'll have a look around. The storm will hit any time now."

"I'm coming with you."

"You should rest."

"We have a mission to finish." She eased herself out of the sleeping bag, testing her body and bracing for the dizziness that didn't come. Relieved, she reached for her clothes.

"You're damn stubborn."

"So I've been told." None of the clothes were totally dry, but they weren't wet, and the inner layers were mercifully warm as she carefully dressed.

"Here's your ComDev," Tanner said. "Luckily these things are waterproof."

She took it from him and clicked on the light app. This part of the cave was about twenty feet wide, ten feet high, and ran about a hundred feet back into the mountain before it split into two different tunnels.

"Do you hear running water back there?" she asked.

He stilled for several seconds. "Faintly. I'll check it out. Could be how the tile got to the lake."

"I'm coming too."

"An hour ago you were passed out from the cold. You should rest and regain your strength. There are some protein bars in my pack."

"I'll take one of those bars, but I'm going with you." She flicked the screen of her ComDev to a locator app. It worked even when a GPS signal wasn't available. "I'll set our present coordinates and track our route in case we get turned around back there."

He shook his head and muttered something under his breath.

"I brought a light Ancilon bag that can be worn like a pack. We take just what we need—some climbing equipment, flares, knives—and pick up the rest of the gear on our way out. If those caves get too narrow, we'll have to take it off anyhow."

"Fine." She didn't care about the sleeping bag or stove, but she wasn't leaving any weapons, digging tools, or heat packs. She tucked what she could from her backpack in her jacket and pockets. "Ready when you are."

Handing her a headlight and turning on his own, Tanner took the lead. They paused where the cave branched into two tunnels. "The medicine man and priest's trail goes that way." He shone his ComDev light into the tunnel to the right.

The ceiling was not as tall as in the main cave, but still high enough for both to walk upright. The temperature was moderate here—forty-five or fifty degrees, she'd guess. Not unlike the caves where wine was stored in France.

"Do you hear water?" she asked.

"Yeah. Also in that direction."

"Lead on."

The passageway ascended into the mountain twisting in one direction and then another until Chantal became disoriented. In some sections they could walk upright, others required they duck or bend over. She'd never been claustrophobic, but she was glad she could glance down at her ComDev and see the path they'd come so far. When the tunnel opened into a comfortable passage, she stood erect and stretched.

"Damn," Tanner shined the light ahead where the wall had partially collapsed, dumping stone and gravel into the passageway. He drew closer and examined the debris. "This happened a long time ago and no one has been here since the priest and shaman passed through. We could close it up completely and leave."

"Not when we've made it this far. You are still picking up their trail, right?"

He didn't answer right away.

Unease prickled the back of her neck. "Tanner, what are you getting?"

"The energy trail goes in, but they didn't return this way."

"There could be another way out. Maybe the tunnel loops around and joins the other tunnel."

"Maybe. By the time they got here, the priest was afraid, the Indian too—but not of each other. Something vague and oppressive weighed them down."

Chantal shuddered. "We have a mission. To complete it, we need to find that box. Help me move some of these rocks and I'll climb through."

"No. We both go." He bent and began lifting stones and piling them out of the way along the wall. "The water is louder. We're close to it."

When the opening was large enough, they climbed through and continued for another twenty feet where the tunnel opened into a cavern so vast the light from their headlights barely penetrated it. The roar of falling water echoed around them.

Chantal shined her light around the ragged wall of rock until it landed on a waterfall that started someplace far above their heads. "This place is amazing."

"Let's take a look." Tanner pulled a battery-powered emergency flare from his jacket pocket and lit it.

Light filled the cavern and Chantal gasped. The space was at least fifty feet wide, and its jagged stone walls rose so high above their heads and so far below their feet, they disappeared into the darkness.

"I've never seen anything like this." He wedged the flare between a pair of rocks and pulled out his ComDev.

"Me either. I wonder why no one has discovered it—a lot of people come through this park."

He shrugged. "Maybe it has been discovered. There could be other access points above or below us."

"It wasn't on any map or in the park guides."

"Then you can report discovering it and maybe get a concession stand named after you."

She stuck her tongue out at him and he chuckled. "So are you getting any sense of where the box is? I'm guessing close to the water, but there's a lot of water."

Slowly he walked along the edge of the drop-off and stopped. "The energy ends here. It looks like there was a ledge along here extending toward the waterfall at one time, but it's long gone."

Chantal shone her ComDev at a dark shadow next to the rushing water. "Is that an alcove in the rock?"

Tanner's ComDev light joined hers. There was definitely a hollow big enough for a person to crawl into.

"I'm going to take a look," Chantal said.

He took off the Ancilon pack. "No, I'll do it."

"No, you won't. I'm smaller and lighter and just as good a climber as you are."

He took a rope and a couple pecker pitons from the pack. "It's too dangerous."

"Damn it, Tanner, use some common sense. If you slip and get in trouble, I can't haul you up by myself. We'll put the line on me and if anything happens, you can save me." She threw him a mock scowl. "Unless you decide to let me fall to the depths of hell or wherever this cave goes."

"Don't tempt me," he muttered. "All right, we do it your way, but if you get hurt, don't blame me."

Tanner secured a ring into the limestone, ran a line through it, then tied the end to Chantal.

She took the pitons from him and examined them. "Good old multiuse stand-bys. Nice choice."

He helped her put on the Ancilon pack. "The Ancilon will protect you from trancing if you find anything and need to bring it back. I put in tongs too that you can use to pick things up."

She retrieved Ancilon gloves and varying sized pouches from inside her jacket and stuffed them in the outside pockets. "If whatever's in that box is as powerful as I think it is, it's going to put this miracle fabric to the test."

And he might not be able to get to her in time if something went wrong. He reached for the pack. "We both go."

She pulled away. "I can take care of myself. If I run into trouble, I'll back off."

"You promise?"

She slipped on the headlight and saluted him. "Yes, sir. I promise."

"Be careful. I'll try to coach you on footholds and handholds where I can. You'll have to rely on your headlight until you reach the cave. The flare isn't as bright as I'd like it to be."

"It's what we have. Let's do this." She inhaled deeply and slowly let her breath out, focusing on the task ahead. The first eight feet were simple, the next forty she'd have to feel her way and hope the striated limestone held her weight. She reached for her first handhold and Tanner caught her arm.

When their eyes met, his held a tenderness she never expected to see. He raised his hand and brushed his fingertips down her cheek. "I mean it, be careful."

Her pulse spiked at his touch. She couldn't read too much into his gesture. Not now, when she couldn't afford to be distracted. She could do this—it was what she was trained for. "Yeah, I know. If anything happens to me, Mark will kick your ass." She grinned, grabbed the rock wall and jammed her foot into the first crevice.

# CHAPTER SIXTEEN

Tanner held the safety rope loosely so as not to impede Chantal's progress along the rocky wall. That didn't mean his entire body wasn't poised to act if she slipped. Each time she groped for her next handhold or jammed her toe tentatively into a crevice in the limestone, his heart stopped and kicked back into operation when the stone held her weight.

As she neared a smooth section, he flashed his ComDev on the face of the rock, searching for her next purchase. She ran her hand on the surface.

"There's a small ridge about twenty inches to your right and eight above your shoulder," he called to her. "The only foothold is a crack two feet to your right and about ten inches below where you are now."

She followed his directions and paused. "Thanks. Where next?"

He coached her along until she was only a meter below the alcove. "Directly above your head. Easy. The stone may be brittle."

She climbed smoothly and then he watched in horror as the outcrop beneath her left foot crumbled away just as her right foot lifted to find its next foothold. "Chantal!"

She hung by her hands until her right foot found a jut of rock to take her weight. A couple of dozen heartbeats later, she pulled herself to the alcove where she sat to rest, her feet dangling.

Tanner's ComDev buzzed on walkie-talkie mode. "You good?"

"Thought for a moment you were going to have to haul me out of the abyss," she chuckled. "Remind me to never complain about Protector boot camp again."

"That was some good climbing."

"Ah. Thanks." She stared at him across the chasm for several beats then cocked her shoulder behind her. "There's more of a cave here than I expected. About eight feet wide and goes back twenty-five feet or so. I'll send you video as I check it out." She pulled on her gloves then squirmed onto her knees and crawled into the cave with the headlight illuminating the way and her ComDev transmitting video back to him.

The roar of the waterfall on the video muted the further in she crawled. The cave was big enough for her to move steadily, but not to stand. The more he considered, the less likely it seemed that the priest had hidden the box there. The image wobbled as she moved, and came in and out of focus, making it impossible for him to see the details.

"*Merde.*" She'd stopped and aimed the camera lens at a pile of skins against the wall. Slowly, the image zoomed in. A mummified body that had once been clothed in leather and fur slumped against the cave's wall. "I think I found one of our guys. The shaman, most likely."

"Don't touch him. I'm coming over."

"No. Let me look for the box. If it's here, it doesn't matter what happened to him."

Tanner clenched his jaw down on his argument. He hated unresolved mysteries, but she was right. The mission was to retrieve the box, not risk his life and hers to investigate an ancient death. Still, the urge to find out what happened to the men whose trail he'd followed here was almost impossible to resist.

"The cave doglegs toward the falls ahead." She shined the light into a small cavern and gasped. "I found it."

As she inched closer, the camera caught three ledges carved out of the rock and a spout of water splashing down next to them from the ceiling. A rolled up skin lay on the uppermost ledge and a box sat on the ledge beneath it. She crawled closer and he heard her choke.

"*Merde.* This thing is broadcasting some serious mojo." The image shook. "No way I can make it back to you with it, even in Ancilon."

"On my way." He pocketed his ComDev and secured the second

line to a boulder, then to his safety belt. The flare used conventional batteries, but would stay bright for a few hours, plenty of time, if everything went smoothly.

The climb to the cave was strenuous and he was glad he'd pushed his rehab over the last year. When he finally pulled himself up on the ledge, he was breathing hard and sweat rolled down his back. High-definition images hit his psychic perception in rapid succession— the recognition of betrayal, staring into black eyes fill with hatred, acceptance of death. The shaman's greed had outweighed his fear and he'd pushed the priest to his death.

"Tanner?" Chantal's floodlight found him. "You okay?"

"Yeah." He pulled himself into a more comfortable sitting position. "The shaman killed the priest. Pushed him into the abyss."

She crawled closer and directed the light behind her. "Wonder why the medicine man didn't make it out."

"Not sure I want to know." Not if he had to experience another death right now.

"If there was something lethal about the box or its contents, better to find out now," she said.

"I want to take this slowly just in case…" No need to finish the thought. She understood the hazards of using his gift.

She handed him a pair of protective gloves and he pulled them on before shifting into a crouched position. He brushed past her, slowly approaching the grisly corpse. Any blood or obvious cause of death had been obscured by time. He wished there was a knife handle or a spear protruding from the mummy's chest. There wasn't.

"You didn't touch him, did you?" he asked.

"Hell, no. I avoid being slammed by murder whenever possible."

"It might not be murder."

She shuddered. "It might be something worse."

Great. Not what he wanted to hear, even if he knew it already. "I'm going to open my senses a little at a time and see what I can pick up. If I get into trouble…"

"I know what to do. It isn't like we haven't been here before."

He let his defensive shield slip away gradually and sensed the energy around him. Instantly, a throbbing light filled his mind and he felt like his entire body was expanding. His heart beat harder, his blood flowed faster. He could track electrical impulses along his nerves and felt the hair growing on his face, head, and arms. His senses were heightened until the infinite number of sights, sounds, and smells overloaded his brain and he knew he was about to die.

A sharp crack across his face snapped his shield defensively back into place. He blinked repeatedly until Chantal's face came into sharp focus.

"What just happened?" she asked.

"I'll be damned if I know. Whatever killed the shaman wasn't human." He told her what he'd experienced.

"Death by sensory overload," she said. "That's a new one for me. Something must have caused it. Whatever's in the box?"

"That's a reasonable guess. He was an intuitive, but his psychic abilities were limited. It's hard to say what proximity to a power object might have done to him."

"Or what it will do to us."

"Yeah. There's that." And they were running out of time before the snowstorm hit. "We have two choices—go get this thing, whatever it is, or blow up the cave and bury it forever. As First Order Durand, you make the choice."

"Or we can call Mark."

"Go ahead. This isn't a decision I want to make."

She spoke into her ComDev, "Call Mark."

The electronic voice responded, "No connection is possible at this time due to external interference."

She swore under her breath. "What do you think we should do?"

"We *should* blow up the cave."

"But?"

"We've come this far. Don't you want to see what's in the box?"

A grin spread across her face. "Absolutely."

"Me too."

He reinforced his psychic shield and led the way to the back of the cave. It was taller than the rest of the area, allowing them to stand upright in the section near the ledges.

The box was too large—a cube of about six inches on each side—to pick up with the tongs alone, so he used his gloved hand to balance it and set it on the floor. Chantal stood several feet back.

"Three of the tiles are missing where the water splashed on its side. Whatever's inside may be damaged." He poked at an oddly shaped tab of yellow metal on one edge of the top and the lid sprung open. The beam of his headlight fell on the contents. "What the fuck?"

Chantal moved closer and peered over his shoulder.

Tanner stared down into the box, hardly noticing the air shifting around him. In the middle of a wooden frame was a translucent red stone that glowed in the bright light. He diverted the light and the stone seemed to glow brighter.

"What is it?" Chantal asked.

His vision sharpened and he could see that the stone wasn't merely translucent, but so clear the texture of the wooden indentation showed clearly through it.

"It looks like a small glass animal heart," she said. "With light behind it."

He reached for it. Even with the protective gloves, energy pulsed at his hand, sucking it closer. His fingers tingled with the invitation to caress the red stone, feel its power. He snatched his hand back, inhaling unsteadily. "Shit. This thing *wants* me to touch it."

"*Wants?*"

He searched for a better word and failed. "Yes."

"Seduction with power," she murmured softly.

"It isn't evil."

"You can't know that."

And yet he did. "Its power feels welcoming, not malevolent. I'm not afraid of it."

Once again, he reached for the heart, this time without hesitation. His gloved fingers closed over the polished stone and lifted it from the box. It felt warm, even through the Ancilon. He turned it around to view it from all sides. "Definitely a heart, but I don't think it's made of glass. The color is too consistent and true for glass this old."

"A ruby," she said. "I've seen some spectacular ones, but this is the clearest and the largest. It's amazing."

As he stared down at it, the stone shimmered with energy and promise. So beautiful, it almost looked alive. Mesmerized, he removed a glove and dropped the stone into his palm.

"What the hell are you doing?" Chantal cried, and jumped back. "Are you crazy?"

Warmth filled him and power surged through his body. His senses sharpened and expanded. The rush of the water as it fell on rocks, the tingling of the spraying droplets. The smells of metal, mold, Chantal's soap and sweat, the mummy, the leather scrolls. Even his sight had improved, allowing him to distinguish details in the dim cave.

"I'm fine. Great. The ruby has amazing energy properties." He held it out to her. "Go ahead. Touch it."

"No! This isn't something we should mess with, especially in a cave in the middle of a mountain."

He stepped toward her and she pressed herself against the cave's wall. "There's nothing to be afraid of."

The shadows on her face exaggerated her frown. "Maybe you should be. Maybe we should leave it. Blow up the cave and bury it forever."

A wave of panic rolled through him and electricity pricked at his skin. "No! The heart and the box go with us."

"It killed the medicine man."

"Trust me. I know what I'm doing." He couldn't explain why he felt invincible or why the prospect of putting the ruby back in its box repelled him. It was as though the heart spoke to him and refused to be locked away again.

"I'll carry it." He opened his jacket and slipped the stone into his shirt pocket.

She stepped forward, planting her hands on her hips. "That's not a good idea."

"I don't remember asking you."

"Tanner, what are you doing? Is the stone affecting you? Is it doing something to your mind?"

"Just because you don't want to touch it, doesn't make it dangerous. In fact, I'm getting benevolent vibes from it."

She exhaled loudly. "All right. What about the skins up there?"

Using the tongs, he removed the rolled leather on the highest shelf and laid the roll on the floor. He opened it carefully and revealed another skin rolled like a scroll. It was covered with tiny pictograms organized in blocks, intricate symbols he didn't recognize at all.

"We'll take that and look at it later. With the storm coming, there's no time to try to examine it now." Chantal said. "Put the box and the scroll in the pack. Our mission is to deliver them for examination by experts. And that's what we're going to do."

He nodded, but didn't move. Any sense of danger or urgency had melted away and he was confident nothing could harm him.

He filled the pack. "Fine, let's go."

The climb back across the abyss was so easy he wondered why he'd ever been concerned about it. His hands knew their next move without him even thinking about them, and his feet had the dexterity of a squirrel. Or a rat. He smiled. His body was stronger and surer than it had ever been, proving the time he'd spent in the Mexican dungeon was no longer an issue.

Behind him, Chantal made her way across the cliff with more caution. At one point she grunted as she pulled herself up a long space.

"Need any help?" he called to her.

"No, I'm fine. Just caught a slippery rock."

When he climbed back onto flat ground, he heard the scurrying of a small animal in the cave and the water running down the rocks. The shaman had experienced heightened senses before he died too. Tanner shook his head. The shaman wasn't a Durand. The shaman wasn't a trained psychic.

Inside his jacket, the ruby felt like a live heart beating against his, filling him with strength and power. He could read the history of the cave through his boots—generations of Native American holy men with sacred gifts coming to this place long before the priest and medicine man. The last had been the man who had died in the cave. After him and the priest, no one had set foot in this place until today.

The flare flickered, throwing the abyss and the waterfall into shadow. Chantal stood on the rim of the abyss and stared back at where they'd been. "Maybe the box wasn't ever meant to be found."

"No, it wanted to be found."

"Don't be ridiculous. You don't know that." She knew more about sacred and magical objects than most of the Durand.

"Yes, I do. It's been waiting to be freed."

The words came out before he'd thought about them, but they were true. He felt like he could sense the essence of objects, and that his ability had expanded and would continue to expand as long as he held the ruby.

The realization jolted him. He had so much untapped potential locked up inside and the Durand rules had always limited him and kept him from exploring it. He saw that now. The Protector code was based on teamwork, the individual was secondary. No one questioned Mark and Adrien's right to rule—they were the most powerful of the Durand, and two of the most powerful psychics in the world. Or were they? Maybe that could change.

Chantal laid her hand on his arm and he could feel her concern through her touch. Her lips parted slightly and her blue eyes stared into his. "Is something wrong? Maybe you should put the ruby back in the box."

"No."

"Just until we get back to the cabin."

"I said no. Let's get going if you're so worried. When we get back, you can go off to Paris and I'll take the stone to the repository."

"Those aren't our orders. We go together."

"I don't need you."

"Too bad. Mark sent me on this mission and I'm on it until it's over, are we clear?"

"We'll see," he snapped. "Mark has too many rules and I'm not ready to concede yet."

"I'd like to see you say that to his face," she muttered. With a huff, she turned her ComDev searchlight into the passageway they'd come through earlier and headed back.

He only hesitated a moment before following her. His energy surged and he slowed his pace impatiently. He almost looked forward to a harsh and difficult trek back to civilization, the deeper the snow the better. There was no need to prove his power to anyone but himself and yet, showing Chantal how much stronger and more fit he was had its attraction.

In the semidarkness he could hear the steady rhythm of Chantal's breath, the soft thud of her boots on the rock, and the swish of the fabric of her jacket against her pants. The air changed as she passed through it, absorbing the scent of her skin, her shampoo, and fresh sweat—the musky scent of a woman. His heightened senses broadcasted what they received through his body straight to his cock. The need to take her then and there—down and dirty—blurred every other thought. He reached for her and caught himself. What was wrong with him?

He adjusted himself and tried to clear his head. She stopped abruptly and he almost plowed into her.

"What the…"

"Sh," she whispered. "Something's not right. Do you feel an odd energy?"

He'd been so occupied with not taking her that he hadn't focused on what was ahead. Stepping in front of her, he extended his enhanced senses. The faint echo of footsteps reached him first, followed by the stench of dark majik.

"We have company," he said softly. "Maybe a Dissembler, more likely, whoever killed Johnny."

"I don't smell Dissembler majik. Or any magic."

"I do."

Her eyes narrowed at him. "So what now?"

"I'll check it out." He drew his Ruger from the inside of his jacket. "He probably thinks the element of surprise gives him an advantage. You stay here unless I need you."

She stuck out her gloved hand, which held an Ancilon pouch. "Then give me the ruby. We can't let it fall into the wrong hands."

"No. I need it." He took the pack off and removed the box and scroll. Using the handle of his hunting knife as a hammer, he crushed the gold latch on the box to make opening it more difficult. He put the box back in the backpack.

She studied him suspiciously. "Why do you need the stone?"

Because it enhanced his psychic abilities. A dangerous reason a First Order Durand wouldn't accept. He tried to push past her but she caught his arm.

"Johnny's killer already knows about the tile," he said. "If the worst happens, I'll offer him the box."

"You didn't answer my question. Why do you *need* the ruby?"

"It enhances my senses. Maybe my reflexes, but I don't know." He removed her hand. "Whoever murdered Johnny has tricks I don't, and you don't."

"And the ruby levels the playing field?"

"I don't know." He glanced toward the entrance cavern, unable to hold her gaze. She was too smart and too perceptive not to see he was lying.

"When we get out of here, we talk about this."

"Sure."

"I mean it."

"I know."

He didn't wait for a reply. Whatever was ahead was waiting for them. Adrenaline surged through his body at the prospect of facing a murderer who wielded so much power. He walked lightly, careful not to make any noise. The tunnel required him to hunch over in places, but that didn't slow his pace. He turned off his ComDev light and listened for any sounds. Ahead, a small rodent scurried away as the smell of majik grew stronger. So this is what Chantal and the other First Order Durand picked up so easily. Other Protectors had developed that talent to varying degrees—very handy when fighting an enemy who didn't look any different from an average person.

Light glowed at the mouth of the tunnel. Whoever was out there had killed Johnny without even using a weapon. He'd frozen Jason and made himself invisible. And now Tanner was going to face him alone. His heart beat harder.

He drew in a deep breath and concentrated on the ruby in the pocket next to his chest. Power surged through him and charged the air around him—energy he knew Adrien could command at will. He'd never felt it before, not like he did now. Was this what made the Durand Sentier what he was? For several seconds, he let the power flow and focused on the energy. His mind took in the feel of it and with a jolt he realized he was able to taste its nature. Yes, he was ready to meet the man in the cavern. Hell, he was ready to meet Tolian himself.

Holding his gun at his side, he stepped into the cavern, which was still brightly lit with the electric flares. A man stood in the center of the space.

"So we finally meet," the man said. "While I've been waiting, I've amused myself trying to figure out how this little gadget works" He pointed at the cooking mat. "Very ingenious."

"Who are you?"

"Aaron Greywolf. And you're Tanner Hays."

Tanner wasn't sure what he'd been expecting, but Greywolf wasn't it. He was almost as tall as Tanner and looked to be in his late thirties except for the short salt and pepper hair that stood up straight from his head. Instead of the western style winter clothes most of the locals favored, he wore high tech cold weather gear that emphasized his lean frame. At this close of a range, the scent of majik rolled off of him in waves.

Tanner swallowed his revulsion. "You've done your homework."

Greywolf's smile didn't reach his cold black eyes. "I assume Ms. Durand is waiting in the tunnel. Please call her."

"Why would I do that?"

Greywolf raised a sleek Remington hunting rifle and pointed it at Tanner's chest. "I'm not a patient man."

"What do you want?"

"Ms. Durand. Then we talk."

Chantal emerged from the tunnel empty-handed. She glanced from Tanner to Greywolf. "The weapon isn't necessary."

"We'll see." Greywolf lowered the rifle, but kept it ready. "What are you looking for?"

"Just out for a hike and a little exploring," Chantal said.

"Bullshit. Where's the tile Hank gave you?"

Chantal frowned. "What tile?"

"You know damn well. The one Johnny Hawkswing found."

"The artifact? We left it in the Tahoe," Tanner said. "Why would we bring it on a hike?"

For an instant, Greywolf's confidence seemed to waver. Tanner saw his opening and moved. He raised his Ruger and before he could pull the trigger, a deafening report echoed in the cavern.

"Tanner!" Chantal rushed at him.

Searing pain pierced his shoulder and his Ruger fell at his feet. The world shifted into slow motion as his mind processed the pain and fought it. He shook his head to clear it.

"Stand back," Greywolf ordered. "I only need one of you alive."

Chantal whirled on him. "What do you want?"

"Hays, kick the gun over here. Then take off the pack and set it on the ground."

Tanner did as he was told. Greywolf was trying to read his mind—he felt the distinct tapping on his psychic shield—and the man's face registered surprise when he was blocked. He then shifted his gaze to Chantal who smugly stared him down.

"So are you going to tell us what you want?" she asked. "Obviously you're not going to use your telepathy on us."

"How did you find the Naato'si Cave?"

Tanner recognized the name. "The Naato'si Cave? Why was it named for the Sun God?"

Blood ran down Tanner's arm and dripped on the floor. The

pain was making him sick to his stomach while it sharpened his mental acuity.

"You're wasting time. How did you find the cave?"

Tanner glanced at Chantal who was poised to act, which might make their situation worse. "There's a first aid kit in that pile over there. Let her stop this bleeding and we'll tell you what we know."

"You'll tell me anyway."

"Not if I'm dead."

"She'll tell me."

Chantal shook her head. "I don't know. I fell in the river and was unconscious."

Greywolf adjusted his hold on the rifle and motioned for her to move. "Get the first aid kit. Any tricks and I kill you both."

While their captor tracked their movements, Tanner concentrated on directing his energy to read the other man's thoughts. Greywolf didn't have a shield in the way the Durand did, but as soon as Tanner probed into his mind, an icy darkness repelled him back out. Nothing in Greywolf's expression or stance indicated he had done anything consciously or that he was aware of Tanner's invasion.

Chantal retrieved a small red and white plastic box and knelt next to Tanner. "Take off your jacket and lay down."

"No. Hand him the kit and get back over there." Greywolf used the rifle to nudge her away.

Tanner took off his jacket and outer shirt, stealthily moving the ruby from his shirt to his pants pockets. The blood had soaked through his undershirt and run down the long sleeve.

"Let me help him," Chantal pleaded. "I've removed bullets before and dressed plenty of wounds."

"No."

Getting to the wound without removing his shirt was tricky, but there was no way he was going to expose his body to Chantal and Greywolf. He cleaned the wound as best he could through the neck opening and applied an antibiotic bandage DT marketed as *new skin*.

"There should be some antibiotic capsules in the kit," Chantal said.

"I'll bleed out before infection sets in."

"Shut up," Greywolf snapped. He picked up the Ancilon pack containing the box and opened the top.

"No!" Chantal leapt to her feet and lunged for the bag, knocking Greywolf backward. He stumbled and his rifle discharged into the ceiling of the cavern causing gravel to shower down on their heads.

Everything seemed to happen in slow motion. Chantal reached for the rifle and Greywolf brought it down on her head. She sank to her hands and knees then rose up, her face twisted in fury. Tanner tried to scramble to her aid, caught Greywolf's boot in the jaw, and fell back on his wounded shoulder. Pain ripped through his face and body. He blinked to clear his vision.

Chantal lay at Greywolf's feet, his rifle pressed against her chest. "I'm done fucking around with you. Give me a reason not to kill you right now."

"Her cousin will pay to get her back alive," Tanner said. "He owns Durand Tech."

"How much?"

"Twenty million, thirty million. Name your price."

"What about you? How much are you worth?"

Tanner chuckled. "In dollars? Not much. But I know you used telepathy on Johnny Hawkswing and it killed him. You also used majik to hide your presence from his grandson."

Greywolf paled. "You made that up."

"Did I?"

"People around here know me, have known me all my life. No one would believe you. They'd think you were crazy."

"Maybe." He glanced at the pack. "Why did you have us followed?"

"I want the tile."

"What do you think it is?"

Greywolf frowned. "A piece of a treasure stolen from the gods. It gives extraordinary power to whoever possesses it."

Tanner could certainly attest to that. "Why was it hidden in the cave?"

"The holy men fought over the treasure, which made our gods angry. It was given back to the gods in their sacred cave where it would never be found."

The story tracked with everything he and Chantal had learned. Best of all, this guy had no idea what the treasure was. "What does that have to do with the tile?"

"The old man's vision was ice and snow."

"Can I please get up?" Chantal asked.

"No." Greywolf slid the barrel of his rifle to her throat. "Hand me that bag. Very slowly so I don't accidentally pull the trigger." The pack lay next to her right arm. She fumbled with the strap then lifted it high enough for him to reach. Having to cover both of them made it difficult for Greywolf to open the pack and look inside.

Tanner braced himself to move if Greywolf shifted the rifle away from Chantal for an instant. She'd be ready to act too.

Awkwardly prying the top of the pack open, Greywolf tipped it to dump the contents on the ground.

"You don't want to do that," Tanner warned.

"Why not?"

Tanner remained silent.

"Why not?"

Tanner shrugged. "Suit yourself."

He stuck the bag between his knees and reached inside. His expression changed from confusion to awe as he drew the box out. "What the fuck?"

Even from ten feet away, Tanner felt the fallout of Greywolf's psychic connection to the box. The air vibrated with a disturbing energy, as though the box rejected the man holding it. His weapon fell to the floor, freeing Chantal. She grabbed the barrel of the rifle as she rolled from him and crouched into a defensive position.

"Hands up." She aimed at her former captor.

Greywolf didn't seem to hear her. He stared at the box, mesmerized.

Careful not to jolt his shoulder, Tanner slowly rose to his feet. He slipped his fingertips into his pocket and touched the ruby. A shimmer of electricity climbed up his arm and melted through his body. His vision shifted and the bubble of dust hovering around Greywolf came into focus and filled his head with the scent of rotting jungle undergrowth. It looked alive, undulating in the flickering light of the cavern, and he knew what it was. Majik.

"I said raise your hands," Chantal said. "Now."

There was no sign that Greywolf was aware he was in the sights of his own weapon. He began to shake and the majik expanded and thinned.

"He's in some kind of trance." Tanner could feel the effect of the majik on his skin, like a swarm of crawling insects. He stepped back, but the creepy sensation remained. "Shoot him."

"What?"

"Shoot him—in the leg, arm, just debilitate him."

Chantal stared at Greywolf. "What is he doing? I can smell magic, or is it majik? There's something odd…"

Tanner picked up his Ruger and aimed it at Greywolf. "Put the box on the floor."

Drawing a skinning knife from a sheath at his waist, Greywolf bared his teeth and jabbed in Tanner's direction. "Now you die."

Tanner pulled the trigger. Nothing happened. The pin didn't fall, the hammer didn't work, and the bullet stayed in the clip. "My gun jammed. Shoot him."

This time Chantal pointed the rifle at Greywolf and fired. Except nothing happened.

"What the hell?"

"It worked before," Chantal said.

Tanner had proof the weapon had been operational—the throbbing of his wound. What was happening?

Greywolf smiled. "It seems this box has powers it acquired from its maker. There's a protection ward that won't allow you to hurt me as long as I have it in my possession."

"The majik is dissipating," Tanner observed. "Once it's gone you'll be vulnerable again."

Greywolf laughed. "What do you know of majik? I've studied the arts all my life and learned from my father. You know nothing."

"And yet, we found the box and you didn't. We found the cave, you didn't. And we know where that box came from and you don't."

Greywolf frowned. "We've been looking for the cave for generations. You were just lucky."

Chantal laughed. "Luck had nothing to do with it. We tracked the men who hid the box."

"Impossible. They've been dead for centuries."

Tanner nodded. "They died in the cavern, one murdered and the other by his own greed. You don't know who or what you're dealing with, Greywolf."

For a moment the professor studied them, box clutched to his chest. "It doesn't matter how you found it, it's mine now and I control its power."

"Really?"

Greywolf stepped back toward the entrance to the cavern. "Tom," he called. "Is everything in place?"

Tanner and Chantal exchanged glances.

"Tom," Greywolf shouted again. "I'm coming out. Is everything ready?"

Tanner attempted to shoot him again, and again the weapon didn't fire. "Shoot him!"

Chantal raised the rifle. "It won't fire."

Greywolf laughed as he backed toward the entrance. "Next time you go hunting be sure your equipment is in order."

Chantal charged him, rifle raised to use as a club. Tanner followed, gun raised, ignoring the pain shooting through his arm and shoulder. Five feet from Greywolf they hit an energy barrier and were propelled backward. Chantal screamed in frustration. Tanner grabbed his shoulder to protect it as he fell.

Greywolf took off into the dark passage. Tanner rose to follow while Chantal found her Glock in her pack. "Son of a bitch isn't getting away if I can help it."

He ducked into the entrance tunnel and was thrown back by a blast that shook the cavern until sand and gravel rained down on them. The dirt shower was unmistakable. Tom had indeed made everything ready.

Tanner waited for the dust to settle before he shone his ComDev into the passageway. Rubble filled it from floor to ceiling.

"How bad is it?" Chantal asked.

"The tunnel collapsed. We're trapped."

# CHAPTER SEVENTEEN

Chantal studied Tanner. Something was off aside from his bleeding shoulder and their current dilemma. He somehow seemed *more* than he had always been, and yet she couldn't define the change. "Sit down and let me look at that shoulder."

"We have bigger problems."

"Bigger than you bleeding to death?" she asked.

"I'm not bleeding anymore and we need to find a way out of here."

"Of course you're bleeding."

"No, I'm not. It stopped." He took the ruby from his pocket. "Because of this."

The stone glowed in his hand. She shivered and dread pooled in her stomach. "You're asking for trouble. We don't know what it is, but we know it killed the medicine man."

"And it's healing me. Without it, I won't make it out of here."

And he had to make it out. They had to make it out. "What just happened?" she asked.

"Tom, whoever he is, blew the entrance to the tunnel."

"That's not what I meant. What happened with Greywolf? You saw something I didn't."

He didn't meet her eyes. "What did you see?"

"Him holding the box and going into some kind of trance. There was some kind of magic or majik—it had a smell and taste that was different from Dissembler majik. I couldn't tell if it was neutral or negative."

"Like the box itself," he said.

"Why didn't our weapons fire?"

"I can only guess." He picked up a canteen from the gear piled along the cavern's wall and unscrewed the spout. "The box's magic initially repelled Greywolf, but something shifted and it began feeding on his power. Did you see the aura it created?" He took a drink and offered the canteen to her.

She shook her head. "No. What kind of aura?"

"Particles of light and energy. I think that's what stopped us from shooting him."

"I've never heard of that kind of magic before." But that wasn't totally true. What she'd heard wasn't magic at all. "Do you know anything about the Shalamov Source?"

"It's the center of an underground world in Siberia. Shalamov psychics often have telekinetic abilities—the genetic result of the properties of their Source's energy." He replaced the canteen and took a flannel shirt from his hiking pack.

"Don't you want to take off the bloody undershirt shirt before you put that on?"

"It's too snug to take off without opening the wound." Tanner shoved his injured arm in one sleeve and wrangled his good arm into the other. "This is fine."

She looked away and recovered her train of thought. The guns hadn't fired. "Aside from its remote location, the Shalamov Source itself is responsible for the primitive conditions of the domain. Its properties prevent electrical, mechanical, and technical devices from operating."

"Like guns?"

She nodded. "If the protection ward, or whatever it was, originated with the Shalamov, that might explain the guns not firing. But why didn't it affect our ComDevs when we transported it out of the cave?"

"Looked like Greywolf triggered its majik."

She took her ComDev from her pocket and checked its functions. "Light works, temperature and humidity readings, internal memory, internal apps. Call Mark." The message that appeared on her screen confirmed her worst fears. *No Signal.*

"We're still too far under the mountain, aren't we?"

And trapped. "It worked in the Outback where no one else had service. It worked in the middle of the ocean. Lex used to joke that a ComDev worked everywhere on earth and probably Outer Space."

"Guess we proved that wrong." He reached for a light jacket that normally served as an insulated lining for a waterproof shell. It was neatly folded next to the sleeping bag. "Can you give me a hand with this?"

"Sure." She held the jacket while he slipped his arms in. Automatically, her fingers freed the collar that got tucked inside, her skin brushing his neck and hair. He didn't jerk away. Progress or resignation? She hoped the former.

"Guess we'd better check out the other tunnel," he said. "See if there's another way out."

The flares would provide light for another thirty hours or so, but Chantal turned two of the three off to conserve their conventional batteries and picked up the other. "In case we're here for a while."

"Good point." He'd already started for the tunnel they hadn't explored earlier. He ducked his head and entered. "Humans have been here, but not for a very long time."

Chantal turned on her headlamp, glad the bright LED light warned her of low-hanging rocks and the uneven floor. About fifty meters in, the tunnel widened to room size—thirty feet by thirty feet, she guessed—and ended. It was tall enough for Tanner to stand upright, but not much more. Her heart sank. Not a way out.

"Look at these." Tanner approached the far wall and his headlamp and ComDev revealed stylized paintings covering the relatively smooth rock. "These are much older than three hundred years."

He was right. They reminded her of the paintings in the Lascaux Caves in France. She'd only seen the reproductions—the caves having been closed to visitors before she was born—but the colors and style were surprisingly similar. "I'd guess they're more than three thousand years old. What are you picking up in here? What was the room used for?"

"Talking to ancient spirits. The holy men believed the spirits created the pictures so men would be able to see their forms."

"Can you tell who made these and how long ago?"

"There's centuries worth of human energy and lots of it. At some point, people lived here." He shone his ComDev slowly around the room to illuminate the paintings. "No people. Only animals."

"Like the Guardians," Chantal murmured.

"Who are the Guardians?"

She bit her lip. She wasn't going to explain her family's most guarded secret to him. "A lot of cultures believe their gods take animal form when they come to earth."

"Aren't you curious?" he asked.

"Of course."

"Touch the wall." The eagerness in his voice reminded her that he, too, was a scholar who studied the past through what it had left behind.

She hesitated before moving forward. The paintings didn't give off any indication of magic and nothing about the cave felt hostile. Slowly, she extended her hand. "I don't expect this to take me down."

"I'm right here to catch you." His voice came from close to her ear—he was only inches behind her.

Her fingers brushed the wall and a rush of impressions filled her head. Ancients grinding pigments, making primitive brushes from leaf fibers, chanting as they drew the charcoal outlines and filled in the color, worshippers, petitioners, wise men, fools. Suddenly, everything shifted. She was enveloped in energy and heat, her palms pressed against the rock and held there by a force she couldn't fight.

The reception amped up and intensified, as though the painted figures were singing their memories, showing her their past. Her legs gave way, but she didn't fall. The power around her held her up when her body went limp and her mind sizzled on overload. Everything went dark.

Gradually the lights came on again. Her mind rose from its fog and her body registered the warm softness beneath her head and body. Her right hand was still imprisoned by the same heat and power that had held her at the wall. She opened her eyes and pulled away—the power was in Tanner, the warmth was his hand.

"Take even breaths." He knelt next to her where she lay on the sleeping bag in the main cavern.

"What the hell did you think you were doing?"

He had the sense to look guilty. "I wanted to experience what you were picking up. The ruby…"

Understanding of what she felt dawned on her. "The damned ruby let you use my abilities, didn't it? And you were willing to risk my sanity and maybe my life without even asking me."

"I wouldn't have done it if I'd thought you were in danger," he replied defensively.

"Oh, right. And you know all about the ruby's power? You held me against that wall until I passed out. What the hell is wrong with you?"

His eyes threw daggers at her. "You don't understand."

"Enlighten me."

The muscle in his jaw tightened and his lips pressed together. "The power. It's unimaginable."

"So you're entitled to use it for your own purposes regardless of who you hurt? Is that it?" The hardness of his stare began to frighten her. He had this new power and he hated her. And they were trapped in the cave together.

"The First Order Durand have never hesitated to use their power. How many Protectors have Adrien and Mark sent on missions that they have never returned from? Or returned so damaged that their lives were ruined?"

She pulled her hand back. "You arrogant son of a bitch. You and Luke volunteered for the assignment in Mexico—nobody forced you to go. You'd still be there, or dead, if Mark hadn't risked his own life to get you out."

"And Javier got killed because you were above following our agreed-upon plan."

Something inside her snapped. They were never getting out of here anyhow and she was tired of protecting his feelings. "Javier was working with the terrorists. He was a traitor who led you into a trap."

"That's a fucking lie."

Her hand shot out and slapped him across the cheek. The loud crack startled them both and fury rolled off him.

"If you were a man," he growled.

"You'd what? Fight me for telling the truth?"

His mouth tightened. "Javier was my best friend. I would have known if he was a traitor."

"Maybe you didn't want to know."

"That's bullshit."

"How many times did he complain about Adrien and Mark and the rest of the Durand? How many times did he tell you we had no right to have so much while so many Protectors lived modestly?"

His fierceness waivered. "That was just talk. It doesn't mean he was a traitor."

"And yet, he suggested you two deserved more, and if you left the Protectors you'd be better off." She saw she'd hit a chord and continued. "He sold us out—you, me, and all those people in the Underground."

He leaned into her face. "I don't believe you."

"Deep in that stubborn head of yours, you know the truth. You just don't want to hear it from me."

His bark of a laugh held no humor. "Yeah. And why am I only hearing this now—seven years later?"

He inhaled sharply. Realization dawned on him. "Mark and Adrien didn't trust me. You didn't trust me."

She shook her head slowly. "I trusted you. Even though you blamed me."

"But the Sentier thought I was a traitor. Does he still?"

"No, or you wouldn't be here." Adrien hadn't specifically forbidden her to discuss her orders to kill the Dissembler terrorists before they escaped. Still, it was Adrien's call when and whether he was briefed. "But you and I are here on a mission to take that ruby back to the Durand vault, where it can't fall into the wrong hands."

He laughed. "And how are we supposed to do that? We're trapped inside a mountain with no way to communicate with the outside world and it would take an earthmover to dig out the tunnel Greywolf blew up. We have a few protein bars, a day's worth of dried rations, and about a quart of water left."

"And you were shot." She glanced at her watch. It was nearly midnight and she was cold, hungry, and tired. They still hadn't discussed what her mind had processed about the wall paintings, but that didn't need to happen right away. "It's late and I need food and a few hours of sleep to think straight."

He nodded and his expression softened a little. "You take the sleeping bag and I'll stand guard."

"Stand guard for what? We're trapped in here. Nobody's coming in." She remembered how warm and cozy she had been tucked against his body. "We can share the sleeping bag and both get a good few hours of sleep."

"That's not a good idea." His gaze slid down her body and back with an intensity that made her forget she was pissed off at him.

"Because I'm so irresistible? Believe me, I'll have no trouble keeping my hands to myself."

# CHAPTER EIGHTEEN

Mark pulled his Maserati into his space in the Durand hangar at Paris Orly Airport. The Dassault Falcon was ready and the crew and passengers were waiting for him.

Before getting out, he checked his ComDev for messages. Nothing from Chantal or Tanner. "Call Chantal," he said. His call went to voicemail. "Locate Chantal." UNABLE TO LOCATE DEVICE appeared on the screen. "Shit."

His unease wasn't quite worry, but it had been sixteen hours since their last message and they'd expected to be back at the cabin hours ago. "Current weather, Glacier National Park, Montana." The report popped up on the screen: BLIZZARD, TEN INCHES OF SNOW, TEMPERATURE TWENTY-TWO DEGREES FAHRENHEIT.

Both Tanner and Chantal had been trained for harsh conditions and would have taken the proper gear. Even if they had to wait out the storm in a cave, they'd be fine.

He got out of the car and headed for the plane. His copilot, decked out in full uniform, waited for him at the bottom of the stairway. "Good morning, sir. Everyone's aboard and we're ready to go."

Mark nodded to the flight attendant and the two Protectors catching a ride home as he boarded, then settled in the pilot's seat. The cockpit smelled of fine new leather and the flight deck was a pilot's wet dream. An outsider might consider the jet an extravagance, but as much as he traveled it was a luxury he savored. Plus, the cost didn't even put a ding in his vast fortune.

His ComDev buzzed and he glanced at the screen before answering. His father. "What's up?"

"Are you still in Paris?" Georges rarely called and never for chitchat.

"Taking off for New York in a few minutes, why?"

"Got a minute?"

Mark smiled. Between his companies and his philanthropy, his father was constantly busy, and yet, he was always considerate of everyone else's time.

"Sure, Dad, what's up?"

"I got a call last week from Theresa Powell. She used to work for me in legal."

"I remember her." She'd been a no-nonsense attorney who had given him advice when he was starting Durand Tech.

"Her daughter and two friends disappeared somewhere between Paris and Nice about three weeks ago. The American embassy hasn't been very helpful and the French authorities less so. I was wondering if you have anyone who could investigate what happened."

Mark frowned. His father had been the Durand Field General before Adrien took over and was one of the most connected men he knew. "You know more agents in the CIA, Interpol, French government, and American diplomatic corps than anyone in the family."

"In the last week, I've exhausted my contacts. The consensus is that they've been abducted. No clues as to who did it or where they might have been taken. No activity on their credit cards or passports. They just vanished."

Mark closed his eyes and rubbed his right temple where a headache had lodged. "Let me guess. College girls, pretty, well dressed, great figures. How many blondes?"

"Two of the three. Long hair, multilingual, and smart. According to Theresa, they're also cautious. They wouldn't take up with strange men, or accept invitations to villas or yachts."

As much as he respected Theresa, he also doubted the young women were as careful as she thought. Too many women had jumped at his invitations over the years. "Human trafficking is big business. Pretty girls that age can bring a lot of money. We have

Protectors undercover in the major cities along the Mediterranean specifically investigating possible smuggling organizations. Send me the girls' photos and any details you have. I'll make sure they're on the lookout for them. That's the best I can do."

"Thanks, son. I know it's a long shot, but I had to ask." Georges Durand cleared his throat. "Have a good flight. Stop in and see us one of these days."

"Sure. Soon." Mark hadn't seen his parents in months. Exhaustion rolled over him—the deep fatigue of too much failure and the feeling of helplessness in the face of overwhelming evil. He couldn't remember his last good night's sleep—eight hours with no nightmares or guilt.

His ComDev pinged—the message from his father. He'd deal with it during the long flight. He called up the tracking system to check on Tanner and Chantal. Still offline.

"Pre-flight inspection has been completed." Ian, his copilot for this flight, stood in the doorway. "Are you ready to take off, sir?"

"Let's do this," Mark replied, forcing himself to push the weight of his responsibilities into the darkness in the back of his mind and focus on the one thing that he still loved—flying. Tanner and Chantal were on their own. There was nothing he could do but trust they'd surface—preferably with whatever treasure or curse the Shalamov had sent to the New World.

# CHAPTER NINETEEN

In spite of hot food, dinner was a cold affair. Neither of them said much that didn't have to do with cooking, serving, and eating the reconstituted stew. Tanner usually avoided dried rations and was pleasantly surprised to find they weren't bad at all.

He ate slowly, postponing the inevitable. Sleeping in a tent with Chantal had been bad enough. In the same sleeping bag? Agony. She'd been right, there was no reason to keep watch and they both needed a couple of hours of rest before they went searching for another way out. Unfortunately, the temperature in the cave hovered at forty-five Fahrenheit—warmer than outside—but too cold to sleep on the ground in only his jacket and pants.

"So are we going to talk about this?" Chantal asked.

"About what?"

"The two-ton gorilla."

He scowled at her.

She looked to the ceiling as though petitioning a higher power. "The sleeping arrangements neither of us is happy about."

"Oh, *that* gorilla." He shrugged. "I spent two weeks in a rat-infested dungeon with slop to eat and filthy water to drink. I think I can make it through a night in a clean sleeping bag next to you."

Her expression softened. "I'm so sorry that happened to you."

"I don't want your sympathy. I volunteered for the assignment knowing the risks. I was just making a point."

She snorted. "That sleeping with me wouldn't be the most horrible experience of your life. I'm happy we got that settled because I can barely keep my eyes open. I'm going to bed—sleep. Feel free to crawl in when you're ready."

He took his time cleaning up and reorganizing their gear, trying to ignore her arranging the thermal ground cover then spreading the sleeping bag on top of it. When a flare rolled away the movement in his peripheral vision drew his attention. He gulped. Chantal wriggled out of her pants and laid them on the edge of the ground cloth, her long legs and perfect ass in thin silky long underwear right there for him to appreciate. And it was one hell of an ass.

He turned his back to her and tried to work up a healthy repugnance. Too bad his body wasn't cooperating. At all.

"I'll turn out all the flares but one," he said.

"Sounds good." Her voice was muffled.

When he finally turned again, she was nestled in the bag, nothing showing, but a few strands of auburn hair sticking out the top.

He planted his butt against the wall, took the ruby from inside his jacket, and held it in his open palm. Why had someone carved it in the shape of an animal's heart? That seemed important. Did the shape give it power?

The stone was warm on his skin and he could almost feel it beating. The power that emanated from it was subtle, having filled him it now worked on his body, making him stronger and bigger. And aroused. As though the need to procreate lived inside the flawless red stone.

He glanced at the sleeping bag and slipped the stone into his pants pocket. No matter how he felt about her past sins, Chantal was a beautiful woman and the chemistry between them was undeniable. Always had been. They were trapped here, might die here, and he wanted her. Deserved her.

Tanner shook his head to reset his mental process. They were Protectors on a mission and they'd find a way out of this fucking cave.

He stretched his shoulder, the one with that had taken the bullet. Sore, but not as bad as he'd expected. With her nestled in the bag, he retrieved the first aid kit and stripped down to his underwear shirt. The blood had dried and pasted the fabric to his skin. Carefully, he peeled it off. The water they'd heated to reconstitute their stew was still warm. Using his ruined shirt, he washed away the blood. The artificial skin bandage was trickier. With his thumb nail he worked up a corner and slowly lifted the "skin." The last thing he needed was to start the bleeding again.

"What the fuck?" He glanced at the sleeping bag. She hadn't moved.

With the corner of his shirt, he carefully rubbed the dried blood from the hole—or what had been a hole. The skin was raw and angry, but the wound had closed. It was impossible, but there it was—proof of the ruby's power. And its connection to him.

He pressed a new artificial skin bandage on the wound and found a clean T-shirt in his pack. In a couple of hours, the bullet hole might be healed. He patted his back pocket to assure himself the stone was still there.

Although the ruby gave him strength, fatigue rolled over him and he could no longer resist. He rose and crossed to the sleeping bag, torn between wanting to crawl into a warm cocoon and wanting to stay awake and plan their escape from this prison. Sleep would clear his head and help his shoulder heal. He'd wake up before Chantal and come up with a plan then.

Kicking off his boots he considered the possibility Greywolf would return, but they were safe from the collapsed entrance. He took off his pants and pant liner and stood there in only his T-shirt and cotton boxer briefs. The air chilled his skin. A couple hours of sleep and he'd get them out of there.

He tucked the stone into the breast pocket of his tee and hesitated before slipping into the sleeping bag. Although it was oversized for one person, he had to stretch out straight and ease her over to zip it up. Nothing like the way he'd held her against his body to warm and revive her. Granted, they'd fit better if they spooned. He grunted and shifted his back to her.

As he relaxed into a doze, the impressions he'd received through Chantal when she touched the wall floated around his mind. Painted dancers gyrating in the firelight, chanting, sacred smoke. Soon consciousness drifted into a sleep filled with fantastical dreams.

Tanner awoke, much too aware of the warm woman pressed

along the front of his body. Her breathing was even and he hoped she was asleep. Sometime in the last couple of hours he had turned over and gathered her into his arms. Worse, one hand cradled her breast under her shirt while the other had slipped into her pants to explore the heat between her legs—and her hands lay on his, guiding him where she wanted him.

He lay perfectly still in spite of the urgent need to move his hips, to rub his erection against her ass. He'd obviously started this while they slept and he needed to stop it before it went too far.

"Quit thinking," she whispered and parted her legs to encourage his hand further.

So she wasn't asleep.

"I'm sorry. I didn't mean to…" At least he hadn't *consciously* intended to touch her, but now his fingers caressed the slickness between her folds and fondled the hard bud of her nipple.

She moaned softly and writhed against his hands. "Don't stop. We may die in here. I can feel how hard you are and I want this too."

The power of the ruby surged through him, aroused him on the most primal level, and he hardened even more. That power was his now. All the animosity of the past shifted and in its place was raging lust. She was so wet and ready for him. His hips surged against her ass, rubbing his cock along the crack, straining to be inside her.

"God, I want to fuck you," he growled.

"Then do it."

He released her breast and unzipped the bag. Cool air rushed in, but he was too hot to care. In one violent pull, he yanked down her pants and in a second pulled down his own. His cock sprung free and he fisted it to guide the head to her opening from behind.

"Yes," she groaned. "Take me hard."

He sank into her, burying himself to the hilt, and his hips took over. Pounding into her tight slick heat, over and over until he felt himself close to exploding. He reached around her to stroke her clit, thrusting hard and fast until she cried out with her release. Half a dozen strokes later he came so hard his roar echoed through the cavern.

He collapsed next to her, their breathing heavy and in sync. He pulled the open sleeping bag over them and folded her in his arms.

"That was amazing," she breathed.

Yeah, it was. No woman had ever turned him on like that before. Dipping his head, he kissed her. She tasted like the honey and oats bar she'd eaten earlier. His tongue flicked her lips and she opened for him, slipped her arms around his neck, and responded with a passion that made him want more.

He pulled her shirt over her head and hungrily kissed a trail to her breasts. They were perfect—not too big, not too small. He sucked on one nipple and teased the other with his fingertips.

She arched into him. "Bite me. Don't be gentle."

He applied his teeth and fingers—biting, pinching, and lathing her nipples to ease the pain—and was rewarded with sexy moans. "Like this, do you?"

"Oh, yeah." Her hand closed around his cock and began to work him. "How's this?"

"So good." He began a southern descent, nipping the tender skin of her stomach. "But I want to taste you and make you come with my mouth."

He took her moan as a yes and closed his teeth over her clit. Her hips rose to meet his mouth and her legs spread to give him full access. He watched her face as he teased and licked her, used his fingers and lips and tongue on her until she cried out his name. He didn't stop until he felt the spasms around his fingers subside.

"I want you inside me again," she panted.

She didn't have to ask twice. He knelt between her thighs, his cock still hard and ready to take her. He looked down at her—her eyes bright in the flare light, skin flushed, lips parted, breasts abraded from his whiskers. The instinct to mark her as his startled him. This was Chantal. Then she reached between them and guided his cock to her entrance.

Any control he still had dissolved and he plunged into her with a grunt. His body took over and claimed her—rough and hard and completely. Her fingers dug into his back and the pain gave his thrusts more power. The sensation was so intense as his climax built, the friction of the thrust and drag so intoxicating, he could hardly breathe.

When Chantal shattered under him, any remaining control snapped and he exploded inside her. When he finally came back to himself, his teeth were latched to her shoulder and he tasted blood.

He pulled back. "Fuck. I'm sorry."

Dazed eyes looked up at him and she smiled. "I like it when you lose control."

He *had* lost control, and his cock was still hard and ready to fuck her again and again in ways he'd never considered before. A warning alarm went off in his head. What was happening? The truth hit him in the gut and it took a long moment for the message to reach his brain.

"It wasn't me," he said.

She ran her hand down his stomach and brushed his erection. "Gee, I could have sworn all those body parts were attached."

He pulled back and fumbled in his shirt pocket. The ruby had fallen out and was quickly located under his knee. He tossed it toward the pile of equipment against the wall. "The ruby did something to me." The stone had changed his thought process, his body's reactions. Climbing out of the sleeping bag, he pulled on his pants and jacket then shoved his feet into his boots.

Chantal sat up and wrapped the bag around her naked body. "What are you doing?"

"Getting dressed."

"Let me look at your shoulder to be sure you didn't reopen the wound."

"I didn't. It's healed, courtesy of the damned stone. I'm ready to find a way out of here."

She stared at him in shocked silence as he picked up a headlight and flare, and headed into the tunnel. He couldn't stay in the cavern where his heightened senses were filled with the scent of sex, especially with her still naked and his erection throbbing to bury in her again. Distance might clear his head or give him enough control to focus on their situation. He licked his lip and the tang of her blood shot an electrical charge straight to his groin.

Thinking with his cock wasn't going to get them out of there and unless they came up with an escape plan, they were going to die in this cave. He ducked into the tunnel, shining the light on the floor until he located the leather roll. It was unlikely it was a map out of there, but it was worth a look.

He picked it up and sat down against the tunnel's wall. Careful not to damage the ancient skins, he unrolled them and studied the tiny pictures filling the inner skin. His breath froze in his lungs, his hard-on forgotten. What the hell had they stumbled onto?

# CHAPTER TWENTY

Chantal curled into the sleeping bag and for several minutes breathed in the heady scent of Tanner on the cloth, on her body. There was a large wet spot under her hip, but she didn't care. In fact, the last thing she wanted was to analyze what had happened between them. Hot sex—raw and rough—the way she'd wanted it. As often as she'd fantasized what it would be like with him, this had been so much better.

Groping inside the bag, her hands closed over her long underwear shirt and pants. She wriggled into them and braced herself to venture out to dress in her damp clothes in the cold cavern. The chill wasn't so bad, maybe because her body was still overheated. She dressed quickly and knelt next to their supplies where Tanner had tossed the ruby.

Carefully, she poked through the pile of gear. The ruby lay on the ground, wedged between the wall and a jagged rock. It seemed to absorb and amplify the light from her ComDev until it glowed from within. As she studied it, the heart shaped gem seemed to beat in time with her own heart. What was it and how did its power work?

The temptation to touch it warred with her healthy sense of self-preservation. Without Tanner to sever whatever connection was formed with the ruby, it could take over her mind permanently. And its effect on Tanner was another disturbing puzzle. Not that she wasn't ready for another round of scorching sex, but only if he wanted her of his own free will. She'd been in life and death situations before and could deal with that. Sex with Tanner was something else altogether.

A familiar leather pouch lay a few feet from the pile. She

donned her gloves and picked it up. He'd carried it for as long as she'd known him. At sixteen he'd seemed like a grown man to her thirteen-year-old self, but he'd never treated her like a child the way Mark and Adrien did.

She ran her gloved hand over the worn deerskin. He'd made it from a hide his grandfather had tanned himself. Did he still carry the stone arrowheads and lucky rabbit's foot? She had no right to pry. They were no longer children and certainly not friends.

She tucked the bag into a side pocket of his pack. Too much time had passed to hope Tanner would ever care about her the way she cared about him, no matter how little time they had left. Even if they escaped from this tomb, they'd go their separate ways at the end of the mission.

A Durand never admitted defeat until all options were exhausted. Chantal was not going to die sitting in a musty cave feeling sorry for herself. She pushed to her feet. If they couldn't go back the way they came in, they'd just have to find another way out.

Some of the climbing equipment they'd brought was in the tunnel near the abyss. She packed what tools and supplies were left in the backpacks, pulled on her arctic pants and jacket, and gathered up Tanner's cold weather gear. Lastly, she wrapped the ruby with an Ancilon mitten, dropped it in an Ancilon pouch and zipped it into the pocket on her jacket sleeve. She allowed herself a last glance at the sleeping bag where Tanner had made love to her. They wouldn't need it if they escaped and it wasn't going anywhere if they didn't. She clicked on her headlight, lit a flare, and headed for the tunnel. And hopefully a way out.

Thirty feet into the passage she saw him kneeling over the leather hide. His attention was so focused that she was almost next to him before he looked up.

"This is amazing. It chronicles the ruby's history and its journey from Siberia in tiny pictures."

"It doesn't have a map out of here, does it?"

He frowned as though he'd forgotten their predicament. "No."

"Then roll it up and stick it in your pack. If we don't find an exit, we'll have the rest of our short lives to study its wonders." She tossed him the pack. "How's your shoulder doing?"

"Sore, but nothing I can't deal with." He hesitated. "Where's the ruby?"

"Safely wrapped and stowed where it won't cause either of us trouble." She hoped. "We need to go back to the abyss. That's the only possibility of finding a way out of here."

He rolled the leather and carefully wrapped it in the softer skin before cushioning it in his pack. "I came to the same conclusion. What do you think—do we climb up or down?"

She watched the way he moved when he rose. He was favoring his wounded shoulder. "You were shot hours ago. Do you really think you can climb those sheer walls?"

"Yes."

"If you're not sure, say so. Don't take chances with both our lives."

He rolled his shoulder and winced. "I'm not a hundred percent, but I've dealt with worse."

"We should eliminate a downward escape route first," she said. "I can repel down as far as the rope will reach, see if there's a tunnel out and you can help me back up if I strike out."

He hoisted his pack over his good shoulder. "Let's do this."

The tunnel seemed longer and narrower than it had when they'd passed through it the last time—the ascent steeper. By the time they finally reached the cylindrical cavern with the abyss, waterfall, and seemingly endless ceiling, sweat ran between her breasts and her confidence had waned. One glimpse over the precipice and the gravity of their situation hit her.

Tanner propped his flare between two boulders and unhooked the rope from his pack. "There are only about sixty feet of rope," he said.

"That will put me below the level of the river. That's far enough." She stashed her ComDev in the inside pocket of her jacket, stepped into her climbing harness, and fastened it at her waist. "Between the headlight and a flare, I should be able to see any caves down there."

He handed her the end of the rope.

As she knotted it to her harness, she felt his gaze on her. An inner struggle played out on his face, one she didn't want to deal with before dropping off the side of the cliff.

"About what happened…" he began.

"Drop it. The ruby made you horny, I get it. I'm not some sixteen-year-old virgin with romantic stars in my eyes. I enjoy recreational sex as much as anyone." Her throat tightened and she swallowed. She couldn't let him see how much he affected her. "I know nothing's changed. We're on a mission and that's it."

"I don't hate you," he said quietly.

His sincerity wounded her and she reminded herself not to read too much into his declaration. "Good. Then I won't have to worry about you dumping me down there. Ready when you are."

He handed her a flare, wrapped the rope around a smooth stone and held it in his leather-gloved hands. "Ready."

Without hesitating, she took the leap and slowly began repelling off the jagged stone wall. Above, Tanner held the rope taut, feeding it out at her signal. Ten feet down she held the flare so she could scan the cylindrical wall for possible tunnel mouths. None of the shadows were large enough for a viable tunnel. She dropped another ten feet, then another. The circumference of the space was narrowing noticeably which made it easier to see all the way around. Nothing worth investigating. Another ten feet and she saw some sort of a hollow to her right. She tucked the flare's handle into the back of her harness, set a firm grasp on the rocks closest, and found footing.

"Give me about six feet," she called up to Tanner.

"Did you find something?"

"Maybe."

Stretching herself against the wall, she pulled her way to the hollow and boosted herself into it. The opening was wide enough for her to rise to her knees and retrieve the flare. Her heart sank. The little cave ended eight feet in.

"Dead end," she called up to him. "Brace for my weight. I'm coming out."

As she descended further, the rock face grew smoother, especially on the side with the waterfall. Finally, her drop ended.

"No more rope," Tanner shouted.

"Haul me up."

She grabbed rocks and found footholds to climb whenever possible to help him. In a few minutes, she was standing on the ledge again. "How's your shoulder doing?"

"Fine."

"Fine enough to climb?" She pointed upward. "No macho bullshit."

He inhaled deeply. "I think so."

"Not good enough."

"What choice do I have?"

They both knew the choice—the one secured in her sleeve. She didn't dare touch the ruby, but if it made him strong enough for them to get out of this tomb, it was their best chance. She unzipped the pocket, took out the wrapped ruby, and held it out to him. "This is our best shot. Use it."

He stared down at it without moving. "It's dangerous."

"No shit, but I want out of here."

"I don't like what it did to me. I was out of control."

"Were you stronger? Your senses more acute?"

"Yes."

"And it healed you," she said.

He nodded.

"So we deal with any side effects. Dying here is not on my bucket list. Take it."

Reluctantly, he took the ruby from her hand and slowly unwrapped it. When his bare fingers closed over it, he jolted. Instantly he seemed bigger, more powerful. "Its energy is stronger than before like it recognizes me."

"Can you direct it? Send it to your shoulder?"

"Not necessary. It's already working." He paused and glanced around him. "I can hear the waterfall hitting the bottom of the abyss, smell the algae on the walls, feel a cold draft from above swirling around me. Hear your heartbeat. Smell myself on your body and you on mine."

His voice was sexy and predatory, and heat surged deep in her body. Wrong time and place to respond to his involuntary lust. "Let's get back to the cold draft," she said. "That could mean an exit somewhere up there."

"Where's your ComDev?"

She pulled it from her pocket.

He shone his above their heads. "Put the light on high and follow my beam."

"We won't be able to see anything from down here."

"You won't." He aimed his light about twenty feet above their heads and slowly moved it around the cavern walls.

She followed his light with hers. There was no way they'd see a cave from here, superpowers or not, but she humored him. Gradually, he raised his aim. She kept quiet until their search reached more than fifty feet and the light did little more than cast shadows on the rock face. "This is a waste of time. We can't see anything from here."

His light beam stopped on a jutting rock. "There. There are particles flashing in the light. Probably snow or sleet from the storm. That's where the draft is coming from."

"I don't see anything."

"You don't have my sight," he pointed out.

This was insane. Her eyesight was perfect and there wasn't anything there. Or, if there was, the light was too dim to see it. Then again, the ruby had healed his shoulder. "Okay, we climb to that point and hope you're right. Greywolf expects us to die in here, but he may come back when he realizes the box was just the carrier and not the power object."

"Then he'll have to dig us out." He stepped forward and gazed down at her mouth, sex and testosterone blasting off him. "Could be worse."

She gave him a hard shove that barely budged him. "Cut the shit. It's just the ruby that's making you horny."

His expression hardened. "Fine. Get on your gear and let's go. I'll take the lead." He hoisted the pack on his back and slid an electric flare between the pack and his jacket to throw as much light as possible. His ComDev went in his pocket and he flicked on his headlight. Without looking back, he began to climb.

# CHAPTER TWENTY-ONE

Tanner's preternaturally keen senses made climbing easy. He knew exactly where to place his hands, the next purchase for his foot. This must be how monkeys and squirrels scurried up trees and walls, he thought, instinctively knowing they wouldn't fall.

He glanced below. Chantal's progress was slower, more deliberate and tentative, but she knew what she was doing. She'd be fine.

Just above his head, the wind carried minute particles of ice that tickled his face. The sounds of the snowfall and branches creaking echoed in the tunnel, which he guessed was short and narrow. And led outside.

With little effort, he made it to the hollow, hung on the edge, and thrust his ComDev inside. Snow drifted at the other end, leaving only a small opening to the night. Moving the snow wouldn't be a problem, squeezing through the narrow tunnel would.

"Find something?" Chantal called to him. Her head was now just below his boots.

"Yeah, an exit."

"Good going! Can you crawl inside so I can come up?"

"No."

"Why not?"

"I'm too big."

"Shit."

"For once we agree." He moved aside and offered her a hand up. "You can make it. Let me have your equipment and I'll push it through after you."

She climbed up next to him and peered into the tunnel. "What about you?"

"I'll climb higher and see if there's another way out."

"I'm not going to leave you here," she said.

"Me or the ruby?"

"You can be a real asshole, you know."

He chuckled. "So I've been told. Mostly by you."

"How much wider does this crawl space need to be for your shoulders to get through? Six inches? Eight inches?" she asked.

"What does it matter?"

"Just answer my question."

He leaned into the mouth of the tunnel to measure. The opening was narrower on this end and widened over the next seven feet to the exit. "On this end, I need about eight inches to get through. More would be better. On the other end, I may be all right."

"Can we use your hunting knife to dig it out?"

"No, it would ruin the knife."

"Which you won't need if you're dead."

He paused to think. "It would take too long. I can't hang here forever hacking at rock. We need something more…"

"Dramatic?"

"Powerful. Like…" He wriggled out of his pack and plopped it in the cave. "DT's plug explosives to quickly fry locks." He took a small cylindrical bottle from the front compartment of his pack and carefully poured out a half dozen plugs the size and shape of a pencil eraser. Then, using the tip of his knife, he bored holes in the rock deep enough to jam the plugs in.

"Nice. How do you detonate them?" Chantal asked.

"With sound waves. Move away from the mouth." He crawled along the rock a few feet to his left and spoke into his ComDev. "Detonate 3477 Go."

The explosion shot rock chips and sand ten feet into the cave. When the dust settled, he climbed back to the mouth to inspect the results. After the debris was removed, the hole was wider, maybe wide enough for him to squeeze through.

"Good work. Let's get out of here." Chantal went first, spreading the shiny ground cloth on the floor to help her slide on her stomach as she crawled. When she got to the far end, she pushed out into the snow then ducked back in headfirst. "Now you."

He nudged his pack and jacket ahead of him and squeezed into the tunnel. The fit at his shoulders was snug and an instant of panic paralyzed him before the ruby reclaimed its power over his mind. His muscles undulated, easing him along the ground cloth like a snake, arms stretched in front of him to minimize his width until he could use his feet to inch forward.

"Almost here." Chantal reached for his hands and pulled him forward over the smooth ground cloth.

As she backed out of the tunnel, he slid along until he could rise to his elbows and crawl the rest of the way.

Emerging from the cave, cold blasted against his face and relief rolled over him. The predawn sky seemed bright and welcoming compared to the pitch-blackness of the caves. Over a foot of snow covered the hillside—manageable, if not optimal—and he could hear the rush of water below. This, he could handle.

Chantal pulled on a fleece hat and wrapped a scarf around her neck, for once not complaining about the snow and cold. She reached into her pocket and pulled out her ComDev. "Call Mark. Speaker."

In two rings he picked up. "Where are you? We've been trying to reach you for hours."

"We're on some mountain in the park now. We got trapped in a cave and had to find a way out."

"How did you get trapped?"

"Long story," she said. "We got the item, but had to let the box it was in go."

"So what is the item?"

She glanced at Tanner. "A ruby shaped like a small animal heart."

Mark chuckled. "Adrien's not going to fucking believe this. So you two okay to bring it in?"

"No problem," Tanner said. "Might take us a few hours to hike out of here, but we're fine."

She glared at him as though she was about to argue, then turned her attention back to Mark. "Any chance you can send a plane for us this afternoon?"

"Sorry. You're getting a break in the weather now, but another front is about to hit. It'll be at least another twenty-four hours before someone can pick you up."

She swore under her breath.

Tanner couldn't help smiling. "No problem. We can hole up at the cabin." Together. The cold had given Chantal's cheeks and lips a pink glow that invited erotic fantasies. Although she'd deny it, her body didn't lie. He inhaled the scent of her arousal and heard the spike of her heartbeat. They'd start with a hot shower.

"Check in with me when you get back," Mark said and the line clicked off.

"Present location," Chantal said and studied the screen of her ComDev.

Tanner took out his ComDev and tapped the nav-map icon that showed location, geography, and conditions in real time. "There's a path to the south about twenty yards that'll take us along the river. From there, it's about seven miles to the Swiftcurrent Motel."

"I can see that," she said irritably. "I'll bet that's also the route Greywolf took to find us."

"Then it's a good thing we're armed and my senses are jacked up. I'll be able to hear snowmobiles from a mile away or more."

"Yeah, about those jacked senses." Her fingers dug into the pocket on her jacket sleeve and pulled out the Ancilon pouch. "We can get out of here without the ruby's power. Time to put it away."

"I disagree. When we're safely back at the cabin, I'll give it to you."

"By then you'll be in too deep. You ramped up much faster this time than the first time you had it. What if it won't let you go?"

Who did she think she was talking to? He was in total control. "That's ridiculous. I can hand it over whenever I want."

"Then give it to me now."

"No." He stood and adjusted his pack on his back. The flare had dimmed, but it didn't matter. The eastern sky was turning from a dark navy blue to deep lavender. It would be light in another half hour. "Let's get out of here."

The path was wide and flat and easy to see, even covered with snow. He picked up residual energy of hikers, but not of Greywolf. Not yet.

He reached a hand to Chantal and easily lifted her the last few feet onto flat ground. "No one has been here recently, but the trail looks good."

"Then let's get moving. I'm cold, hungry, and ready for a hot shower." She took off at a brisk clip. He followed her, keeping open to any new energy as his feet hit the ground. The ruby also enhanced his natural talent and made it easier to read the history of the trail with his shield fully in place. Convenient, and the protection could come in handy if they crossed paths with Greywolf.

Behind the clouds the sun had risen. Tanner checked their progress on his ComDev. They'd covered two miles—the only relatively flat miles on the trail. The next four were uphill and the last one downhill.

Chantal said over her shoulder, "We have five miles of easy hiking ahead that any rookie Protector could handle after a full day of boot camp. You've confirmed Greywolf didn't use this trail. So why do you need the ruby now?"

Because he loved the heightened abilities it gave him. He felt strong and invincible. "In case we run into Greywolf again."

"Bullshit. We can handle him and you know it. You don't want to give up the power, which is exactly why you have to."

"What kind of logic is that?" And yet a part of him knew she was right—the part that didn't crave dominance over his world and the woman confronting him.

"Tanner, let me carry the stone. You don't need it anymore and it's messing with your head. I'll wrap it up so it doesn't affect either of us." She held out her hand displaying the protective pouch. "We can put it in here and stick the pouch in an extra Ancilon bag. Please."

"I can't."

"Yes, you can. Just hand it over."

He didn't want to. The ruby was his. It understood him.

She stepped toward him and reached for the zipper of his jacket. Without breaking eye contact, slowly she unzipped it. His gaze dipped to her mouth, pink and luscious from the cold. Hunger flooded through him and he pulled her against his body and kissed her hard. His mouth devoured hers, invaded, conquered and she surrendered with a moan that went straight to his cock. Her hands roamed his chest and stomach, stopping at the waistband of his pants. He wanted her here, now, snow be damned.

She shoved him away hard and, caught by surprise, he fell backward, recovering his balance just before he went to ground. "What the hell did you do that for?"

She opened a gloved hand to show him the ruby.

He grabbed for it and she skittered away.

"You bitch," he growled.

"Just saving you from yourself. The only reason you fell for that move was the ruby's influence. Normally, if I'd unzipped your jacket, you'd have asked me what the hell I was doing, not stick your tongue down my throat."

"You liked it. I can smell your arousal."

"Listen to yourself. We're Protectors on an important mission, not teenagers on a date."

Protectors on a mission. He knew that. He also knew she was right—her trick wouldn't have worked had he not been blinded by ruby-induced lust. So how had he forgotten the big picture? The jacked up energy simmered through his bloodstream and flowed from his nerve endings and there was nothing he could do to stop it. Nothing except take the ruby back.

"It's like a drug," he said.

"Then the sooner we pass it off, the better." Chantal dropped the stone into a small pouch, and tucked that into a large Ancilon bag, and zipped it into the pocket of her sleeve. "Let's get out of here before Greywolf discovers we have the treasure and comes looking for us."

# CHAPTER TWENTY-TWO

"Goddamn it!" Aaron Greywolf stared into the empty box. It had taken him over an hour to open it. "They have must it." At least he knew they weren't going anywhere.

Tom leaned over his shoulder. "What they got, boss?"

"Whatever was in the damned box."

From the way the skins were molded, the object looked to be egg shaped and small enough to fit in his hand. Or pocket. How could he have been so stupid not to open the box in the cavern?

He glanced out the window. The snow had stopped, but another storm was due to hit this afternoon.

Tom plopped himself on an ottoman in front of the fireplace and began poking at the logs, sending sparks onto the hearth.

"What would it take to reopen the tunnel into the cave?" Aaron asked.

Tom shook his head. "You told me to close it up good. There's ten foot of stone and rubble to get through. If we could get a backhoe in there…"

Aaron snorted impatiently. "How the hell would we do that? The ATVs barely made it on the river trail and now there are a couple feet of snow on it. If the next storm drops another foot, it could be spring before we can open the cave again."

The Durand woman and Hays would be dead long before then and it would be simple to take the prize. Still, he wanted it now, not in the spring.

"Me and Corey and Junk could take the snowmobiles on the high trail and climb down with picks and shovels. Might take a while to dig it out, but we don't have nothing else to do."

"How long a while?"

"Can't say. Couple days, maybe more."

"What if it snows again?"

Tom snickered. "Don't make no difference. Snow don't bother us."

Of course it didn't. They'd grown up in the mountains, sleeping outside in all weather. A tarp or some branches were all the shelter they needed to be comfortable.

"How soon can you leave?"

"Soon as I round up the others and the snowmobiles. A couple of hours."

Aaron tried to do the math, but there were too many variables. The cave might be opened in ten hours or twenty-four. Cell service in that part of the park was nonexistent so Tom couldn't call in a progress report and Aaron had no intention of sitting in the snowstorm watching them work. On the other hand, if they broke through without him, Hays and the girl might get away.

"Okay, call your brothers."

Tom saluted. "Yes, sir."

"And, Tom, tell them to come armed."

# CHAPTER TWENTY-THREE

The huge snowflakes would have been beautiful if Chantal had been sitting at the window of a ski lodge with a cup of Irish coffee. She glanced down at the screen of her ComDev. "I can't imagine how people made it through this country before GPSs."

"They didn't," Tanner grumbled. "They got lost and froze. Or didn't leave their shelter in bad weather."

Only another mile to go to the lodge. The cold had penetrated her damp clothes and her teeth chattered. She was frozen to the bone in spite of the strenuous exercise.

"Redial." Her ComDev called the main phone line of the motel again. It rang and rang until it finally rolled over to a *closed for the season* message. "There has to be a caretaker, right?"

Tanner didn't answer, just trudged on. "The new snow has almost covered our tracks. Doubt any roads will be open until the storm stops, and we still need to pick up the truck."

A few minutes later they emerged from a stand of trees to what, in summer, would be the lawn of a rustic motor lodge complex. To their right were a dozen cabins and the main building was almost dead ahead. A light shone in one of the rooms of the single story building. Relief washed over her. The electricity was on—someone was there.

"Looks like we're in luck," she said.

He paused and slowly surveyed all the buildings. "Yeah, maybe. Or they might have left some lights on for security."

"Such an optimist. I'll stick with my little fantasy for a few more minutes."

His voice dropped. "And which fantasy would that be?"

One that included being warm. And, maybe, him naked. "Let's just go." Her feet sunk into the snow with each step, but she picked up her pace. The cabins were all dark and the shutters closed tight for the winter. This far off the main road, the place probably closed by late September.

"So what's the plan?" Tanner asked. "Knocking on the door could get us shot."

"What do you suggest?"

"Holler first so they don't think we're sneaking up on them."

They approached the room with the light in the window. The step and walkway in front had been clear at some point, but were now covered with two inches of fresh snow. They stopped on the sidewalk where they could be seen from the window. It wasn't possible to see enough of the room to know if it was occupied and she had no intention of looking in the window.

"Hello," she shouted. "Is anyone around? Hello."

A woman's head appeared in the window, a frown on her face.

Chantal stepped onto the step, but not onto the wooden porch. "Hello. We got caught in the blizzard. Can we get a couple rooms until the storm lets up and we can get back to our truck?"

The woman made no move to open the door. "We're closed."

"We know," Tanner said. "We just need shelter until we can get to the main road."

The door opened and a middle-aged woman in a red flannel shirt, denim overalls, and fleece lined slippers stood back. She had a pistol in her hand, but it was pointed at the floor.

"Come in. I'm the winter manager, Nola Bretsky." With a slow once over she assessed their clothes and gear. "Didn't figure on the snow?"

"We had to leave our tent and other gear behind when a landslide trapped us in a cave," Chantal explained. There didn't seem much reason to lie.

Nola scratched her head, ruffling the short cap of wiry gray hair that looked like she cut it herself. "Never much liked them caves. Dangerous. Dumbasses get trapped or lost in them every year."

Great. In less than a minute she'd pegged them as dumbasses. Now they were dropping snow on her floor.

"We just need some shelter until the storm lets up," Tanner said.

"You the hikers left your Tahoe on the fire trail lay-by?" Nola asked. "Park rangers been calling around asking if anybody seen you. They was going to send out a search party to look for you when it stopped snowing."

"If you can give us their number, we'll call and tell them we're safe."

"You can use my phone." Nola nodded toward a '70s era princess phone on a cluttered desk. "Ranger switchboard's number on the sticker. Ain't no cell service up here."

Chantal made the call and got voicemail. She left a message that they were safe and not in need of rescue. She didn't mention where they were. The longer Greywolf thought they were trapped in that cave, the better. "Could we rent a couple rooms?"

"Only got one with electric and hot water. No heat, but it's got a fireplace and there's a woodpile out back."

"We'll take it," Tanner said. "How much?"

"It usually goes for a hundert forty a night, but if I got to clean it and do the sheets and towels…"

"Will two-forty cash cover it?" Chantal saw the calculation in the woman's eyes. That cash would go right into Nola's pocket and no one would be the wiser.

"That should cover it. Come on. I'll show you the room."

• • •

"It could be worse," Tanner said as the door closed behind Nola.

Chantal dropped the set of sheets and four towels on the queen-size bed and surveyed the accommodations. The brown carpet was worn and the pine paneling had seen better days. "Yeah, we could still be trapped in the cave."

"The fireplace will warm the place up pretty quickly."

She opened a door and found the bathroom. Her heart sank.

The showerhead was missing along with the curtain, and rust stains ran down the tub from the faucet. She turned on the water and it came out burnt orange.

"Rusty pipes." Tanner stood close behind her—close enough to feel his warm breath against her ear. "Give it a minute or two. I'll go get some wood."

The outer door opened and closed. Chantal sat down on the closed toilet seat and rested her head in her hands. The adrenaline she'd been running on drained away and her entire body trembled with the cold. Harsh conditions were one thing; cold and snow added a new dimension she hated and—if honest—feared.

The motel room provided rustic shelter, but the temperature in the bathroom wasn't much warmer than outside. They had the ruby and all she wanted was to get the hell out of here. And get away from Tanner. Tears welled in her eyes. She had no delusions that for him the sex had been anything more than a psychic imperative from the stone, but her body craved him.

The front door opened. Facing him like this, having him see her so weak was not going to happen. She kicked the bathroom door closed and stared at the wall it had hidden, or rather the gas heater on the wall. Her giggle echoed in the tiled room. It sounded slightly demented and that made her laugh harder.

Tanner knocked on the door. "Are you all right?"

"Terrific! Ecstatic! Thrilled to be alive!"

He cracked the door and peeked inside. "Hysterical from the cold?"

She waved him in. "Not anymore. Look what I found."

He studied the ancient heater. "Does it work? Looks like it'll blow up if you light it."

"As long as it warms the place up, I'll take my chances." She turned on the gas and pressed the lighter button. Flames danced behind the rusty grille with the promise of one warm place in the cabin. "Let's check in with Mark then I'm taking a hot bath."

Tanner expertly laid the fire and lit the tinder. The dry kindling caught quickly and soon the fire was blazing merrily, even if it hadn't taken any of the chill off the room yet. He stacked another small log on the pile and watched the flames lick it.

"You're good at that," she said. "My father usually fills the room with smoke before he can get a fire started."

He smiled at her and her heart did a little flip. "I've had a lot of practice. Your father has staff to do it for him."

His tone was matter of fact, but his words acknowledged the chasm between their backgrounds.

"I sometimes wonder how he and Armand ever survived their years as Protectors." She took out her ComDev. "I guess things were different back then. Call Mark. On speaker."

Mark answered on the first ring. "Where are you?"

"In a room in a motor lodge that's closed for the winter."

"Did you break in?"

She rolled her eyes. "No, we rented it from the winter manager. It's snowing again. Hard. It may be a while before we can get out of here."

"Someone reported the Tahoe to the park rangers," Tanner added. "They were ready to send out a search party. We confirmed we were safe but didn't tell them where we are."

Chantal filled Mark in on Greywolf and everything that had happened in the cave. "If Greywolf has gotten the box open, he'll know it was only the container. Right now, he thinks we're buried in the cave and the longer he thinks that the better our chances are of getting out of here without him in our way."

"And this ruby. Have you read it, Chantal?" Mark asked.

"No. It's too powerful to risk touching." She glanced at Tanner. "Tanner has. After Greywolf shot him the ruby healed him."

"What else, Tanner?" Mark demanded.

Tanner wouldn't look at her. "It ramps up whatever abilities you have. Heightens senses—sight, smell, hearing are acute. Physical strength tripled at least. You feel invincible." Tanner glanced at her and she held his gaze. There was no way to explain the lust effect without admitting to the sex.

"But the Shalamov sent it away. Why?"

"It's too early to say. We were in survival mode and used its power to get out of the cave. Under normal conditions—who knows?"

"Be careful and keep me posted."

"We will," they replied in unison, as the call clicked off.

"Thanks for not telling him what happened," Tanner said.

"What was I supposed to say? The ruby made you have sex with me?" *And I loved it.*

He winced. "I don't know why I lost control and I'm sorry."

"You know what I think?" she asked.

"No. And I don't want to know."

"Too bad. I think you wanted me. That the chemistry between us is still there, but you're so busy blaming me for something you don't even understand that you're in denial. The stone just jacked up what you already felt and you were powerless to control it."

"That's what you think, huh?"

"Yes."

He picked up his gloves and headed for the door.

She grabbed his arm. "Lie to me, but don't lie to yourself."

He yanked himself from her grasp and walked out the door.

# CHAPTER TWENTY-FOUR

When Tanner returned to the cabin, the water was running in the bathtub and the door was closed. His body was totally up for joining her in a hot bath and his brain was struggling to remember why that was a terrible idea.

He stacked the logs next to the wood he'd brought in earlier and added one to the roaring fire. The blaze had taken enough of the chill off the room for him to shed his jacket. From the battered dresser, Chantal's ComDev played some pop song for a few bars before the call went to voicemail. He glanced down at the screen. *Kara—DT.* There were three voicemail notifications and five *Call me ASAP* texts, all from Kara since he'd been gone.

He knocked on the bathroom door. "You have voicemails and texts from Kara. She seems anxious to talk to you."

Chantal swore. "I'm almost thawed out. What do the texts say?"

"Call me ASAP."

"I hate artifact emergencies," she grumbled. "Is it still snowing?"

"Yes."

"Then she can wait another five minutes."

He chuckled and went to put the electric kettle on.

Fifteen minutes later Chantal emerged from the bathroom, hair in a knot on the top of her head and her skin pink from the hot water. She picked up her ComDev and listened to the first message on speaker: "I have info on the piece of pottery and maybe origin. It's old. Very old. Call me."

Tanner made a low snorting sound. "That's an emergency and this is your expert? We could have told her that."

**160**

"Yeah. Maybe she doesn't want to leave details on my voicemail. She should know it's secure."

He dropped into a beat-up armchair next to the fire. "Just call her."

The call went through immediately. "Chantal! I was getting worried. I couldn't reach you and the Tahoe hasn't moved in 38 hours."

Chantal's gaze flew to Tanner's.

*What the fuck?* He mouthed.

"What do you know about the Tahoe?" Chantal asked.

Kara giggled nervously. "A Tahoe was checked out and left in Kalispell for Tanner to pick up. In your message, you mentioned him so I assumed you were working together."

Chantal frowned. Had she mentioned Tanner? In any case, Kara knew where they were, at least approximately. "Why did you track it? That's strictly against regulations."

"When I didn't hear from you I got worried." Kara cleared her throat. "You usually check in when I'm working with you."

Chantal wasn't buying that, but the Tahoe was on the other side of the park. "We're fine. What do you have for me?"

"The piece of pottery—the symbols appear to be Sumerian cuneiform, my guess is from about 2500 B.C. It's impossible to pinpoint an accurate age of the material without having it in the lab."

"We know," Tanner muttered. "Any idea what the symbol means?"

"Enki—the senior god—but with a variation we think is an honorific. It could be part of an incantation where Enki is being petitioned. There's no way to know the specifics without seeing more of the context."

"We?" Chantal asked. "Who did you confer with?"

"Nobody. I just posted a drawing of the symbol on a Sumerian cuneiform board. It's all anonymous. No one knows who I am."

"Shut it down," Tanner ordered. "You can go back to doing whatever it is you do."

"Thanks, Kara," Chantal said. "We'll take it from here."

"In a blizzard without a vehicle? When I didn't hear from you, I flew to Spokane and drove here. Where are you? I'll come get you as soon as the snow stops."

Tanner shook his head. Normally she'd agree with him, but Kara had been with DT for ten years and had been involved with Protector missions for the last six. She had Secret clearance, which was why she could track the Tahoe. And it wasn't as though they could Uber back to their SUV. "Hold on for a minute." She put the ComDev on mute.

"The sooner we get out of here with the ruby, the happier I'll be," she said.

"Me, too, but we're not going back to the Tahoe. Greywolf had us followed so he probably has somebody watching it. If Kara knows where it is, she can go get it and take it back to Spokane or Seattle or wherever it needs to be next."

"And the tile in the safe?"

"Not important. Greywolf has the box and we have the payload. Once we hand over the ruby, Mark can send someone to take care of Greywolf, which hopefully means putting him in prison for murder."

"And explain that how?"

He gestured at her ComDev. "Just tell Kara to call in a pickup for the Tahoe and we'll check in when we get to L.A."

Chantal took the ComDev off of mute and put it on speaker. "Hey, Kara, we don't need the Tahoe anymore. Call DT and have them send a pickup when the weather clears up. I'll give you a call when we get to L.A."

A male voice was faintly audible in the background before Kara replied. "Are you still in the park? The roads are still closed, but as soon as the plows come through, I can be there."

Alarms went off in Chantal's head. Kara wasn't alone. "Who was talking to you?"

"Just my, ah, boyfriend. He didn't want me to drive alone in the bad weather. I didn't think you'd mind."

"You know the regs. You have security clearance and he doesn't. We shouldn't be having this conversation in front of him."

"He's cool, I promise. I wouldn't date him if he wasn't."

Tanner drew his forefinger across his throat. Chantal had worked with this woman for long enough to know that she liked to show off her knowledge, and that was her strength and her weakness.

"Do you have anything else for me?"

Kara cleared her throat. "Somebody tried to hack into DT—specifically into Tanner's email. The computer had some sophisticated security protocols, but I traced it to the Department of Native American Studies at Montana State University."

"The tile was found by a local man," Chantal said. "Lots of people here know about it. Could the hacker be some curious student?"

"Whoever it was, was good. If we weren't DT, they would have gotten in." A muffled male voice just barely came through. "Want me to run background checks on the department staff?"

"That's not necessary. I've got to go now. Call you from California." Chantal ended the call. "What do you make of that?"

"Creepy. Aside from bringing her boyfriend along, she knows how things work. If she was worried about us, that concern is reported to the Protector hotline and they take over. Research staff never comes looking for agents. Ever." Tanner hadn't moved from his seat, but he'd taken out his ComDev and was busy working on it. "She's already run a check on the department staff."

"Yeah, and she probably knows Greywolf is in the area. She could easily trace his credit card use or cell phone."

Studying his ComDev screen, Tanner frowned. "And she knows he wrote a book called *Legends, Myths, and Magic of the Blackfeet Tribe*. The description on Amazon says it relates stories of an ancient people who once lived in what is now Glacier National Park and the legend of a mystical treasure buried there centuries ago."

"*Merde.*"

"Exactly. And we have Greywolf's treasure," he said.

"Which he's going to figure out sooner or later." Hopefully

when they were long gone. "Our ComDevs are untraceable, so Kara can't find us, but we can find her."

"Mark needs to have her tracked and monitored." He spoke into his ComDev. "Call Mark Durand."

The call went into voicemail so he left a detailed message.

"So what do you propose we do next?" she asked.

"The only thing we can do. Sit tight until the storm stops and we can get out of here." His gaze darted down her body and back to her face. Heat flared in his eyes, which locked with hers for several beats before he turned away.

Chantal let out a soft breath. It was going to be a long day. Maybe even a longer night.

# CHAPTER TWENTY-FIVE

Chantal shifted restlessly on the sofa in front of the fire. The hours they'd spent in the room felt like days. She had texted Mark her own update and checked her messages. She tried to ignore Tanner dozing in the chair next to her, his boots propped on a stained ottoman. Even at rest, his face had a fierceness she didn't remember. Maybe it was the scar or the lines in the corners of his eyes. Seven years had changed them both.

She tore her attention back to her ComDev. The weather forecast predicted the storm front to pass during the night, which would force them to stay in this damned room until the morning at the earliest. She suppressed a groan.

In the distance, she heard the sound of engines. She listened for several seconds. They were getting closer.

"Tanner, wake up." She nudged his arm. "Someone's coming."

He bolted up, instantly alert and listening. "The only thing that can get here through the storm is snowmobiles."

The roar got louder and was definitely headed their way.

"I have a bad feeling about this," Chantal said.

"Give me the stone."

She hesitated.

"Do it now."

The engines pulled up outside the motel and were turned off.

"Damn it, Chantal, give me the stone."

She grabbed her jacket and handed him the pouch with the ruby just as a heavy fist pounded on Nola's door.

Tanner stepped closer to the door, listening. Apparently, the ruby had already heightened his senses.

"What's happening?" she asked.

"They're telling Nola that the park rangers got your message and caller ID indicated we were here. These guys were sent to get us." He paused. "Nola is directing them to our room."

The loud rap on their door came a few moments later.

"I'll get it," Tanner said. "Stay on guard."

"I've done this before." She stepped behind the loveseat and adjusted her hand around the Glock she had taken from her jacket pocket.

Tanner opened the door. Two men in snowsuits, hats, and goggles stood on the porch. She tapped them with her empath senses and stiffened. Devious and greedy, but not menacing.

"You Tanner Hays and Chantal Durand?" one of the men asked.

"Who are you?" Tanner asked.

"Corey and Junk Joseph. We were sent by the park rangers to get you."

"We didn't ask for help," Chantal said.

The men ignored her.

"Come in out of the cold," Tanner backed away from the door to let them pass. Something was wrong. She could feel it, but couldn't identify it.

The men yanked off their helmets. The shorter one had black hair pulled back into a man-bun. The taller had a crew cut and a black eye. They leered at Chantal boldly.

"Do you work for the park service?" she asked, pretty sure the answer was no.

"Sometimes," the taller one said. "You need to put on your gear and come with us, ma'am."

"We're fine here," Tanner said. "You can tell the rangers we'll find our own way out when the weather breaks."

Black-eye drew a semiautomatic from his pocket. "Sorry. Can't let you do that."

"Because you're working for Greywolf," Tanner said.

The two men exchanged panicked glances.

"How do you know that?" Black-eye asked.

"We don't know nobody named Greywolf," Man-bun insisted.

Even from across the room, she could feel the energy rolling off of Tanner. His power was growing before her eyes.

"Here's what you're going to do." Tanner's voice held a new resonance that sent a shiver through her. "You're going to give us your suits, helmets, and cell phones, and stay here until we send someone for you."

The men nodded and started to undress.

Chantal had seen Adrien and Mark use mind control on threatening *ordinaires*, but Tanner's new abilities frightened her. The stone's seductiveness worried her even more.

He picked up the smaller suit and tossed it to her. "We're paying you for the use of your snowmobiles and we'll let you know where to pick them up. Relax, enjoy the fire and take a nap. You have nowhere to go and nothing else to do."

She climbed into the monosuit over her jacket and clothes and zipped it up. It was too big, but not too long. "So the *item* has enhanced your telepathic abilities. Anything else you want to tell me?"

Tanner zipped his suit and dropped black-eye's gun into his pack. "No. Let's go."

"To Babb or to find Greywolf?" She tucked her Glock into the pocket of the suit and pulled on her hat.

"Babb. It's just outside of the park. According to our guests, Greywolf's not far from here at a lodge about a mile detour off route 3. With any luck, we'll be long gone before he figures out his buddies aren't coming."

With a final glance at the two men sitting next to the fire, Chantal and Tanner stepped out into the cold and headed for the snowmobiles parked in front of Nola's apartment."

"Greywolf's figured out there was something in the box and we have it. When those guys don't show up with us, we can expect him to come after us," Tanner said. "The box has power, but we can't risk losing the ruby."

"So we go to Babb and try to get a ride out from there?"

He nodded. "If we meet anyone who's working for Greywolf, I'll know." He slipped an earplug in one ear and his ComDev into his suit. "I programmed the navigation for audio direction so follow me."

"And I have backup." She'd fastened the wrist device linked to her ComDev over her glove. A glance would tell her if they were headed in the right direction and it would vibrate and buzz if they got off course. Unfortunately, it couldn't tell her if there was an obstruction in the road and the snow cut visibility to less than twenty yards. With a turn of the key, the monster engine came to life and adrenaline surged through her. After sitting, she was up for the rush of speed and danger.

"Come on, Hays. Daylight's wasting." She held on tight, stomped the accelerator, and took off into the storm.

# CHAPTER TWENTY-SIX

Aaron Greywolf rested both hands on the box and absorbed its magic into his body. The ward was ancient and powerful. Unfortunately, he had no idea what it was or how to use it. It clearly had a purpose and whatever it had contained was the key.

He stood and stretched. Tom was dozing by the fire, mouth open and snoring. Junk and Corey should have picked up Hays and the girl by now, and be on their way back.

It had been sheer luck that Tom had seen the bulletin to call off the search for the couple, when they'd checked in with the park service. And a phone call had gotten Aaron their location. Their escape from the cave had saved his cousins a lot of work—but how the hell had they done it? Hays had to be in bad shape with an untreated gunshot wound—much too weak to have dug them out.

His iPad showed the snowmobiles were on their way back. GPS trackers were handy little items even when there wasn't an emergency. The temperature had dropped to 12 degrees and the snow showed no signs of stopping—a stroke of luck that had delayed Hays and Durand from slipping away with the treasure. But this was his world, his people. He knew how to function in harsh weather and soon he'd have whatever his box had contained.

Impatient, he glanced at his iPad to check Junk and Corey's location and froze. They'd passed the turnoff to the lodge and were headed for the park entrance.

"What the hell are you doing?" He tried Corey's cell phone and it went right into voicemail. Nausea rolled through his stomach. Something was wrong.

He found the number for the office of the motel where Hays

and the woman were staying and dialed from the landline in his room. On the fourth ring, a woman answered. "We're closed for the season."

"I'm trying to locate my cousins," he said. "They were picking up two of your guests on their snowmobiles. Have you seen them?"

The woman coughed. "Yeah, they're here. That couple—Tanner and Sharon—rented their snowmobiles and paid for them to stay here until the storm stops."

"You sure?"

"Yeah. Just took them some chili and a couple beers. They was watching TV."

"Can I talk to them?"

"Don't have no phone in their room. I can give them a message."

"Tell them to call Aaron. Please." He hung up and immediately dialed the ranger station.

A recorded message answered. "Due to severe weather, this location is open for emergencies only. Please leave a message with your name, details of your location and the nature of your emergency and we will contact you as soon as possible."

"This is Dr. Aaron Greywolf. I want to report an assault and the theft of two snowmobiles by Tanner Hays and Chantal Durand. They're armed and dangerous and headed for Many Glacier Entrance."

He hung up and started to layer on warm clothes. Tom had arrived on a third snowmobile, which was gassed up and ready for action. Now Aaron had no choice but to go after Hays and Durand himself.

• • •

The snowmobiles flew through the deep snow, the roar of their engines shattering the silence of the woods. These vehicles were built for power and speed packing lots more horsepower than most recreational models. Tanner felt invincible—which he knew was the stone's power, not his own—and he resisted the urge to open the sucker up to see just how fast it would go.

The snowfall had almost stopped, improving visibility. The icy wind whipped against his face, but he barely noticed the cold. In spite of the volume of the snowmobile engines, his ruby-heightened senses picked up the scent of deer, the scurrying of a small animal and the groaning of the trees under their burden of snow. Even his new sight instinctively identified shapes under the white blanket allowing him to swerve around a fallen branch without slowing, knowing Chantal would do the same.

The road dropped to run along the lake, mountains looming on either side of it. The late afternoon sun had fallen behind the peaks, leaving their route in shadow. He could smell the snow, its fragrance sharp and crisp, mixed with exhaust, pine and the scent of deep water teeming with life. The snowmobile engines drowned out everything else with a rhythmic roar that hummed through his body even as the machine pounded the track under him.

*Your destination is eight point six miles ahead.* The voice from his ComDev startled him. He checked on Chantal, gesturing the *okay?* sign and got a thumbs up. All was well and they were making good time. A mile later, their luck changed.

A Land Cruiser was parked in one of the roofed gateways on either side of the log gatehouse. The other drive was blocked by heavy-duty metal barrier about eight feet high, and a light was on inside the building. On either side of the entrance, the woods were too thick to ride through.

Tanner stopped and Chantal coasted up next to him. He flipped up his face shield. "Guess we have to go in."

The gatehouse door opened and a uniformed ranger carrying a shotgun stepped out. "You need to come with me."

Chantal followed Tanner inside. The warm air enveloped him and the smell of burnt coffee assaulted his nose.

"Sit down." The ranger pointed at a pair of wooden chairs along one wall.

They sat.

"We got a call to be on the lookout for Tanner Hays and Chantal Durand. I'm guessing that's you."

"A call from who?" Chantal asked.

"I ask the questions," the ranger said. "Where did you get those snowmobiles?"

Tanner focused on Kilpatrick's thoughts. Dr. Greywolf had reported the snowmobiles stolen and named them as the thieves. Armed and dangerous, huh? This was too easy. He shifted in his chair, ready to rid them of this inconvenience and move on.

"We rented them from Junk and Corey Joseph," Chantal said. "They're at the Swiftcurrent Motel. You can call and check our story with Nola, the winter manager."

Kilpatrick nodded. "I'll do that. So why did Aaron Greywolf report the snowmobiles stolen?"

"No idea," Tanner said.

"Them boys are mighty proud of them snowmobiles. Can't believe they'd just let you borrow them."

"Rent," Chantal muttered. "For a lot of cash."

Tanner didn't take his eyes off Kilpatrick. He concentrated on planting thoughts that he hoped would become memories. "We didn't steal anything. You talked to Junk and Corey and they told you they rented the snowmobiles to us. Now you're going to move your vehicle and let us continue on our way."

Kilpatrick crossed to his desk and picked up his keys. "I'll move my truck for you."

"We'd appreciate that," Chantal said.

They followed him outside and he got in the Land Cruiser. Before he closed the door he called to them. "Be careful out there. Not much cell service between here and Babb to call for help if you get in trouble."

Tanner waved to the ranger and climbed on his snowmobile. "Hurry up. Highway 89 is about eight miles west on Route 3 and I want to get there as soon as possible. Greywolf is coming."

"How do you know that?"

"He has the box with him. It's calling to the ruby."

"Shit." Tossing Junk and Corey's phones into a snowbank, she swung onto her snowmobile and started it. "Do you think the link works both ways? Can Greywolf find us with the box?"

"No idea, but he knows this country and we don't. If we don't get a head start, we'll be facing him again in his territory."

# CHAPTER TWENTY-SEVEN

Mark checked the weather report for northern Montana on his laptop once again and superimposed Chantal and Tanner's ComDev locations on the radar map. They were heading out of the park and should make it to a main road before dark. The front should pass in the next eight hours and he could arrange to have an airstrip plowed for him to land and pick them up in the morning.

The sun streamed through the window wall of the Durand family's New York penthouse. He was the only family member who considered the sprawling residence home. His Paris and Los Angeles flats were more current in style and conveniences, but this place held the collection of sacred relics, magical objects, and just plain weird shit that the family had acquired over the last three centuries. Security here was so advanced that even the wiz-kids at Durand Tech couldn't break it—which was critical in a world where the enemy was brilliant and powerful, psychic and soulless.

"Trace Kara Hagen," he said and a moment later a pulsing blue dot appeared on the map. Columbia Falls on Highway 2 just west of the park and not far from where Tanner and Chantal had left the Tahoe. He pulled up her cell history—calls to Chantal, to DT, and to a burner number. The burner was currently in the same location she was. Chantal's message had mentioned a man with Kara.

"Call Vernon at investigations." The call connected immediately. "Vernon, I need to know who the man is with Kara Hagen in Columbia Falls, Montana. Send me photos, history, whatever you can get."

"Yes, sir."

"And Vern, this doesn't go any further."

"Of course. It never does."

Except sometimes it did. Was Kara the newest traitor, or was she being used? The war against the Dissemblers had altered. The enemy was no longer easily identifiable by the stench of majik—something that had changed eight years ago. Greywolf could be a Dissembler. So could Kara's friend.

He focused on the map on the screen. Tanner and Chantal were almost to Babb on the Blackfeet Reservation. East Glacier Park Village was about thirty miles south on Highway 2 east of the park. The highway would be plowed first and was their best chance of finding a ride out of there.

His ComDev dinged indicating he had a new message. It was from Vern.

*Facial recognition software identified man as Carlos Bianchi, a doctor from Buenos Aires. Our database identified that as an alias for Tomas Peralta, a persuasive who has traveled extensively in trouble areas over the last five years. Flagged by analysts as possible sleeper Dissembler. Photo attached.*

Mark opened the photo file and froze. "Call Adrien."

In spite of the late hour, the Sentier answered. "Bonsoir."

Mark cleared his throat and swallowed past the dread. "You're not going to believe who has surfaced in Montana."

# CHAPTER TWENTY-EIGHT

Between her breath and the cold, the scarf covering Chantal's mouth had frozen. The helmet over her hat and the face shield offered some protection from the wind whipping at her as the snowmobile pounded through the snow. Luckily, its heater worked and her feet and legs were toasty. This section of the road followed along the river and was relatively flat and easy to follow. Flying along on the white powder would have been a kick if a murderer weren't chasing them.

Although it was technically still daylight, the storm had darkened the sky. The road veered away from the river and climbed before leveling off. Forest flanked the road for a half mile and ended abruptly where Route 3 ran into Highway 89. Relief rolled over her when she spotted red and white lights ahead—Babb, Montana. Except for the well-illuminated Cattle Baron's Supper Club, the only sign of life was dim lights in a couple of mobile homes in the adjacent fields.

She signaled Tanner to turn into the parking lot, pulled up to the Supper Club, and killed the engine. "I need to use the ladies' room and hot coffee would be nice."

The establishment comprised a large wooden barn-like structure with two smaller buildings attached to one end. Three pickup trucks were parked in front of The Bunkhouse Café, but the action appeared to be happening in the barn.

He climbed off his snowmobile. "Keep your senses open. We're on the reservation. If Greywolf called here we may not get a friendly welcome."

She climbed off hers, pulling the helmet off and the icy

scarf away from her face. "I'll rely on you to read their minds and manipulate them then."

He reached for her. "I had no choice. We have to protect the ruby."

"I'm First Order Durand, remember? You think this is the first time I've seen one of us use telepathy to control *ordinaires*?" She yanked her arm from his grasp. "We do what we must to complete the mission. And right now what I need to do is use the bathroom."

Hot air hit her when she opened the door. The inside of the club was varnished wood—stripped tree trunks, and planks mostly—and at one end was a round bar with wooden barrels as barstools. Four cowboys and a thirty-something bartender in western attire turned to check them out as they came in.

"Didja git lost?" a grizzled old man asked.

"Nope," Tanner said and sauntered their way.

She followed him.

The bartender looked him up and down. Chantal had to admit he looked much better in his borrowed gear than she did in hers.

"What can we do for you?" the cowgirl asked.

"I'd like to use the ladies' room," Chantal said.

Cowgirl pointed to a hallway on the other side of the restaurant. "That way, honey."

Honey. "Thanks," she muttered and headed for the facilities.

Without any effort, Tanner read the thoughts of the men at the bar. Boredom, curiosity, two of them wondered what Chantal looked like under all those clothes. All but the bartender thought they were stupid to venture out in the storm. The bartender wished he'd get rid of his snowmobile suit and Chantal.

"Can we get two coffees?" he asked the bartender, then flashed her a warm smile she could take any way she liked.

"Sure. Want some whiskey in them?"

"No, thanks." He turned to the men. "Anyone know if 89 has been plowed further south?"

"Hell, they won't bother 'til the snow stops," one of the younger men said. "No reason to do it twice."

"What about Highway 2?"

They shrugged in unison.

"Couldn't say. Where you headed?" The guy was just curious. And he thought Tanner was a crazy city guy who didn't know his ass from his hat.

"Trying to get back to Kalispell."

"On them snowmobiles?" The old man chortled. "That's almost a hunert-fifty miles, son."

The bartender set two mugs on the bar and put a pitcher of milk and a sugar bowl next to them. "It's only about 40 miles to Highway 2 if you take 49. Glacier Park Lodge usually closes at the end of September, but you can probably find a motel room until the plows come through."

The cowboys nodded, but they all thought Tanner and Chantal would get lost on 49 and end up frozen somewhere. They weren't going to talk him out of that plan, though.

Chantal appeared and accepted the coffee. She climbed onto one of the barrel seats and sipped it. He was much too aware of her scent and the desire his body felt for her. It was the stone, and yet those flushed cheeks and rosy lips inspired all kinds of erotic impulses there was no way he could act on.

He needed to use the head and log the route south in his ComDev, but he didn't want to leave her here. The younger men were much too interested in her and he didn't want a fight. He pushed aversion thoughts on all the men and friendly ones on the bartender then left Chantal on her own.

Done with the bathroom, he sat at a table far enough from the bar for privacy, but with a view of everyone. The men were talking among themselves while Chantal chatted with the bartender. She'd unzipped her monosuit and slipped it off her shoulders along with her jacket. His aversion push had worked—not one of the guys paid any attention to her.

A message from Mark popped up on the screen of his ComDev. *Where are you headed?*

Mark had no doubt tracked their ComDevs so he replied: *To East Glacier Park Village then to the cabin via Highway 2.*

*And the item?*

*Safe.* He paused for a moment then continued. *The box is calling to it. Greywolf is on our trail.*

*Then get moving. DO NOT ENGAGE. Item must be protected at all costs.* The message paused then continued. *Avoid Kara Hagen. She's in Columbia Falls with a suspicious companion. I'll take care of them when I arrive.*

Just as Chantal and he had suspected. *On our way. Will check in at EGPV.*

Plugging in the route took only a few seconds. The ComDev calculated an hour and twenty-seven minutes based on the weather and their mode of transportation. He headed for the bar. One last task to complete before they left.

"Can I get you something to eat?" the bartender asked. "The cook isn't here, but we have sandwiches and pie."

Chantal was already wriggling into her jacket and monosuit.

He threw a twenty on the bar. "Thanks, but we need to get going."

"Good luck," she said.

"Damn stupid tourists," someone muttered under his breath. "Don't complain when you freeze in a ditch somewhere."

Tanner didn't argue the logic of that last statement. Instead, he concentrated on gathering strength from the ruby. He knew scrubbing multiple memories was possible, but not so sure of the technique. Focusing on the minds of everyone but Chantal, he telepathically tried to dim their memories of the last hour. "We weren't here. No one was here except two kids on snowmobiles picking up a six-pack of beer." He tested their thoughts and found confusion. "No strangers have been here since yesterday. Keep drinking. Don't look back. Nothing happened."

Signaling to Chantal, he backed toward the door, watching the men and the cowgirl. They seemed unaware of him and Chantal, not even turning when he opened the door and the cold wind swept in.

As they climbed on the snowmobiles, Chantal finally spoke.

"You're getting pretty good at that telepathy business. Hope it sticks."

"Me, too. Greywolf will be here soon and he's a telepath too. Let's hope he stays long enough to give us a head start south."

"And the box. Can you tell how far away it is?"

He let his senses work through the ruby. "A few miles, not far. If the box is broadcasting to him the way the ruby is to me, he won't be fooled by my attempt at memory scrubbing for long."

"Then we better get going."

"One more thing. I checked in with Mark. He said Kara's in Columbia Falls with someone suspicious. We need to avoid them."

"Just as we thought." She started her engine. "I'll be right behind you. Try to stay on the road."

# CHAPTER TWENTY-NINE

Aaron saw the snowmobile tracks when he pulled into the parking lot of the Cattle Baron Supper Club. Unfortunately, the snowmobiles were gone. The box in his pack hummed so softly he only felt the vibrations over his snowmobile's engine. They had begun a few miles back and he assumed it had something to do with the treasure it had once protected.

Circling the parameter of the parking lot, he found the tracks leading down US 89. So Hays and the girl were heading for Highway 2. As long as they were on the reservation he had the home advantage so stopping them in St. Mary's or East Glacier Park Village was critical. He pulled up to the front of the restaurant. A pit stop might provide some information, or at least allow him to make his calls.

He recognized the men at the bar and they recognized him.

"Professor! What are you doing out in this weather?" Herb asked.

"Tracking down the couple who stole my cousins' snowmobiles—the man and woman who just left here." He tuned his senses to read Herb's mind. All he got was confusion. The old scoundrel knew nothing about Hays and Durand. He tapped the thoughts of Sheila, the bartender. Again, no knowledge of the two.

"Nobody been here except a couple of kids a while back buying beer," Sheila said. "They came on snowmobiles."

He couldn't be wrong. The tracks from the Many Glacier entrance led directly here. "You sure?"

"We ain't had that much to drink," Herb growled and the others muttered in agreement.

One by one he read each of the other men's minds, probing for some hint of a memory of Hays and Durand.

"How about a drink, Professor?" Sheila asked. "Something hot and strong? Irish coffee? Some brandy to warm you up?"

"Did you hear anything odd? Some snowmobiles in the parking lot?" Maybe the two hadn't come in.

"Nope. And if they was Corey and Junk's monsters, we'd a heard them," Ray said. "Them things are loud enough to wake the dead in St. Mary's."

Everyone but Aaron chuckled.

Was it possible to completely wipe out the memories of five people at one time? He himself could alter memories like he'd done with Jason Hawkswing, but not multiple people. And he certainly could not erase memories completely.

For the first time, his confidence wavered. He'd had the advantage of surprise in the cave and the backup of his boys if things got rough. Hays had a bullet in him. How had they escaped and made it to Babb?

Sheila put a shot of gold liquor on the bar in front of him. "You look like you need this."

He hesitated for a long moment then threw it back. "Thanks." One shot of bourbon wouldn't dull his senses and the burn down his throat reinforced his resolve. Reporting the snowmobiles stolen wouldn't work if Hays or Durand could manipulate minds. Better to find out where they were and deal with them himself.

# CHAPTER THIRTY

Ten miles into the trip on Highway 89, Chantal had to admit she was enjoying herself. Tanner rode next to her most of the time, pulling ahead when the road narrowed or there were obstacles to avoid. The last time she'd been on a snowmobile, she and Lex had raced across a frozen lake in Greenland. Lex had won as usual, and they'd retired to the ski lodge for drinks in front of the fire.

No one had been chasing them then. Certainly not a psychic killer.

She glanced at Tanner. Not many telepaths could scrub memories and very few could wipe clean several at once. His new abilities were getting stronger—maybe too powerful. Would he keep them when he no longer had the ruby? As far as she was concerned, the sooner they handed off the thing, the better.

She checked her ComDev. The miles had flown by. Soon they turned onto MT 49. The map noted this road was closed in the winter and she could see why. Between the mountainous terrain and wooded sections, the road would be treacherous for cars and trucks. Even on snowmobiles, the twists and turns required complete concentration. Tanner had taken the lead and frequently looked back to be sure she was keeping up.

A broken branch over the road forced her to duck and when she looked up all she saw ahead was the sky. Her heart leapt into her throat as she jerked sharply to the right and skidded along the edge of a hundred foot drop-off before veering back onto the road. The pounding of her heart felt like it would burst through her chest and her hands trembled on the steering grips. She let up on the gas and slid to a stop. Ahead, Tanner U-turned and came back.

"What are you doing?" he asked impatiently.

She wanted to throw something big and hard at his head. "I nearly went over that cliff."

"Why?"

"Because I couldn't see it until I was almost over it." Her voice shook a little.

"But…" Understanding dawned across his face. "Shit. My senses are so jacked; I can see, hear, and even taste everything around me. I knew about that drop-off in plenty of time, but you didn't. I'm so sorry."

"Your damned superpowers almost got me killed trying to keep up."

"The ruby's the only reason we got out of the cave and the only reason I didn't bleed to death."

"So don't get me killed now!"

"I said I was sorry. I was trying to put more distance between us and Greywolf, and we have. But I'll slow down."

She hated she couldn't keep up, but with his senses so heightened she couldn't. "Thanks. Let's get going. This road isn't going to get any easier in the dark."

By the time they got to East Glacier Park Village, they'd been riding in the dark for thirty-five minutes. They dropped off the snowmobiles in front of a small motel with a NO VACANCY sign. Luckily, the sprawling Glacier Park Lodge was bustling with activity and their best bet to find a ride or a room for the night.

The log lodge glowed against the snow-covered lawns. Entering the lobby was like going a century back in time. Towering tree trunks supported the structure and roof, creating a several story central space. The place was busier than Chantal had expected. A group of older people, luggage piled next to them, occupied the dozen or so sofas and chairs in the center of the lobby. They didn't look happy.

"Welcome to God's Country," Tanner muttered. "I've never seen so many straight tree trunks before and these are huge."

"Definitely Americana. Let's see if we can get transportation out of here."

A harried young woman stood behind the concierge desk talking to a gray-haired couple in golfing clothes and light jackets.

"What are we supposed to do?" the man asked. "This was a golf package, not a ski package."

"Unfortunately, we have no control over the weather, sir."

"Then we want a refund," the woman whined.

"I'm sorry, I can't help you with that." The young woman smiled sweetly. "You'll have to talk with the lodge manager."

The couple trudged off grumbling and Lex stepped forward. "Hi. We're looking for a ride to Kalispell."

The young woman shook her head. "You and about a hundred other people."

"What about the train?" Tanner asked. "Doesn't Amtrak run in that direction?"

"Stopped running last week until spring. The roads haven't been plowed yet and may not be open until midmorning." The concierge sighed. "The tour group of seniors over there have a bus outside that can't go anywhere tonight, but you might get a ride with them in the morning."

"What about a snowplow?" Tanner asked. "We can pay if they'll let us ride along."

The young woman laughed. "You are desperate. I've never heard of anyone hiring a snowplow, and it would be expensive."

"Not a problem," he said and nodded toward Chantal. "She's got cash."

"I'll make a couple calls. Do you have a cell number?"

Chantal gave her a relay number to reach her ComDev and slipped her a hundred dollar bill. "Thanks."

"How about dinner while we wait?" Tanner said. "I'm starving."

"Me too, but it's too risky to eat there." She pointed to the crowded restaurant. "Room service."

"Do they even have it?"

"Haven't you ever heard of bribing staff to bring you food? When we get the rooms, you alter the receptionist's memory to see a middle-aged couple and two teenaged kids."

He winked. "You're getting good at this."

"No, you are. I've lived with telepaths all my life, and for the record, the Durand do not use telepathic manipulation except when absolutely necessary."

He draped an arm around her shoulders and guided her toward the reception desk. The woman at the desk greeted them wearily. "Welcome to the lodge. You don't have reservations, do you?"

"No. We were caught in the park in the storm," Chantal said. "Do you have two rooms available?"

"Only one interior queen room—no windows." She pointed to the catwalk around the upper part of the lobby. "Up there."

"No adjoining rooms?" Tanner asked.

The woman rolled her eyes. "This isn't the Ritz."

"Nothing else?" Chantal tried not to sound desperate.

The woman shook her head. "We were supposed to close September thirtieth but stayed open for a seniors' wilderness excursion. Then the storm hit and we filled up."

"You're sure there's nothing else?" Tanner asked.

"Not unless you want to spring for the Governor's Suite. It's *expensive*. Got a bedroom, bathroom, kitchenette and a living room."

"We'll take it." They said in unison.

The woman studied their clothes and lack of luggage. "It's six hundred dollars a night."

"A bargain." Chantal dug her wallet out of the inside pocket of her jacket and chose a European Visa card and Norwegian driver's license for one of her aliases. She handed the cards over.

The woman sighed wearily. "I'll need to run this for approval. Computers are slow today. It could take a couple of minutes."

And in the meantime, they were standing in the middle of a crowded lobby. "Think you could make us invisible?" she whispered to Tanner as the woman stared at her screen.

"Sorry. Haven't got that down yet."

• • •

The suite turned out to be rustic, but large and cozy. The concierge called ten minutes after their food arrived.

"Sorry I couldn't help you," she said. "County plows can't take nonemployees because of insurance, and the tribe's plows only carry two people, both drivers who take turns on the run. The roads should be open by afternoon and if you don't mind paying, there's a limo service that uses an Escalade with snow tires that will take you."

"Fine, book it and charge it to room 825. And thanks." Chantal ended the call.

"Greywolf will be here long before tomorrow afternoon," Tanner said, cutting a piece of rare steak. "If the ruby *feels* the box then the box may be able to track the ruby."

She really wanted a glass of wine. Or a bottle. A waiter from the restaurant had been happy to take a hefty bribe to bring food up. She hadn't thought to order wine.

"How far away is the box now?" She pushed a piece of asparagus around her plate. "Can you tell?"

"Still on the road. He didn't take the same route we did. Stuck to the main road where we turned off on 49."

"Then he has to find us once he gets here." She took a bite of pasta and chewed. She had a good idea how he was going to react to her next suggestion. "If the box can track the ruby, wrapping it in Ancilon will disguise it and buy us time."

Tanner froze with his fork halfway to his mouth and lowered his hand. "Then I won't know where the box is."

"This isn't about the damn box, is it? It's about your newfound telepathy and enhanced senses. What other abilities has the stone given you?"

His mouth tightened. "Besides physical strength and the ability to heal from a gunshot wound?"

"Tanner, this thing is dangerous. You can't gain power without paying a price. The Durand have known that for centuries. Even Adrien…" She stopped herself. Adrien's fall and redemption wasn't her story to tell.

"Even Adrien has limits? And Mark?" He lowered his voice and his eyes darkened. "Does it bother you that I might become more powerful than either of them? Or does it turn you on?"

She tried not to react to the way he was looking at her, but her body betrayed her.

He gave her a slow, sexy smile that didn't help the heat spreading in inconvenient places. "Thought so."

She pulled out her ComDev. "Call Mark."

He answered on the third buzz. "How's the lodge?"

"You're tracking us? I thought ComDevs were untraceable."

"They are unless you're Adrien or me. Am I on speaker?"

"Yes."

"Then fill me in."

She glanced at Tanner, who had resumed eating. "We made it here with no incident. As a result of possessing the ruby, Tanner has acquired some impressive new abilities. Advanced telepathy—he scrubbed the memories of everyone in the bar where we stopped—enhanced senses, increased physical strength and the ability to heal himself. Oh, and he can feel the box the ruby was in calling to the stone. He can even tell how far away it is." She stared at Tanner. "Is that it or is there anything you want to add?"

"That's pretty much covers it."

"Can the box track the ruby?" Mark asked.

Tanner tore off a piece of roll and dipped it in the steak sauce. "I don't know. Maybe." He popped the bread in his mouth.

"Where's the ruby now?" Mark asked.

Tanner just chewed.

"In his pocket," Chantal said. "I think we should put it in Ancilon to hide its energy from the box. He disagrees."

"Why?" Mark asked.

Tanner glared at her. "If it's wrapped up I won't know where Greywolf and the box are. He snuck up on us in the cave. That's not happening again."

She glared at him. "If it isn't emitting its power, then he won't find us. Stop being so damned stubborn."

"The power isn't yours," Mark said. "And using it may burn out the abilities you have. The Durand have discovered other amplifying objects over the centuries and used them to fight our enemies. In the end, the psychic who used them always suffered and often died. The Shalamov are a power-hungry lot. If they sent the stone away, there was a reason. Protect yourself before it's too late, Tanner."

"Is that an order, *sir*?"

"Yes. A direct order."

"This is fucked up." Tanner took the ruby from the pocket of his shirt and laid it on the table. He glowered at Chantal, his lip cocked in a sneer. "Take it. When Greywolf shows up and uses his magic on us, remember I told you so."

She put on her protective gloves and picked up the stone. A tingle of energy shot up her arm and hit her in the chest before she dropped it in a pouch. To be extra careful she put the pouch inside another Ancilon pouch. "It's in double protection and I'm putting it in the room's safe."

"Good. Leave it there until you head for Kalispell tomorrow," Mark said. "I'll pick you up when you get to town and we'll get the hell out of there."

"What about the box?" Tanner asked. "Do we just leave it behind?"

"Your first priority is to get the ruby out safely."

The muscles around Tanner's eyes tightened and she thought he might argue with Mark. The field general was usually cool with questions and even a discussion of options, but he reacted badly to his orders being challenged. Very badly.

"We'll text you when we're on our way, and get your ETA and where to meet you," she said. "Anything else?"

A long moment of silence followed and she checked if Mark was still on the line.

"No. Be alert and stay put tonight," Mark said. "See you tomorrow." He clicked off.

Tension hung in the air. "Why did you tattle to Mark?" Tanner demanded.

"I didn't *tattle*. I *briefed* him since you obviously weren't going to."

"My enhanced abilities saved us and you made me sound like a power-hungry asshole."

"No, I didn't. I just stated the facts."

He leaned back in his chair and crossed his arms over his chest. "You decided you were right and I was wrong. You presented the situation to Mark to get him to back you up."

"I didn't hear you making a case for yourself."

"Two First Order Durand. Would it have mattered?" He shook his head. "The rules apply to everyone but you, and certainly not to Mark or Adrien. I've had a taste of the power they were born with, abilities they use at will for their own agendas."

"Their *agendas* are to stop the Dissemblers from destroying civilization and to stop Tolian from controlling the world. You've been a Protector since you were eighteen—isn't that your agenda too?"

"Greywolf isn't a Dissembler."

"No, he's a murderer who left us to die in that damned cave. If he got the ruby, god knows what he'd do with it, but I guarantee it wouldn't be good works and charity." She rested her hand on his forearm and he didn't pull away. The heat of his body warmed her palm and felt all too intimate. "The stone gave you the ability to save us. You're a good man. I don't want to see it destroy you."

"It won't."

"We don't know what it will do. The priest and medicine man both died because of the ruby. Power like that is destructive and not worth risking your life over."

The aggression drained from his expression. "The stone's power beginning to fade already and yet my senses are still ultra-acute. I can hear people moving around, toilets flushing, the dripping of water in the shower in our suite. I can feel your breath and the heat of your skin, smell the cheap soap from your bath, the perspiration on your skin—your arousal."

She drew her hand back, and he caught it and held it against his chest.

"Why are you doing this?" she asked.

"So you'll understand that my abilities aren't gone, just because the ruby is tucked away. Dimmed a little, but still strong."

She nodded, not trusting herself so close to him. He was right—her body reacted to being near him, touching him. Her hand wanted to explore his chest, touch his mouth, and trace the scar on his cheek.

He breathed in deeply and gave her a slow, sexy smile. He knew that she wanted him. He pulled her from her chair and effortlessly lifted her to straddle his lap, pressing her sex against an impressive erection.

His mouth closed in on hers, gently at first, then with more heat. She opened her lips to welcome his invasion and he pulled her hard against his hips, his tongue exploring and claiming her mouth. His taste filled her head—the intoxicating spice of him she'd never forgotten. She held on to his massive shoulders and shifted so his cock rubbed exactly where she wanted him. A growl vibrated deep in his chest and she rocked against him again.

His hands snaked under her shirt and he broke the kiss to lift it over her head. The cool air hit her flushed skin as his hungry gaze caressed her body.

"Damn, you're gorgeous." His fingers brushed the tops of her breasts and his thumbs teased her nipples until she arched into his palms and moaned. "And so hot."

Her fingers explored his chest and shoulders, tracing the solid muscle under his shirt. She tugged at the fabric, desperate to get to skin. "Take this off."

He pulled back and his body tensed. "Why?"

"I want to see you, touch you."

"Do you?"

"Yes. Do you want me to beg?"

"No." A swift pull exposed tanned skin and a sculpted torso.

A torso so scarred, she gasped. A terrible ache filled her chest and she could barely whisper around the sorrow that squeezed in her throat. "Oh, Tanner."

"Not what you were expecting." He reached for his shirt and she caught his wrist to stop him.

"Don't," she pleaded. "I never imagined they'd done this to you."

"I survived."

He sat stiffly as she traced a thick white scar that ran from his right shoulder across his chest and brushed her palm over the mutilated pink skin on his pec. Her eyes filled with tears. "How did you bear it?"

"I didn't have a choice." He didn't move, just watched her caress his body.

She pressed kisses on his chest and shoulder and flicked her tongue on skin puckered by a burn. She tasted sweat perfumed by a masculine musk that was uniquely his.

"You're not repulsed?"

"By your body? Not at all. It's a warrior's body." She ran her fingertip over the smooth skin where the bullet had entered his shoulder. "I want you to tell me about Mexico, but not now."

"Good." He slipped a hand behind her, unhooked her bra and watched hungrily as her breasts sprang free. He dripped his head to capture a nipple with his teeth and sucked until she groaned. "And so fucking sexy."

Chantal arched her back for him as his mouth worshipped one breast and then the other. Her fingers entwined in his hair to hold him where he was, grasping as the pleasure ricocheted from her nipples to between her legs and back. When he began to rock his erection against her sex she thought she might come.

"I need to be in you," he rasped. "Tell me to stop now or…"

"Don't stop!"

In a single motion, he lifted her to her feet and stripped off her pants. A moment later, his were gone too. Palming her ass, he lifted her off her feet and she wrapped her legs around his waist. He pressed her back against the wall and drove into her. She met his thrust and dug her fingers into his shoulders. He filled her so completely her entire body shimmered with pleasure. Again and again, he plunged into her, the slick friction so exquisite she never wanted it to stop.

"Come for me, baby," he groaned.

And she did. "Oh, Tanner!" Wave after wave of pleasure rolled over her, punctuated with her cries. And moments later he roared and came too.

Remaining deep inside her, he finally stilled. "Sorry I couldn't take it slower. It's been over a year and a half since I've been with anyone."

She didn't correct him, just enjoyed the pounding of his heart against hers.

He went on. "Will you let me make it up to you?"

"Now?"

"Got anything else on your schedule?"

"Nope."

He brushed her lips with his then settled in for a long, sensuous kiss. Every cell in her body lit up, wanting and needing everything he could give her. When he finally came up for air, he looked almost as dazed as she felt.

"Any objections to a bed?" she asked.

His eyes gleamed wickedly as he carried her to the bedroom. "Whatever you want, baby. As long as you want it."

She wished that was true.

• • •

Chantal's breathing slowed and her eyes closed. When he was sure she'd fallen asleep, Tanner slipped out of bed and into the bathroom. He needed a long hot shower to wash the scent of Chantal and sex off his body before he lost control and took her again. And there was no doubt he would if he didn't get himself straight. He'd never had that kind of stamina before, not even in his randy college days. And thanks to the ruby's residual effects, the erection he still sported was more than ready for another round.

He flicked on the bathroom light and squinted against the

fluorescent glare off white tile and porcelain. This bathroom had a walk-in shower with a bench that fueled his imagination. His cock bucked. "Enough. We have work to do."

The water was hot and the soap was some special spa shit that thankfully had only a faint, herbal scent. As he lathered up, the suds tickled his skin when the tiny bubbles burst. His senses were still preternaturally acute and the sensations of everyday activities felt new and strange. The mint shampoo tingled on his scalp and the hot water slid sensuously down his body to rinse the suds off. He let the water pour over his head for several minutes to clear his mind then shut it off and reached for a thick towel to dry himself.

For the first time in months, he stepped in front of the mirror and studied his naked body. Chantal had been shocked at first by the extensive damage, but not disgusted. He could still feel her lips and mouth on his mangled skin. And there had been no pity in her reaction. Would any other woman have handled the massive scarring as she had? He doubted it. Then again, no one but Chantal and the Durand doctors had seen him naked since Mexico.

He finger-combed his hair and wrapped the towel around his waist. His beard had passed the stubble stage and, combined with the scar down his cheek, gave him a decidedly menacing appearance. A shave would take care of the beard, but the scar was a souvenir he'd learned to live with. Mexico was over and he was alive. And a murderer was out there looking for him and Chantal.

His pack was in the living room and still held a clean pair of jeans and a white T-shirt. He dressed and settled on the sofa with his ComDev, his Ruger, and a beer from the minibar. Closing his eyes and focusing on locating the box, his consciousness no longer had the link to feel its call. Was that good or bad? Unease prickled the hair on the back of his neck. They could be sitting ducks here or safely hidden. Which was it?

He logged his ComDev into DT's system and searched: *Dr. Aaron Greywolf cell phone*. Two numbers popped up on the screen. "Locate," he commanded.

Two tiny cell icons appeared on a map, one in Missoula and the other less than a mile away. He zoomed in on what appeared to be a residential street off route 49 and watched the icon for a couple of minutes. It didn't move. If Greywolf was coming for them, he'd left his cell phone behind. Somehow, Tanner didn't think the professor would abandon his phone at this point.

The shower went on. Chantal. Naked. Her sexy moans replayed in his head. The memory of her hands on his body, her mouth on his, the pure ecstasy on her face when she came—his body roared to life. He adjusted himself and took a swig of beer. The sex had been spectacular, earth shaking, but there were still issues they needed to resolve. The ruby had boosted his performance, but he couldn't attribute the attraction to the stone anymore. He'd wanted her long before London and never stopped. She'd been right—the stone had only ramped up feelings that were already there. No other woman had ever rivaled her in his heart.

No matter how well she'd performed on this mission, she was still holding back information about what happened the night Javier died, and until she came clean, he couldn't completely trust her.

"Hey, mister." Chantal stood in the bedroom door wrapped in a white terrycloth hotel robe. "Did you happen to see the Mac truck that hit me?"

He laughed. "That bad?"

"That good. You're very talented, Mr. Hays." Barefoot, she padded across the carpet and curled up in the chair across from him. He let out the breath he was holding. Had she snuggled up to him, she'd be naked again in three seconds.

"Only with you." Had he said that? It was true, but so not cool.

Her grin managed to be both innocent and seductive. "I doubt it." Her expression sobered. "Any idea where the box is?"

He told her about tracing the cell. "I'll keep an eye on his phone and be ready for any visitors if you want to catch some sleep." He patted the Ruger on the sofa next to him. "But I think we should be fine until tomorrow."

"Thanks. I'm not tired." She tugged the robe tighter around her slim body. "Tell me what happened in Mexico."

He'd repeated the story enough times to have it down. "Luke and I got ID'ed by the border drug lord, Juan Miguel Medina. We'd infiltrated his organization and were thrown in a dungeon with the rest of his enemies. His business partners and enforcers included Dissemblers with sadistic skills. By the time Mark got to us we were in bad shape, but he carried Luke out and half carried me."

"I know the abridged story. Tell me what they did to you, how you survived."

He hadn't even told Mark the full scope of the torture, and pride wouldn't allow him to tell her all the humiliating details. But she'd seen his body and not turned away. The ordeal played back in his head like a gory horror movie, not like an excruciating part of his life. "Someone knew who we were. The Mexicans used fists and whips on us—crude and uncontrolled beatings that would have killed us sooner rather than later."

She winced. "They're the ones who ripped up your back?"

He nodded and the muscles of his back and shoulders twitched with the memory. "The Dissemblers were into inflicting max pain that stopped just short of being fatal. They were good—knife wounds filled with salt then cauterized with a hot poker, branding, stretching, even a form of crucifixion. One motherfucker was a master at breaking bones with a baseball bat." And had taken glee in sodomizing Luke. Tanner had been luckier. "The dungeon was cold and wet. They gave us slop to eat. When Mark found us, Luke was unconscious and I was delirious and could barely stand. I don't know how he got in and can't imagine how he got us out."

"I've heard the Dissemblers call him *Espectro da Morte*. Specter of Death."

"Yeah. I know he uses telepathy to become invisible, but it was like he just touched the guards and they dropped." He searched her face for some indication she understood. "Is that possible?"

"You know I couldn't tell you if I knew. Mark isn't like anyone else, not even Adrien. He does what has to be done." She fiddled with the ends of the robe's sash. "How did you bear it?"

"I wanted to live and I believed someone would come and get

us. At the time, all I could think about was survival. Afterwards was harder—the memories and pain."

"I'm so sorry." Her eyes were filled with compassion, not pity, which made him want to tell her everything. "You had a flashback up on the ridge, didn't you?"

"You knew?"

"I suspected. We all have demons in our line of work."

"Adrien offered to scrub the memories, but nothing could change the damage to my body, so in the end, I couldn't do it. If I didn't remember how I got the scars, I'd hate them. Instead, they remind me how lucky I am to be alive."

"Thank you for telling me." Her smile was kind and accepting.

A weight lifted from deep in his chest. He was glad he'd told her. His head had been fucked up since he got back, no matter how much he tried to convince his Durand shrink he was fine. But they still had business that wasn't going away.

"Now tell me about that night in London."

# CHAPTER THIRTY-ONE

According to the GPS devices on the snowmobiles, they were parked in front of the Dancing Bears Inn, but the woman at the front desk said the place had filled up the night before and the NO VACANCY sign had done its job. Aaron called the other motels. Most had already closed for the season, but he'd gotten the same answer from the two that were open—the surprise blizzard had caught people in the park and their rooms had been snatched up yesterday and that morning.

His former colleague at the university only lived in East Glacier during the summer these days, but because of the cold weather had to keep the electricity and heat functional during the winter. And he kept a key under a rock near the back door. Aaron had made himself at home, charging his cell, and cursing the lack of Wi-Fi. At least the cabin was warm and private.

His cell buzzed. Maria Naranjo.

He answered. "What did you find out?"

"That the computer system at the Glacier Park Lodge sucks."

"Did you find them?"

"No one named Hays or Durand has checked in. Neither used a credit card in the hotel or any motel in town."

"What about cash? Maybe a couple checked in under a false name and paid cash. They had cash."

"Checked that too. I verified the identities of almost everyone who checked into the Lodge since noon. Had a problem with a group of Japanese tourists—the alphabet thing is a bitch—and a Norwegian family who checked into a suite."

"I need you to track them down."

"Have you been to the Lodge? We're not talking a high tech

operation. In fact, I'd say they cultivate their rustic ambiance. I was lucky they have a computer system at all."

He huffed impatiently. "Durand and Hays can't get away."

"If they're in East Glacier Park, they're not going anywhere. The roads are all still closed. You have plenty of time to catch up with them."

"Let me know if you find out anything else." He hung up.

So close, but he wasn't going to underestimate these two again. Anyone who could delete memories could manipulate what someone saw. He had to disable them and get whatever they'd taken from the box.

He took one last gulp of coffee and wished there'd been something more substantial than a chicken potpie in the freezer. He was tired and that was dangerous. The two psychics he was looking for were more powerful than anyone he'd ever faced alone. One of them was a telepath and Hays had not only survived the gunshot wound, but in spite of his injury, escaped the cave. What else could they do?

His phone buzzed, indicating he'd gotten a text. The sender read Unknown. What the hell? Who had sent this?

*You'll find them at the Glacier Park Lodge, Room 825.*

He called Maria. "Did you just text me from another cell?"

"No. Why?"

"Don't bother looking for Durand and Hays. I found them."

He hung up. Why would someone text him their location? Was it a trap? It didn't matter anymore. The treasure was within his reach and nothing was going to stop him from fulfilling his destiny.

He laid a blanket in the center of the living room floor and sat down cross-legged with the box. He cleared his mind of everything but the box and his two foes and began to chant. The words were in an ancient language he only partially understood, taught to him by his grandfather. He called on the spirits of his ancestors, the elements, and the weather. They would strengthen him and focus his power.

Energy filled the room, swirling around him and filling him

with light. But laying hands on the box did not bring it back to life. Four hours ago the thing had gone silent, which either meant Hays and Durand had gotten away, or they were somehow hiding the treasure.

A fever crept through his body, beginning with his hands resting on the box, filling him with a holy madness. The box wanted its treasure and it was going to drive him until the reunion—or until it killed him.

• • •

"Tell me something I don't know," Tanner snapped. Every Protector knew the history of the Durand, no matter how distant their relationship to the Sentier.

Curling further into the chair, Chantal pulled the robe closer around her body, but her toes still poked out the bottom. He tossed her a woolen blanket from the sofa.

"Thanks." She snuggled under the blanket. "Did you know that fifteen years ago, Mark faced off with Tolian in the Andes?"

"And lived?" That got his attention. Tolian, the Brazilian Sentier who controlled the Dissemblers, had killed his predecessor in a psychic duel to win his title. He'd been eighteen at the time. His power was as legendary as it was evil.

"Just barely. I don't know the details, but I know Tolian was waiting for him—tipped off by someone in our ranks."

Tanner did the math. He'd only been twenty and Mark had been twenty-one. "Did they find out who?"

"Yes, a Protector sold him out. Mark traced the payment to an offshore account."

"Who was it?"

She shook her head. "I don't know. That was the beginning. In the old days, Dissemblers were easy to identify by the smell of their majik, but a new breed of Dissembler spies didn't use majik. They befriended Durand, Protectors, and DT employees undetected."

"Whoever tipped off the Mexican cartel about Luke and me was one of these?"

"Dissemblers are masters of mind control. Sometimes they use psychic abilities, other times simple psychology. If someone feels unappreciated or used, they're easier prey. If they're jealous of other Durand or resent the hierarchy, they're ripe for recruiting."

Which brought them to her accusation against Javier. "You think Javier was recruited?"

"I know he was."

"I don't believe it. He didn't like the First Order—said you were a bunch of privileged aristocrats who thought you were better than the rest of us—but that doesn't make him a traitor."

She laughed. "We *are* a bunch of privileged aristocrats, but we're also the strongest psychics of our generation, especially Adrien and Mark. We don't ask anyone else to do anything we don't do ourselves. In fact, we get the most hazardous assignments. Mark pulls off impossible missions, as you well know, and risks his own life in the most dangerous situations."

"I know and I'm grateful, but Javier was my closest friend for years. I can't believe he was working with Dissemblers."

"Think back. When we heard the attack, we were outside the embassy. Do you remember why?"

After Javier's death, he hadn't thought again about why they'd been there so it took a moment to recall their circumstances. "Javier had a tip on an assassination attempt on a visiting African dignitary—the President of some new government."

She nodded. "Yes. We were only blocks away from the bombsite when it went off. When we got to the blast site, I caught the scent of two Dissemblers and tracked them to the warehouse."

Those moments were etched in his memory—so much smoke, wailing, screaming, the bleating London sirens. Running through the streets and alleys, the stares of the stunned and frightened people followed them as they sprinted by. "I remember."

"When we got to the warehouse, Javier was already there, talking on his cell and immediately ended the call."

"He was talking to Mark, wasn't he?" Tanner recollected the call, but after what happened later, it seemed unimportant.

"No, he wasn't. I wanted to report in to Adrien, but he insisted you go in with him immediately."

"There wasn't time."

"Wasn't there? Why not? You know procedures as well as I do. If we knew the Dissembler terrorists were in that warehouse, we were supposed to call in for backup."

Cold nausea rolled through his gut. He'd never forget her insisting they call for backup and Javier telling her to shut the fuck up and stand guard.

Her gaze didn't leave his. "He didn't want back up because he was working with the Dissemblers. Adrien had been watching him for months and intercepted hard evidence against him. The Wild Card was you."

"Adrien suspected me?"

"He didn't know. You were Javier's best friend and he was very vocal about his resentments."

"So you barged in and got Javier blown up."

"I was ordered to kill the Dissemblers before they got away. And, if I hadn't shot them, they would have gotten away."

He tried to recall his friend's plan. "We had them in our sights. Javier and I could have handled them."

"Then why didn't you act?" she asked. "Why did Javier leave you in the middle of the warehouse and take cover near an exit on the far side?"

"There wasn't an exit!"

"Yes, there was. I could see it under the stairway when I came in. You couldn't from your angle, which is probably why he stationed you there."

He stared at her, the air locked in his lungs. Was it possible Javier had intended to set him up?

Chantal continued. "When the firefight started, it was clear the shots were coming at you and me, not Javier. Then I got shot and you pulled me out of the line of fire into the alcove."

"The *ordinaire* terrorists blew Javier up and escaped. If he was working with them, why kill him?"

She shook her head. "Maybe he'd become a liability. Perhaps it was an accident."

"Why didn't you tell me this before?"

"I tried that night. You refused to listen and said no excuse would ever be good enough."

The memory of his words, his scathing tone seared through his brain and he gritted his teeth to bear the pain of it. He'd wronged her then, and over and over in the last seven years. "I'm so sorry. His death was a terrible blow. But why didn't you tell me later?"

"I was hurt. And pissed off. Really pissed off." She shrugged. "Besides, Adrien wanted to keep an eye on you after it happened."

"He didn't trust me."

"No. By the time you were cleared of any part in the plan, our feud was common knowledge and eventually, I ended up in Australia."

He swallowed past the tightness in his throat. All these years he'd blamed her for getting his best friend killed when she'd been following orders. He'd been so sure he knew what happened that night because he'd been there. "It wasn't fair to either of us."

When she spoke her voice was soft and sad. "Would things have been different if you'd known the truth?"

Would they? Would their lives have taken a different course—together?

A wave of anguish rolled over him. Then, he felt it—the box's desperation to find the stone. His breathing turned loud and labored and echoed in his brain. The box was calling, and the residual power in his body responded.

"It's awakened," he rasped.

"What has?"

"The box. It's been quiet since we shielded the ruby. Now, it's as though the volume has been turned up and I have a heavy metal band blaring in my veins." His hands and arms trembled badly.

"Can it find you?"

The energy shifted to a different pitch, a lower key and volume he could think through. "Maybe. If it can sense the remaining energy in my body, but I don't think so."

"What should we do?"

"Get dressed and ready to move out." He stood and tested the stability of his legs. Strong and stable. "The box is moving in our direction. If Greywolf is coming here, we need to get ready for him."

Chantal unfolded from the chair and picked up her clothes from the floor where they'd fallen earlier. He forced himself to look away as she dressed.

"I'll make sure all the guns are loaded," she said as she pushed her feet into her boots.

"Let's avoid a gunfight if we can. This hotel is full of people."

"No shit. But I'm not ruling it out, not if he opens fire."

"Fine." He dumped his pack on the table to inspect its contents. A couple of chemical flares and several clips of ammo were the most promising of the items. "Any ideas? Go to him? Ambush him here?"

"I'm not much on taking a defensive position," she said.

"Me either."

"And clearly, we can't let Greywolf keep the box now."

"Agreed."

"So we become the predators."

He smiled. "Two of us and one of him. I like the odds."

"And we have the bait to lure him wherever we want him to follow." She opened the safe in the living room closet and took out the Ancilon pouch. "What do we do with the ruby? We can't leave it behind and we can't risk losing it."

"Hide it in your sleeve. I still have enough power to face Greywolf, but if I'm hurt, you may need to use it." A voice in his head insisted he take the stone for himself. Which would lead the box directly to them.

"I afraid of touching it," she said. "What if I trance?"

"Hopefully it won't come to that." Her gift might prove to be her curse if the ruby incapacitated her. "Only use it as a last resort."

She reached up and traced the scar on his face with her fingertips.

He froze, holding himself rigid so he didn't reach for her. Their mission depended on them both having clear heads. "We're going to do this, and deliver the ruby and the box to the Durand vault."

Her hand dropped. "I know. I'm just ready for it to be over."

The box was getting closer. "We need to go now."

She reached for her jacket and a loud knock on the door made them both jump. Tanner telepathically scanned the hallway. Two men. A second knock. They were curious and a little put out and their thoughts weren't focusing on their purpose.

"Tanner Hays, Chantal Durand, please open the door." The voice was authoritative, but not hostile.

He glanced at Chantal and she shrugged. He turned the handle and stepped back as two men in puffy down coats with police patches on the arms and front, pushed in the door.

"Police," the taller officer announced. "You're under arrest for felony theft of two snowmobiles and gear."

There was little time to waste and the box was getting closer. Tanner focused on the officer's thoughts, suggesting they were looking at a middle-aged couple and they'd made a mistake.

"Get your things," the man said. "You need to come with us."

It wasn't working. His ability to manipulate minds was gone.

Chantal cleared her throat and he glanced at her. An eyebrow rose expectantly. He shook his head subtly and her face fell. At least the ruby was hidden in her sleeve.

"This is a mistake," she said, pulling on her jacket. "We rented the snowmobiles. They're parked at the Dancing Bears Inn across the street. We left the keys, a note, and a bonus payment with the front desk downstairs. You can check with them."

"We will." The second officer had a potbelly and a scraggily moustache that needed trimming.

"This is a mistake," Chantal said.

"Park rangers posted a bulletin a few hours ago about the stolen snowmobiles with your names and descriptions," moustache said. "Lodge security spotted you when you arrived."

"Why did you register at the lodge under a false name with a fake credit card?" The taller man stared at Tanner's facial scar.

Tanner didn't like the guy's tone. "She's being stalked by a local man and the credit card is hers and perfectly good."

Moustache poked his head in the closet with the safe. "Here are the snowmobile suits and helmets. There's a note and a fifty dollar bill." He read it out loud. "These belong to Junk and Corey Joseph. There's a phone number. Please call them to pick up their gear."

The first officer called the front desk of the lodge from the room's phone. Reception confirmed Chantal's story and he hung up. "We still need for you to come with us."

Chantal stepped back so she and Tanner stood side by side, arms touching. He recognized the maneuver and knew what was coming next.

"I don't think so," she said.

Moustache lunged for her. As one, Tanner and Chantal did what they'd been trained to do—quickly and efficiently take the men down without causing serious injury. In less than a minute, the officers were lying on their stomachs and Chantal was snapping their own handcuffs on their wrists.

"You're not going to get away with this," moustache groaned. "You've got nowhere to go."

"Sorry about this," Tanner said as he ripped a piece of adhesive bandage and pressed it across the guy's mouth. "We were set up, but there's no time to prove it. A murderer's looking for us and you fellas have led him right to our door."

He retrieved his pack and slung it over his shoulder. "The box is close, almost to the lodge. Let's get out of here."

They made it to the emergency exit without being seen. At the bottom of the stairs, he grabbed her arm before she opened the door to the outside. "The alarm will go off when we go out this way."

She shook off his hand. "We just left two tribal officers handcuffed in our suite. Don't you think it's a little late to be stealthy?"

"Fuck." He pushed the bar and sure enough, the alarm blared over their head. "Run."

Clouds blocked the moonlight and only low-watt landscape lighting dotted the grounds and gardens. Chantal took the lead, nimbly dodging snow-covered obstacles around the periphery of the lawns and across a road.

He almost tripped on a buried log fence and swore. "Where are we going?"

"There." She pointed to a long, low building ahead.

There were no lights on and it took him another thirty yards before he realized it was the train station. "The trains have stopped for the season. No one's there."

She picked up her pace. "Exactly."

The station had been designed for summer visitors with deep overhangs and a small, enclosed shelter for protection from sun and rain. Dim yellow security lights glowed at each corner of the roof creating more shadows than illumination. Railroad tracks ran along one side and an open field stretched from the station to Highway 49. On the far side of the tracks lay Highway 2 and a strip of rustic buildings that were dark for the night. No one was going to sneak up on them.

"The box is getting closer," Tanner said. "Want to go inside, out of the wind?"

"Sure."

The door locks were easy to pick and there wasn't much inside that a thief would want to steal anyway. "It isn't any warmer inside than out," she said. "Except maybe for the wind chill."

Tanner picked up a water bottle from a case behind the counter. It was frozen solid. "Back in the cave, remember when Greywolf said the box has powers it acquired from its maker? That its protection ward wouldn't allow us to hurt him as long as it was in his possession?"

"Yes. So why are we luring him out here?"

He stared out the window facing the lodge. "To take possession of the box."

"How's that going to work?"

He dropped the bottle on the counter and the noise echoed in the log station. "Think about it. The box protected him against us trying to shoot him. He perceived the danger and we projected the intention to do him harm. The ward isn't intelligent. It doesn't protect against chance occurrences or the water wouldn't have been able to carry away the loose tiles. It requires psychic energy of some sort to recognize danger. If there is no intention or fear, it doesn't protect."

"That's your theory? What if you're wrong?"

"Then we have to get away and figure out another angle. We can't let him keep the box and he'll keep coming after us as long as we have what was in it."

"You're right. He won't give up. So do you have a plan?"

He smiled, and her traitorous heart melted. "We'll have to work quickly." And he explained what they were going to do.

Fifteen minutes later, Chantal had forgotten about the cold. She surveyed the station, which looked exactly as it had when they arrived—or almost exactly. A lot of Tanner's plan involved *winging it,* but it was a good plan.

He stood next to her, their arms touching. "I'm ready for a showdown. What about you?"

"Let's get this done and get the hell out of here."

She unzipped the pocket on her sleeve and withdrew the pouch with the ruby. She dumped it from the double pouches onto the ticket counter, careful not to make direct contact with the stone. The heart glowed as though it was lit from within.

Tanner moved closer and removed his glove. "May I?"

She nodded. They needed every advantage they could get, which meant Tanner needed a recharge while they waited for the box to find them—before Greywolf arrived.

He held the ruby on his open palm. The effect was clearly visible, as though he'd grown taller and more muscular as she watched. His eyes closed and his nostrils flared. "The box is humming now. I can feel the connection. The vibration is high-pitched and deep at the same time."

"How far?"

"Outside. Not far."

A round of bullets came through the window and past her ear. "Shit."

They dropped to their knees behind the counter and Tanner rested his back against the drawers. "He's out there and has no problem with being heard."

"So what do we do? We can't just start shooting into the dark. There's a motel across the highway."

"And we can't sit here and get shot at. The box is picking up the ruby, not us."

"We should wrap it back up," she said. "Then the box won't detect it, right?"

"Right." He closed his hand around the stone.

Not a good sign, but he had to give it up. "I'll take it outside," she said. "You can wait for Greywolf to come out from his cover."

Tanner grimaced. "He's not as subtle as we expected. I'd rather not get blown up in here."

"Do you think he has explosives? He wouldn't risk destroying the ruby."

"He doesn't know what was in the box. And he probably assumes its power is so great it can't be destroyed."

She thought about that. "What kind of weapons do you have on you?"

"My Ruger, flares, and a couple knives."

"No explosives?"

He shook his head. "No. Nothing that will cover any area and nothing that will do much damage."

She held out the protective pouch for him to drop the ruby into. He hesitated, then let it go.

"You're jacked up again, right?" She tucked the pouch into her sleeve pocket.

"Yeah. As much as when I had it for a longer time. It seems to recharge my abilities faster each time I touch it."

Which meant his senses were operating on overload. "So where's Greywolf?"

He remained perfectly still and she tried not to breathe or distract him.

"In the bushes, on the right side of the field. I can hear him moving and the box is almost screaming in frustration."

"You can hear the box?"

"Yes. Not with my ears, in my blood."

She inhaled sharply. His new abilities both impressed and frightened her. "I'm going out and hunkering down on the platform. It's your show now."

"Then I'll do my best not to fuck this up."

She grinned at him. "I'd appreciate that and so would the rest of the Durand."

Crouching so Greywolf wouldn't spot her silhouette through the window, Chantal made her way to the rear of the station and slowly opened the door. A frigid gust caught her in the face and took her breath away.

Another round of shots shattered the rest of the windows on the lodge-side of the building and some on the trackside. She ducked against the outside wall. Trying not to make a sound, she crept along the log-wall until she reached the corner. If the ruby heightened Tanner's senses, the box might do the same for Greywolf. That would certainly complicate the situation.

Dropping her butt on the wooden floor, Chantal propped her back against the wall and listened to two more rounds of fire. Several seconds passed without a sound and then she heard a rumbling along the road. A snowplow headed south on Highway 2, its lights shifting shadows on the snow. She scurried to the corner of the building and peeked out toward the field. Greywolf lay in the snow, aiming a large weapon at the station. She had to warn Tanner.

Pressing against the wall, she spoke as softly as she could against the logs. With his senses jacked, hopefully, he'd be able to hear her.

"He has a launcher of some kind. It's aimed at you."

The vibrations on the wooden floor from his body weight moving assured her he'd heard. Where he'd gone for cover was another matter.

The missile came at them quickly, shattering the glass still clinging to one of the window frames and landing inside. She waited for the explosion and a couple of seconds later, it came—but not the explosion she expected. Tear gas.

She covered her nose and scooted to the back of the platform. The wind was coming from the trackside of the building through the broken windows. No coughing. Where was Tanner?

"Come out with your hands up and you'll walk out of here," Greywolf shouted. "Stay where you are and you're dead. I have all night and plenty more ammo."

She ran her hand over the sleeve that held the ruby. Using it herself was the last resort and a risky one given her abilities. Nothing happened for over a minute. What was going on?

Peeking through one of the windows, she spotted Greywolf trudging through the snow toward the station, guns in either hand.

She ducked and crawled backward towards the edge of the platform, listening for any sound and watching the building for some sign of Tanner. Had he been hit? Was he dead? A shiver racked her body. Was it possible for her to take down Greywolf without him?

Her toes hit the edge of the platform the same time Greywolf's boots hit the front steps. She slid backward off onto the tracks. Powerful arms caught her before she hit the ground. A voice hissed in her ear, "Shhh. I've got you."

Greywolf called out, "Give me what I came for and I'll let you walk away."

"Bullshit," she muttered softly. "You okay?"

"Fine. Good thing that was tear gas and not a grenade," he whispered.

"He's trying to kill us."

"No shit." Tanner brushed his lips across hers. "Time to finish this."

A minute later, Chantal crouched beneath the trackside of the platform while Greywolf stood above her, shining a search light up and down the track. His footsteps creaked on the planks over her head, showering dust and dirt on her.

"You won't escape," Greywolf shouted. "We'll find you sooner or later."

Her heart beat so loudly she barely made out Tanner's faint tread inside the building. Her fingers readjusted around the grip of her Glock, ready for action. She waited, senses on high alert. The platform shook—boom, boom and a loud crash followed by a surprised grunt and the loud thud of a body hitting the floor.

She didn't dare call out and give away her hiding place. Above her, a weight moved. Tanner or Greywolf? A scraping sound and another thud. What was happening?

A moment later, a backpack landed on the track not twenty feet from her. Tanner's pack lay by her side. This was Greywolf's.

Unraveling from her awkward position, she crawled from her hiding place and grabbed the pack. Instantly, the box's energy assaulted her and she dropped the canvas bag before it sent her into a trance.

"You still there?" Tanner called to her.

"Yes." Her eyes had adjusted to the dark and Tanner stood over Greywolf. She pulled on her Ancilon gloves, tucked her dirty Ancilon long underwear around the box inside Greywolf's backpack, and left it on the tracks. "Is he conscious?"

"No. I taped his hands and feet, but I won't be surprised if the duct tape he brought doesn't hold him very long."

"As long as it holds until we're done." She bent to retrieve Tanner's pack and handed it up to him. He then lifted her up on the platform.

Greywolf was sprawled face down on the floor and the heavy door that Tanner had rigged to hit him lay a few feet away. Blood slowly seeped from a cut on the back of his head. Had his hair not been short and white, it wouldn't have been noticeable.

She glanced at Tanner who watched their captive intently. His face showed no emotion. Part of her wished Greywolf dead. That would be less dangerous than what they had planned, even if the police got involved.

"Are you up to this?" she asked.

"If something happens..."

"I'll break the link. You'll be fine."

He nodded and knelt next to Greywolf. A quick motion turned the unconscious man onto his back. Tanner laid his hands on Greywolf's head and closed his eyes. His shoulders began to tremble and an eerie keening reverberated in his chest.

He was trying to scrub Greywolf's memory of everything that had happened since they met him—the box, the power, the cave. He grimaced and clenched his teeth. Greywolf was fighting him. She braced herself to break the link, to free him. Then she smelled it—majik.

Tanner's face paled and he seemed to shrink. "My box. My box. My box."

His words turned her blood to ice. He was losing. If she broke the link now, who would he be?

Chantal fumbled with the zipper on her sleeve. He needed the ruby to resist Greywolf. The stone glowed in the pouch, its power ready to expand. Tanner needed its power.

Or did he? Was he still Tanner?

"My ruby."

She froze. The voice was his and yet, it wasn't.

"My ruby. My ruby. My ruby."

Fear filled her. Could she do it? Would Greywolf defeat them both? Was there any other choice?

She dumped the ruby into her palm and prepared for the trance of her life. Warmth and light filled her and, instead of a trance, she experienced more clarity than she'd ever known. The stone's power pumped through her veins, vibrating along her nerves until her senses knew no bounds.

The psychic battle between Greywolf and Tanner became tangible. The energy exchanged, visible to her. The majik eating into Tanner's body manifested as a foul slime.

Her hand became an extension of the ruby and at the touch of her fingers, the majik sizzled to smoke. She touched Tanner's cheek. *Be strong, my love.*

The trembling stilled and, gradually, the color returned to his skin. Her empath senses felt him grow stronger, the clouds in his mind dissolving to let in her light.

Then, it was over. Tanner opened his eyes and their gazes locked. He'd seen the love in her heart and the intimacy was painful.

A siren screeched in the distance. "We need to get out of here," she said.

Greywolf had yet to regain consciousness, so it was impossible to know if Tanner's reprogramming had been thorough. She hoped so.

"I'll free him." Tanner used a knife from his pack to cut the tape from Greywolf's wrists and ankles. "There's nothing we can do to cover our tracks so we better hurry to get a head start."

She dropped the ruby into its pouch and slipped it back into her sleeve pocket. "Let's go."

Tanner jumped onto the tracks and helped her down, holding her against his body a little more closely and longer than necessary. He picked up Greywolf's pack and slung it on his back. She slipped her arms in Tanner's pack's straps and they started to run.

They followed the railroad tracks for a while, falling into a steady pace despite the extra effort required to run through the snow. When they were out of sight and hearing from the station, Tanner took out his ComDev to check their position.

"The track veers off from Highway 2 in about a hundred yards," he said. "If we're going to catch a ride to Kalispell, we'll need to take the road."

"A snowplow came through earlier. I saw it from the Amtrak station. The police may come looking for us."

"*Ordinaires*?"

She giggled. Actually giggled. The cold was affecting her brain. "Your telepathic abilities still jacked up?"

"And fueled with adrenaline."

She grinned. "Then maybe they'll give us a ride to town."

He took her hand and they crossed the short distance to the road. One lane had been plowed, making walking easier. They went another three miles with no sign of a vehicle traveling in either direction.

"How far to Kalispell?" she asked.

"Too far to walk."

"No kidding. But how far?"

"Eighty-two point three miles."

"Damn."

He chuckled. "We should have thought this plan out better."

"Too bad the ruby doesn't give us superpowers like being able to fly."

"Maybe it does. Have you tried?"

She grabbed his arm. "Are you serious?"

"No." He shook his head. "Someone is bound to come along sooner or later. Worse case, we can rest at the Summit Mountain Lodge. It's less than seven miles ahead."

Seven miles. With nothing to do but put one foot in front of the other, the last two days were catching up with her. The ruby had given her the strength to run and now that boost was wearing off. Her arms and back were stiff and her legs ached. She slipped her hand into Tanner's. He held it firmly.

What was going to happen between them after all of this? Would they go their separate ways? "What do you want to do first when the mission is over?"

"Sleep for ten hours straight. You?"

"Hot shower and clean clothes, then sleep for ten hours straight."

He grinned wickedly. "We could do that together."

Her heart skipped a beat. "We don't seem to be very good at *sleeping* together."

"We'd get around to it sooner or later."

The memory of *not sleeping* with him sent a wave of heat to her core. He was still under the influence of the ruby. Would he feel the same when it wore off? It was foolish to pay attention to what he said now, and yet, she couldn't bear the thought of him turning away from her again.

• • •

"Dr. Greywolf, you need to answer our questions."

Aaron tried to focus on the man's words and make sense of them. His head pounded.

"What were you doing out here, sir?" The man dropped to one knee.

He squinted at the officer, a distant cousin, like most of the tribe. "I was following Chantal Durand." An urgent life or death undertaking.

"Why?"

"I'm in love with her." Was he? Of course. Obsessed with her since the first time he'd seen her.

The two officers exchanged looks. "She and her companion assaulted us at the Lodge and escaped custody. The man…"

"Tanner Hays," Aaron said.

"Tanner Hays told us she was being stalked and they were forced to check in under false names. Would you be the stalker?"

"No!" A stalker? Him? "We were in love."

"Then why was she running away from you?"

Such hard questions. His mind, usually so sharp, was fuzzy. "He made her. Hays wants her for himself and…" Memories rushed at him like a tsunami. "I only shot at them to scare him."

"Did they shoot back?"

"No. I brought lots of weapons and plenty of ammunition. I kept shooting so they had to take cover in the station."

"What happened next?"

"The tear gas. I thought it would flush them out so I could shoot him."

His cousin cleared his throat. "Are you confessing to attempted murder?"

"Murder? No. He needed killing for stealing her away from me."

The other officer spoke up. "Did he kidnap her? They seemed to be together at the Lodge."

"He stole her. She was mine. She came here because she couldn't stay away." The more he repeated the story, the more agitated he became. They were wasting time. "Why are you here instead of going after them? They'll get away and I'll never see her again."

The officer took his arm to help him to his feet. "Your head is bleeding. You may be in shock. We'll take you somewhere you can have it looked at."

He tried to pull away, but his cousin held him firmly. "They're on foot. You can catch them."

The second officer took hold of his other arm and they guided Aaron through the train station. His launcher was where he'd left it, in the snow along with his rifle. His handguns were somewhere. No matter. What was important now was to find Chantal and bring her back to him.

• • •

"This is the longest night in history," Chantal complained.

Tanner had to agree with her. It seemed like they'd been walking for days—uphill then downhill and uphill again. He looked at his watch—a couple of minutes past 7:00. "It'll start getting light in about a half hour. How are you holding up?"

"Wouldn't say no to a cup of coffee."

Headlights appeared coming toward them, the first vehicle they'd seen since East Glacier Village. As it got closer, they stepped to the side of the road. A truck with a plow on the front scooped snow to the far side of the highway, creating a pile mirroring the one they stood on.

"He's coming fast and the wrong way," Tanner observed.

"Can you persuade him to turn around?"

"I'm not sure. We're almost to Summit Mountain Lodge. With the roads clear and the temperature predicted to rise above freezing by midmorning, we can probably get a ride there."

She waved her arms to get the truck to stop. When its headlights hit them, the snowplow slowed to a halt.

"What are you doing way out here?" The driver was a young man—probably in his twenties—in a plaid flannel shirt with the sleeves cut off.

"We got lost in the storm," Chantal said. "Could you give us a ride?"

"I'm headed for East Glacier. That where you want to go?"

"We want to go to Kalispell."

The guy laughed. "Good luck. It's a long walk." He waved and took off.

"What?" Chantal exclaimed. "How could he do that?"

Tanner chuckled. "Step on the gas and go."

Her ComDev buzzed. She took it out of her pocket and checked the screen. "Kara. Mark's text said to avoid her."

"See what she wants."

Chantal answered on speaker. "What's up?"

"Just checked the roads. Highway 2 will be open in a couple of hours. Want me to come get you?"

His pulse tripped and picked up at double pace. Chantal stared at him wide-eyed and speechless.

"Where do you think we are?" he asked.

Kara laughed nervously. "Since the East Glacier police are looking for you for questioning, I'd guess East Glacier Park somewhere. I can be there in a couple hours."

*Avoid Kara.* Was that a suggestion or an order? Having her come for them would solve their transportation problem. If he used the ruby, he could easily neutralize any threat she or her companion posed.

"Don't bother," Chantal said. "We have a rental SUV. Head back to Spokane."

"Are you sure?" Her voice held an odd inflection, almost panic.

"Back to Spokane, Kara. Now." Chantal ended the call, her brow drawn grimly. "Something's wrong. There's no reason for her to monitor police activity unless she was expecting to hear something."

They started walking again. A lot of what had happened in the last few hours niggled at the back of his mind. Things didn't completely add up. "Does it make sense to you that Greywolf would have sent the police looking for us at the lodge?"

"They said security spotted us."

"In that mess?" He shook his head. "No way. Somebody called them, but it wasn't security. Greywolf was so close, why would he want the interference of the police if he hoped to kill us and steal the stone?"

"You think it could have been Kara?"

"Does she know about the credit card and driver's license you used?"

She frowned. "It's possible. I used them once before and planned on retiring them. I may have been a little sloppy with my report."

"Even if you were, you uploaded it to a secure portal. Kara's targeted you specifically. Why?"

"I don't know." She glanced down at her ComDev. "We're only a mile and a half from the lodge. Let's hope we can get a ride from there."

The mile and a half was up a steep hill and took them another half hour. The sky was turning pink as they trudged into a driveway leading to a cheery clapboard building with gingerbread trim. A small sign reading OFFICE next to the double wooden doors assured them they were at the right place.

A middle-aged woman sat at a computer behind a stout wooden

desk. She looked up wide-eyed when they entered. "My, oh, my. Where did you two come from?"

"It's a long story," Chantal said hoping not to have to elaborate. "We're trying to get to our cabin near Whitefish."

"You look plumb worn out. How about a cup of coffee?" The woman stood and held out her hand. "I'm Ava."

Chantal shook it. "I'm Chantal and this is Tanner." No reason to lie. If there was trouble, they'd have to adjust Ava's memory anyhow.

"I didn't hear your car? Did you leave it out on the road?"

"We're on foot," Tanner said. "We hoped to find a ride here."

Ava shook her head. "Don't know about that. None of our guests are planning to leave today. Come on into the restaurant and we'll think about this."

They followed her through a lounge to a simple, but charming room with tables and chairs. "Nice place," Chantal said. "Is it yours?"

"No. The owners took their kids to Disney World and I'm looking after the lodge and restaurant." She gestured toward a sideboard laid out with a continental breakfast buffet. "Help yourselves to whatever you want."

They got coffee and muffins and all three settled at a table by a picture window that looked out to the mountains. The view of the sun rising to illuminate the snowy summits lifted his spirits. "Sure is beautiful."

"You should come back in the summer. Purtiest place in America." Ava winked at him. "There's a quiet cabin for two tucked away from the others. Private and romantic, it is."

Chantal choked and had to cough to clear her throat. "Sorry. The muffin went down the wrong way."

"So you two are heading for Whitefish, are you?"

"Yes. We have a flight out later today from Kalispell," Chantal said. "Do you know anyone who could drive us? We can make it worth their time."

Ava studied them. "You the two the police called about last night?"

He focused his mind on reading her thoughts. His abilities were fading and all he got was curiosity and a hearty dislike of the officer who called.

He shrugged. "Don't know. What did they say?"

"They're looking for a couple in their thirties. Want them for questioning."

For questioning only? The memory planted on Greywolf must have worked. "Is this couple dangerous?"

"Didn't say one way or the other." She smiled and her eyes twinkled mischievously. "I'll call Handsome Harry and see if he can take you. His truck is beat up, but it runs good and he can use the money."

"Handsome Harry?" Chantal asked.

Ava laughed. "It's just a name. He's not handsome like Tanner here. Not handsome at all and never was. Finish your coffee and I'll call him. How much you want to pay?"

"A hundred dollars?" Tanner said.

"A hundred now and two hundred more when we get to Whitefish," Chantal corrected.

Ava grinned. "Well, missy. I think you've got yourself a ride."

• • •

The body of Handsome Harry's pickup truck was almost as beat up as the man's face. Obviously, the nickname was a cruel joke that had stuck. Tanner had given up trying to make conversation by the third mile and soon nodded off to the steady hum of the engine. His head lolled against the window and he jerked awake. Maybe the driver was trustworthy, maybe not. A quick nap wasn't worth losing the box in the backpack jammed between his feet or the ruby in Chantal's sleeve. The sleeve on the arm resting on his thigh.

She snored softly, her head against his shoulder.

After all the danger and physical exertion of the last two days, his body was coming down hard from the adrenaline rush, not to mention the ruby-induced psychic high. His muscles twitched and his nerve endings sizzled. As much as he tried to convince himself they were on the home stretch, until they handed the box and ruby over to Mark, their mission was very much alive.

Careful not to disturb Chantal, he pulled his ComDev out of his pocket and tapped out a message to Mark.

*Mission completed. Heading back to the cabin to pick up our things. What's your ETA?*

Mark's reply came back almost immediately.

*In the air now. About an hour out. Will pick you up at the cabin. Send coordinates.*

Tanner sent the requested information and eased back against the seat to watch the scenery as the miles ticked off. Did he and Chantal have any chance together, or did too many years and hurtful words lie between them? It was easy to get carried away on a dangerous mission—it happened between Protectors from time to time. Life and death situations were an aphrodisiac to people like them.

She stirred in her sleep and he wrapped his arm around her to let her rest against his chest. His heart squeezed just looking at her curled up to him. He brushed a kiss on her forehead and turned his attention back to the landscape.

When they finally reached Columbia Falls, most of the roads were cleared of snow and the sun came out to melt what was left.

Tanner gently woke Chantal. She stared at him in confusion then sat up tall when she remembered where she was.

"Have a nice nap?" he asked.

She nodded. "We're there already?"

"Not yet. Since we don't have to go into Whitefish to get to the cabin, I thought you might want to stop at an ATM here for cash."

"Holler if you see a bank," Harry said. "I don't come to the big city much."

The first bank they came to was closed and the drive-up ATM was out of order. It took forty-five minutes for Chantal to withdraw cash to pay Harry and for them all to get coffee and pastries to go from a local coffee shop.

"Are you sure Mark's going to pick us up?" she asked when they all climbed back into the truck.

"That's what he said." Tanner checked his watch and cringed. "He was only an hour out when he texted, so he might be at the cabin by now."

"Then we'd better hurry. Mark isn't much for waiting."

• • •

Chantal was relieved to see the driveway of the cabin empty when they pulled up. Mark hadn't arrived yet and Tanner's surveillance showed there had been no visitors in their absence. She paid Harry the promised two hundred dollars, plus an extra hundred to forget where he'd dropped them. He happily agreed and went on his way.

"Home sweet home," she said. "Hard to believe we were only here two nights."

"Maybe I'll stay again if I come back to visit Hank."

A heaviness settled in her stomach. He wasn't inviting her. Maybe she'd overreacted to their time together. They weren't enemies anymore, but they weren't lovers either.

"What's your cabin in Jackson Hole like?" Her cheeriness sounded false in her ears, but she doubted he'd notice.

"Simple, comfortable with an amazing view of the valley. You should come see it." He smiled and her heart sputtered and kicked into double-time.

"Don't say things you don't mean."

"Why wouldn't I mean it? I'd like for you to visit sometime."

Visit. Not stay.

He continued, all the while piling gear on the kitchen table to pack. "Spring's the best time before all the tourists come to see Yellowstone. I've got three horses. We can ride up into the mountains—you still ride, right?"

She nodded. He'd taught her to ride Western and she'd taught him to ride English. She'd loved him then and dreamed they'd be together one day. A short visit to his home would be agony.

"Then it's settled. Spring in Jackson Hole. I know you'll love it there."

"Me too." If she could be with him, she'd love pretty much anywhere. Her eyes burned and she pretended to straighten the pillows on the sofa. It was almost easier when he hated her. Then she knew there was no chance they'd ever be together.

"I'm going to pack and shower," she said. "Clean clothes will feel so good. These need burning."

He laughed. "I'm sure you have a closet or two back at Valtois with all the latest fashions."

"Not anymore. A few years out of Paris and I'm woefully behind the times."

"You'll catch up."

And there it was. He'd built that wall again. Her world and his world, the two would never meet.

"Maybe not. I need to move my stuff out of the guesthouse now that Isabelle and her family own it. It's time I had a home base."

"It's good to have a place of your own to come home to."

"Like your cabin."

He nodded, and her heart broke a little more.

"Pack, shower, wait for Mark. I think my immediate future is settled." She hurried into her room and closed the door a little harder than she intended. Tears welled in her eyes and she blinked them away.

She loved him. He didn't love her.

Without paying much attention to folding and packing, she stuffed the bag she'd brought with everything but the clothes she intended to wear on the plane and the jacket with the ruby. She stripped, leaving her clothes in a pile on the floor, and headed for the shower. The water was hot and the bathroom filled with steam in minutes. She stepped in and immediately waited for the tension to dissolve under the hot water. Seconds turned to minutes and still, she felt like a rubber band stretched to its limit.

Outside, a car pulled up. Mark was here. She needed more time with Tanner and simultaneously wanted to be anywhere but here.

The car door slammed. Was Tanner in the living room? Had he gone out to greet Mark? No voices so probably not. Dragging a brush through her hair, she scanned the bathroom counter for a clip and twisted her damp hair up off her neck.

"Make yourself at home," she called out. "I'll be ready to go in a couple minutes."

"Take your time," he grunted.

She dressed quickly and slipped on flats instead of her boots— the Chanel boots Tanner had made fun of—and went out to greet Mark.

The two people in the living room stood with their backs to her, rooting through the gear she and Tanner had left behind when they'd gone to find the box. She recognized Kara immediately.

"What are you doing here?" Chantal demanded.

Kara turned. "Surprise. You and Tanner have quite at cozy love nest here, but not your usual five-star style, is it?"

"What are you doing here?"

The man slowly turned to face her. Her heart stopped and her blood turned to ice. He'd changed. His once handsome face had aged badly, or perhaps, taken too many punches, and his hair was more gray than black. His eyes, however, were as cold and mean as ever.

"And we meet again, Chantal," Javier said. "It's been what, seven years?"

"Where's Tanner?" she demanded.

"Sounds like he's in the shower."

Sure enough, the sound of running water came from his room. He couldn't get ambushed the way she had.

"Tanner! It's a trap!" she shouted.

Javier lunged for her and grabbed her arm. She resisted, but he was too big and too skilled for her—and had been through the same Protector training. Evenly matched, he had the advantage of size, surprise, and a nasty looking dagger.

Tanner's door flew open. Barefoot, dressed only in jeans,

Tanner aimed his pistol at them. It took him a long moment before he recognized his old friend—and saw the dagger at Chantal's throat.

"Let her go," Tanner demanded.

"Whoa, man. What happened to you? Looks like you had a run-in with a pack of wolves. No wait—that was a couple of my compadres down in Mexico wasn't it?"

"Let her go," Tanner repeated.

Javier chuckled. "And I'd heard you hated Chantal for getting me killed. Kara told me all of DT was whispering about how cruel it was for Mark to pair you up for this mission, so I figured it must be something big. We all know Chantal's the General's favorite."

Chantal tried to jerk her arm from his grip. "Shoot the son of a bitch."

"Shut up. He won't shoot me." Javier shoved her in front of him. "I'd rather take her to Tolian alive, but I'll get plenty of mileage out of killing her too. So it's up to you. Put down the gun or watch her bleed out. Your choice."

"You work for Tolian?" Chantal sneered. "Impressive step up from hanging with third rate Dissembler terrorists, isn't it?"

"The Brazilian Sentier is very generous when he gets what he wants. And inside information about the Durand and, especially the First Order, is always rewarded well."

"So why hasn't he taught you majik yet?" she sneered. "Have you even met him?"

"You always did have too much to say." Javier squeezed her arm painfully and the knife nicked her throat. A drop of blood rolled down her neck and landed on the wooden floor.

Tanner was poised to spring. Their eyes met and she mouthed *not yet*. Mark was on his way and would see the strange car when he arrived. If they could stall, there was a better chance nobody would get hurt—nobody but Javier.

Javier pushed the blade a little harder against her neck. "What did you find out there?"

"Nothing," Tanner said. "It was a dead end."

"Then why was Aaron Greywolf chasing you? For years he's

written about an ancient sacred treasure lost centuries ago." Kara approached Tanner. "Is that what you came here to find?"

"No." He glared at her. "We came for the tile and that's all we got."

"You're lying," Javier sneered. "We know the East Glacier police want you for questioning and Greywolf's in custody."

"Just a little misunderstanding." Tanner stared Kara down. "He's using you like he uses everyone. He's a traitor and a murderer."

"You hurt my feelings, Tanner," Javier said with mock indignation. "We were best mates until this Durand bitch shook her slutty ass in your face."

"Fuck you," Chantal spat.

"Language," Javier chided. "We're not here for a Protector reunion. I want whatever you two found and I want it now."

Tanner didn't move. He'd taken the pack with the box into his room and the ruby was still in her jacket sleeve. Giving Greywolf the box had bought them time and now that they knew about the box's attraction to the ruby, they could use it again.

"Give it to him, Tanner," Chantal said. "A stupid clay box isn't worth dying over."

He nodded. "Let her go and I'll get it for you."

"How about you get it or I slit her throat? You know I'll do it."

"Then you'll let her go." Although Tanner didn't raise his voice, the threat was clear. He was taller and more muscular than Javier and the massive scarring on his body made him appear invincible. If it hadn't been for the dagger at her throat, she didn't doubt he would have torn his old friend apart.

"Bring me the box. If it's of any value, I'll *reconsider* her future, or, lack of a future." He drew the sharp tip of the blade along her jawline making a shallow cut.

Tanner growled. "Before this is over, I'm going to kill you."

"Sure. Now get the fucking box."

Tanner ducked into his room and returned with the backpack. "Here you go." He held it out to Kara by the strap.

She took it and reached inside. Kara was *ordinaire,* but she was what the Durand called a mild receptor, with no abilities of her own.

Chantal held her breath and exchanged anxious glances with Tanner.

Kara withdrew the box, carefully opened the Ancilon wrapping, and held it in her bare hands. "It's beautiful. The markings are even more intricate than in the photo you sent of the tile." She ran her fingers over the ancient squares and along the golden edges of the box.

Chantal glanced at Tanner who shrugged. Apparently, the box didn't affect *ordinaires.*

Javier's hands trembled—almost imperceptibly—but the knife at her throat no longer pressed firmly. Chantal knew why. The box excited him and his gift, the ability that got him assigned to several high-level missions. Javier could read the spell, ward, and power of written symbols by touching them.

"Put the box down on the coffee table and tape their wrists," Javier ordered. "The duct tape is on the dining table. Him first, hands in front where I can see them, then hers."

Kara did as instructed. When both were secured and seated against the living room wall, Javier approached the box. He sat on the sofa and examined the markings without touching them. "Did you read this artifact, Chantal?"

"No."

"That's still your function on the team, isn't it?"

"You know how my gift works," she said. "There wasn't any reason to touch it once we found it."

"Weren't you curious?"

No was the wrong answer if they wanted the box to incapacitate Javier. Would it reject him or give him its power? "Of course," she replied. "Who wouldn't want to know its origins?"

Javier laughed. "That's right, you can only read history, not power." Slowly, he leaned into the box and reached his hands toward it.

"It isn't going to bite you," Kara snapped.

His fingertips barely brushed the sides and he went rigid. A loud keening pierced the quiet, its high pitch and volume so jolting that it took Chantal a few seconds to understand that the sounds were words in some ancient language. His eyes went back in his head and his body shook violently.

Tanner grabbed the gun and hopped to his feet in the same moment as Kara yanked the box from Javier's hands. Chantal tried to stand, but her foot slipped on a smear of blood and she had to catch herself on the doorway.

"It's over." Tanner held the Ruger with both taped hands and trained it on Javier. "Both of you, up and over there." He gestured toward the center of the room.

Dazed, Javier struggled to rise and Kara helped him to his feet. With a lightning quick movement, he yanked Kara in front of him and held the dagger to her throat. "Not a Durand, but she'll die unless you let us walk out of here with that box."

Chantal stood next to Tanner. "Why should we care? She betrayed us. Kill her, then we'll kill you."

Javier glared at Tanner. "Are you willing to let this woman die? Would you really shoot me? I don't think so. I think whoever did that to your body, took away your nerve. You were always a bleeding heart. Now you're a broken man too."

The color had drained from Kara's face. "Don't let him kill me, Chantal. I'm sorry for spying on you. I only meant to give him enough information so he'd stay with me."

And Javier had used his psychic abilities on her as well as his well-honed powers of persuasion. "You made a bad choice," Chantal observed.

Javier pushed his hostage forward, keeping close behind to use her for cover. "Pick up the box and put it in the bag. Do exactly as I say and I'll let you go when we get to where we're going."

Chantal glanced at Tanner. His expression was hard, his gaze riveted on his old friend, his gun raised. Had he lost his nerve? Could he shoot Javier given the chance?

Kara hesitated, throwing Chantal a pleading look before

bending to reach for the box. Simultaneously, Javier ducked behind her and a shot exploded, blowing off the side of his face. He fell backward with a terrible crack onto the hardwood floor.

Kara screamed and let the box fall back onto the coffee table. Chantal tried to grab her arm, but the tape around her wrists was too tight. "You're okay. It's over."

Kara stared down at her former lover, sobbing hysterically. Gore splattered behind him on the floor, wall, and chair.

With a sharp yank, Tanner tore the tape on his wrists then unwound what bound Chantal.

"Handy trick," she said.

"Saw it on YouTube."

"You could have gotten loose at any time?"

"Yeah, but I figured unless I got the upper hand, he'd just bind me with something I couldn't get out of." He nodded toward the body on the floor. "I was aiming for his shoulder and he ducked. I didn't mean to kill him."

Chantal laid a hand on Tanner's arm. "Are you all right?"

He nodded. "I didn't want to believe he was a traitor, but seeing him again I knew you were right."

"I'm sorry you had to be the one to pull the trigger."

He brushed a strand of hair from her cheek. "Not me. I've lost too much sleep over the son of a bitch. And more." He gestured toward Kara. "What's going to happen to her?"

"That's up to Mark."

"What's up to me?" Mark's huge frame filled the front doorway. His attention fell on Javier. "Fuck. What happened?"

They told him.

"We thought you'd get here before us," Chantal said. "When I heard them, I thought it was you."

"I went looking for Javier in Columbia Falls," Mark said. "Our people identified him traveling with Kara so I went there first to handle the situation. Obviously, I was too late." Mark addressed Kara. "Did you steal the car outside?"

Kara nodded. "Are you...?"

"Mark Durand," he snapped. "You're quite the little hacker, aren't you?"

Her eyes filled with tears. "I didn't mean any harm. John said he wanted to talk to Tanner, that they were friends, but Chantal had spread lies about him among the Durand."

"How did you meet him?"

She frowned. "At the gym. No, it was…I don't remember."

Chantal laid a hand on Kara's shoulder. "He manipulated you. He was a bad guy, a very bad guy." She glanced at Mark. "You'll fix this, right?"

"Yes." Which would entail scrubbing everything related to Javier and what had happened here from her memory so she could go back to work.

"What about him?" Tanner nodded toward the dead man.

"I'll call in a team to take care of everything." Mark leaned in to inspect the box where it had fallen on the coffee table. "Any problems handling it?"

Tanner grinned. "You'll want gloves." He got a pair of Ancilon gloves from the kitchen table and handed them to the Field General.

Mark donned them and inspected the box, turning it slowly. "Impressive. Where's the other *item*?"

"In my room," Chantal said.

"Good." Mark wrapped the box in its Ancilon protection and carefully placed it back in the pack. He removed the gloves and handed them back to Tanner.

"Ancilon turned out to be one of DT's better inventions," Chantal said. "Too bad it doesn't have much commercial application."

"You never know." Mark took Kara by the arm and gently nudged her toward the door. "We'll wait in the car. Get your things and let's get the hell out of here."

• • •

On the way to the airport, Tanner sat in the front seat with Mark while Chantal spoke quietly with Kara in the back. He caught enough of the conversation to understand what had happened in the Jeep while Mark and Kara waited for him and Chantal to gather their belongings. Kara believed she'd come to Montana on Chantal's orders to deliver a new laptop and set up personalized security. With one quick call, Mark had already arranged a commercial flight for her back to Seattle.

"You can debrief me on the stone on the flight back to New York," Mark said.

"I'm not going back yet." Until he said it, he hadn't realized he had unfinished business in East Glacier Village. "Greywolf killed Johnny Hawkswing. I can't prove that, but I'm not letting him get away with it. I'm pretty sure he confessed to trying to kill me. A charge of attempted murder may have to do."

A cocked eyebrow was the only indication of Mark's surprise. "The item allowed you to convince him of that, did it?"

"He tried to kill us; I just nudged him to confess. And to forget his own *talent*."

"Are your abilities still enhanced?"

Tanner shook his head. "My senses are more acute but that's it. I can't do what you did for Kara anymore."

"But you could?"

"Yes."

"Shit."

There was so much to tell the Durand Field General, but not with Kara in the vehicle. "Chantal can tell you almost everything that happened. I'll come to New York when I finish here. Or to Paris."

"New York." Mark glanced at him and back to the road. "Are you and Chantal good to work together again?"

"Sure." Whatever happened between him and her wasn't anyone else's business. Hell, he wasn't clear on what had happened himself except she'd been the best partner he'd ever worked with. "Why didn't anyone tell me about Javier?"

"At the time, Chantal wanted to. Adrien and I weren't convinced you didn't know what he was planning. We were young and new at making command decisions. We talked to my father and he suggested we wait and watch you."

"You didn't trust me."

"Not at first, but you proved your loyalty over and over."

Dozens of assignments, including the hellhole in Mexico. All that time, he'd blamed Chantal for something she hadn't done. "I wish somebody had told me about Javier seven years ago. Even five years ago."

"Because of Chantal?"

"Partly. That kind of anger has a way of tainting a person's outlook on life."

Mark pulled the rented Wrangler into the commercial terminal of the airport and stopped at the drop-off to Alaska Airlines. He turned in his seat. "You have reservations on the four o'clock flight. Your boarding pass was sent to your phone." He handed her a couple large bills. "Take a cab home and get some rest."

Kara took the money. "Thank you, sir. What about the bag I left at the motel?"

"We'll have it sent to you." He nodded at Chantal.

Chantal hugged the other woman. "I'll call you in a couple days about those hieroglyphics. Thanks for bringing the laptop."

Kara got out of the car, heading for the terminal entrance and Mark eased away from the curb.

"She wasn't to blame," Chantal said. "Are you going to fire her?"

"No, transfer her into an area where her skills will help DT and won't jeopardize the security of Protectors." Mark took a right toward the general aviation entrance. "You're coming with me and Tanner's staying to take care of the Greywolf business. You have the ruby?"

She unzipped her sleeve pocket and handed the pouch to him. "Do you want me to stay too, Tanner? Another witness?"

He wanted her with him for so many reasons he didn't quite understand yet. "No. We can't take the chance someone will recognize you from the media and find out you were in Australia the past few years."

"And in jail where I couldn't have met Greywolf. Got it." She fell silent and stared out the window.

There was so much he wanted to say to her, but not in front of Mark. They had a lot to talk out about what had happened between them the last few days and that conversation couldn't take place on the fly while Mark was getting the jet ready to take off. "You were an excellent partner out there," he said. "Nobody else could have done what you did."

She smiled at him, but her eyes were sad. "Back at you. I'm just glad to be rid of that box and the ruby. Maybe the scroll will throw some light on why the Shalamov sent it away."

"What scroll?" Mark asked.

He'd forgotten about the skins. "There were rolled skins with the box," Tanner said. "The pictures on them appear to be some sort of history. They're in my backpack."

Mark stopped at the security entrance to the Glacier Jet Center. "This is where we get out. Take the Jeep—all the rental paperwork is in the console."

They all got out and Mark took charge of the packs and bags to be loaded on his plane. "Good luck," he said. "See you for a debrief in New York."

Chantal stayed behind until Mark had entered the security entrance to the building.

"Be careful." She laid her hand on his arm. "You don't have the stone anymore."

"And happy to be rid of it. I just want to be sure Greywolf doesn't go scot-free for Johnny's murder." He brushed a stray strand of hair from her cheek, grazing his thumb across her skin. He didn't trust himself to say what he was feeling, to tell her how sorry he was they'd missed the chance of something more all those years ago. Her eyes shone with emotion and her lips parted.

It took all of his willpower not to take her in his arms and kiss her until they were both delirious. Instead, he brushed her lips with his and stepped away. "I'll call you when this is over." Then he headed for the Jeep and East Glacier Park Village.

# CHAPTER THIRTY-TWO

Chantal stretched out on a chaise overlooking the clear blue water of the Caribbean. "I need to go to Paris eventually. You and Bodie have been the perfect hosts, but it's time I decide what I'm going to do with the rest of my life."

Lex Durand waved to her husband, who was hauling a zodiac dinghy up on the snowy beach below. "We love having you here. It's not as though you don't have your own guesthouse. Besides, it's the family compound, you have as much right to be here as we do." Lex peered at her over her sunglasses. "He still hasn't called?"

Chantal sighed. "No." She'd told her cousin about her mission with Tanner the day she arrived—nothing about the box or ruby— but what had changed between them and that he'd said he'd call her. Three weeks later—not a word. If he'd run into trouble in Montana, Mark would have told her. At first, she worried. Now she was despondent. And more than a little pissed off—whether at him or herself fluctuated hourly.

Lex laid a sympathetic hand on her arm. "The last year and a half have been hard on him. Blowing Javier's face half off had to be traumatic."

Chantal shrugged. Lex had always disliked Javier. "Yeah. He didn't seem devastated at the time, but maybe remorse hit him later."

"Or maybe he got tied up with the case against Greywolf. An outsider with a strange story versus respected local academic. He had to come up with a story that included the provable facts but nothing about your mission, and make it sound plausible."

"I know," she sighed. "But he didn't even text an emoji. A thumbs up or happy face, even."

Lex laughed. "Somehow I don't see Tanner texting kissy lips."

"It's time I face the truth—I'm in love with him and he doesn't hate me anymore. I have to chalk up what happened to mission mania."

"Give him time."

"I waited seven years." She swung her legs off the chaise and planted her feet on the floor. "As soon as I can get a flight to Paris, I'm going home to see Adrien and talk to him about doing something important with my life."

"Can we talk first?"

That voice. She whirled around to the end of the terrace where Tanner stood with Bodie.

"I found this guy wandering around looking suspicious," Bodie said. "He says he's a friend of yours, Chantal."

Lex hopped up and hugged Tanner. "So glad to see you. We hope you're here for a nice relaxing vacation."

"We'll see." His eyes met hers over Lex's shoulder.

"Oh, my, Bodie and I are late for…a…a conference call." Lex took Bodie's arm and he gave Chantal the thumbs up behind Tanner's back as he was dragged into the villa.

Tanner sat down facing her on the chaise Lex had vacated. Her heart pounded just sitting this close to him. He'd shaved and the scar on his cheek seemed less fierce than it had when she first saw it. "You found me."

"I wanted to call dozens of times, but just hearing your voice wasn't enough. I needed to see your face." He took her hand. "Touch you. Breath you in."

"You said you'd call." She heard the hurt in her voice and hated that he did too. "I didn't ask you to."

"I know. I'm sorry." His fingers intertwined with hers, sending a tingle of excitement up her arm.

"Is Greywolf in jail?" she asked.

"Yes. And likely to stay there for a while. He hasn't remembered his abilities yet and hopefully won't." His eyes never left her face, as though he was drinking her in.

"Hopefully not." Her heart pounded. Why had he come? Why had he waited so long?

"I told Hank about the cave with the paintings. He was shocked and excited. Between now and summer he's going to work on getting permission to go in and study them. Asked if we'd come for July and August to lend a hand. What do you think?"

"I think it's too far out to decide now." Couldn't he feel her pulse race? The small talk was making her crazy. "It's been three weeks without a word. Why are you here, Tanner? Not to plan a summer dig."

"I wanted to come right away, but I needed to think about us—not just what happened on the mission, what I did to you when I had the ruby."

"That was consensual on my end, so get over any guilt."

"It's not guilt." His thumb stroked the top of her hand. "I studied the skins when I was in New York debriefing Mark. The drawings were cryptic, especially where they described the ruby's power. Mark and I concluded independently that, in addition to enhancing existing and latent abilities, it causes the possessor to act on suppressed traits and impulses—greed, lust, hatred, belligerence—he otherwise would control. That's why the Shalamov sent the heart away."

"Go on."

"I've always wanted you—since you were a teenager and I knew it was wrong to even think about you that way." His grip tightened.

"It was never wrong between us."

"Wasn't it?" His dark blue eyes bore into hers. "Javier rode me relentlessly. Jeered that I was making a fool of myself. Then later, that night I kissed you—do you remember?"

"Of course."

"I wanted you so badly my body was on fire. I thought you wanted me too."

She remembered all of it. The kiss, the heat of their bodies, and the anticipation of finally having the man she'd always wanted. "And then the world fell apart."

"I never stopped wanting you and the guilt ate at me and stroked my resentment. I've always craved you and the ruby removed any civilized restraint. It didn't change what I wanted, it compelled me to act on it."

The sex that she'd wanted as much as he had. Hope bloomed in her chest. "What do you want now, Tanner?"

"For us to be together. Whatever that takes, I'm willing to work at this."

"The sex is fabulous and god knows I've fantasized about being with you since before I knew what sex was." She ran her fingers down his scarred cheek. "But I love you, and no matter how hot we are together, that's not enough for me."

He brought her fingers to his lips. "It's not enough for me either. I've always loved you, even when I hated you. Come back to Jackson with me. I'm damaged goods, but if you're willing, I'll do whatever it takes to make you happy."

"Would you kiss me?"

Grinning, he pulled her onto his chaise and claimed her lips, firmly at first, then with a hungry passion that stole her breath. She kissed him back, tongues dueling, teeth grazing lips until the spice of him intoxicated her. He pressed her into the cushions and stretched out next to her. Breaking the kiss, he gazed into her eyes with so much emotion it took the air from her lungs. His rough thumb grazed her cheek and her lips, leaving a thrilling tingle.

"I love you, Chantal," he said. "I always have and always will."

And Chantal knew she was finally home.

# EPILOGUE

Mark stared out of the penthouse window at Central Park glowing in the golden light of the setting sun. From so high up the people blended into the fabric of the landscape and the park lights flickered like fireflies frozen in place. Such a peaceful scene in contrast to the frustration that raged inside him.

"He rescued seventy-six girls before the fighters killed him." Even through the speaker of his ComDev, Adrien's grief resonated in his voice.

"I should have gone."

"Bullshit. Nesh spent a year infiltrating their organization. He spoke their language with the local accent and blended in."

"I can speak any language with the local accent and I can be invisible when I want."

"Not 24/7," Adrien said. "You're six foot five and white. You would not blend in. We didn't send him in, Nesh begged to take on this mission and would consider his own life a fair price to pay to save those girls from sexual slavery to those monsters."

And Mark had approved the operation himself. He and the Sentier had far too many calls like this in the last two years. "We're losing this war, A. Dissemblers used to be the primary force behind most of the atrocities—the violence, depravity, evil. With this new breed of *ordinaire* devils, do we even know who we're fighting anymore?"

"Evil—in whoever and wherever we find it." Adrien's voice was filled with determination. "We'll never win, but we can't lose, not if civilization is going to survive."

Which summed up the stakes in the war they fought. His

responsibilities as Field General had never weighed so heavily on him before and he knew Adrien felt the same burden. "Get some sleep, man, and we'll talk tomorrow."

"You too." Adrien was silent for a long moment then added. "You and I are the most powerful of our generation. We've both been to hell and survived. We'll figure out what we need to do and do it."

"We always do. Night, A." Mark clicked off.

The silence in the penthouse was almost a tangible presence pressing in on him. His dark gift stirred and threatened to assert itself. He and Adrien *had* been to hell, and he'd lost a large piece of his soul along the way. It was too late to change the past, but he could still do something about the future.

He hurried to the Durand Museum and fulfilled all the security procedures to enter. Passing through the Curiosity Salons—the rooms with objects whose mystical properties were either benign or too weak to impact anyone encountering them—he made his way to the secure vault designed to hold items still under investigation. A retinal scan opened the door and he entered.

The Shalamov box sat in the middle of an ancient oak table dating back to the Druids. Each of the box's tiles had been carefully documented and the loose tile was sent to DT for material analysis. An insulated storage container sat next to it, ready to be filled, sealed, and lowered into the crypt deep below the building where no one, not even he or Adrien, could ever retrieve it.

He pulled on a pair of Ancilon gloves and opened the box. The ruby lay in the middle, glowing faintly. He reached for it and the closer his hand came to it, the brighter it shone until he picked it up.

Even with the glove, the stone heart felt alive—warm, pliable, pulsating. It had been waiting for a powerful psychic for centuries—for him. He stared at it, enthralled. Every instinct shouted it was his. It would give him the power to fight the Durand's enemies, to destroy Tolian once and for all, to clearly see what needed to be done, to finally win the war.

Gently, he set the heart on a leather cushion on the table,

then closed its box and placed it in the stainless steel container. He pressed the palm of his hand on the fleur-de-lys on the wall and the panel slid open revealing a metal door the size of a large safe. The combination of his fingerprints and body heat tripped the lock and it popped open.

The sophisticated dumbwaiter yawned at him, large enough to hold a medium-sized trunk. His pulse thrummed in his ears and the air in his lungs grew heavy. He knew what duty dictated and yet, all the power in the subterranean vault churned in his blood, the energy so vast the Durand had no choice but to lock it safely away from all of mankind.

He turned back to the table and froze. The shadow image of a white ermine shimmered around the heart staring at him. "Use my gift, revenant," it whispered and then dissolved.

What was left of his conscience howled in protest. His revenant tattoo burned as it always did in the face of danger. His dark gift surged through his blood in eager anticipation. The ermine was real. Its ruby heart called to him.

So be it.

Mark picked up the container, placed it in the dumbwaiter and slammed the door. Without hesitation, he pushed the red on button on the wall and the mechanism began its soft hum. The box began its descent into the crypt.

Empty.

LARK BRENNAN's love of reading, writing, and travel has led her to a string of colorful jobs and a well-worn passport—as well as a few years spent sailing and diving in the Virgin Islands. Her travels have inspired her stories—romantic adventures set in some of her favorite destinations around the world. When not travelling, she lives in Texas with her brilliant husband and two adorable canine "children."

CPSIA information can be obtained
at www.ICGtesting.com
Printed in the USA
BVOW09s0520310717

490584BV00001B/24/P